DEAD
MEN'S
WATCHES

The New Age/
Le Nouveau Siècle
X

DEAD MEN'S WATCHES

A NOVEL

HUGH HOOD

Anansi

Published in 1995 by
House of Anansi Press Limited
1800 Steeles Avenue West
Concord, Ontario
L4K 2P3
Tel. (416) 445-3333
Fax (416) 445-5967

Canadian Cataloguing in Publication Data

Hood, Hugh, 1928–
Dead men's watches

(The new age; pt. 10)
ISBN 0-88784-168-6

I. Title.   II. Series: Hood, Hugh, 1928–
The new age; pt. 10.

PS8515.049D4 1995 . C813'.54   C95-930018-X
PR9199.3.H66D4 1995

Cover Design: Bill Douglas/The Bang
Computer Graphics: Tannice Goddard, S.O. Networking
Printed and bound in Canada

*House of Anansi Press gratefully acknowledges the support of
the Canada Council, the Ontario Ministry of Culture,
Tourism, and Recreation, Ontario Arts Council, and
Ontario Publishing Centre in the development of
writing and publishing in Canada.*

For Michael and Elizabeth Bliss
and their very handsome family
with my fondest admiration

I

The funeral fell on a Saturday in the week after Easter, April 12th, 1980. In contrast to my father's obsequies a decade earlier, the occasion was very private, going unnoticed in the papers, thank God. A time arrives in everybody's life when attention from journalists becomes unwelcome; this was one of those times. There were some unanswerable questions about my mother's last rites. I wasn't in the city when she died. Neither was Uncle Philip. Poor Andrea, only twenty years old, had to organize everything in a few days, with ineffectual assistance from Amanda Louise, who arrived in the city on Thursday afternoon, in time to sit in on the discussions with Marshall Estcourt about "the arrangements." Flowers, what kinds, how many, where sent, how acknowledged? Which church?

My mother died in a nursing home and hadn't been able to go to church for years. Fortunately, Lindsay and Estcourt, the undertakers, had professional contacts with every Catholic parish in the Toronto archdiocese. Marshall Estcourt remembered our family links to Our Lady of Perpetual Help, which went back to the early 1930s. He suggested our former parish church as the appropriate location for the requiem, and that's where it was celebrated. There was plenty of space in the family plot at Mount Hope Cemetery — why do these matters always seem so funny?

Ishy was buried next to Dad after the requiem mass at OLPH, a service that seemed unassuming, casual, almost improvised. On the whole, I think Andrea managed the small private ceremony very well. It took place quite early in the day too, allowing plenty of time for the customary post-interment brunch.

Now that does sound comic! When I was growing up there was no such thing as a post-interment brunch. By the beginning of the 1980s it had become the recognized windup to a funeral. Marshall Estcourt actually employed the phrase in my hearing, after the inhumation — to use the appropriate professional term — when he asked Andrea if any of us would like to be taken back downtown in one of the limousines. I can feel a satiric tone creeping into this account of the event, almost against my will. My mother was as much entitled to a formal farewell as my father. I felt that it needn't have come, in the end, to a discussion of the terminal brunch. We don't feel about funerals as we did at one time; there isn't the old formality. We accepted poor Marshall's proffered limousine, and had the driver drop us off on Bloor Street near Bay. Andrea, Amanda, Emily and me. Emily looked at me with a grin and said something about Macbeth and the weird sisters; her mother broke into unwilling laughter. Post-funeral hilarity is simply a tension-reducing mechanism, but it always charms me. I enjoy a good funeral.

We picked a place on Yorkville not far from my mother's nursing home that was actually serving what it called a Saturday brunch. We could have gone to the hotel or to the apartment, but we all wanted to be waited on and even coddled a bit. There were only the four of us. Tony never came in from London. Nor Edie. Anthony and John were occupied with their studies in the U.K. Almost all of my father's associates had faded from the scene in the decade following his death. We were plainly moving into a new phase of life. When your mother dies, you sever the most intimate, binding tie of your life. I had no wife, no lover, to mourn with me. I had a wife who was no wife, and a lover who had been dead less than a week. I sat with the three women who were left to me, in some crazy Swedish smorgasbord brunch-house, and enjoyed myself with little thin pancakes and scrambled eggs and syrup and buns. My feelings were layered and mixed. And where was Uncle Philip? He was the one among us all who had hoped to be united with my mother at the end. If ever I knew a man haunted by hankerings after a brother's wife, he was that man. Now the funeral was behind us, flowers already beginning to droop in the cool April sun. The mourners had all gone home, and there hadn't been that many of them anyway. A new phase, yes.

We chatted amiably, at one level of feeling highly pleased with ourselves. It had been Andrea's first funeral, in the sense in which we speak of somebody's first Holy Communion or first big dance. I deliberately select examples not now considered exciting. Young persons no longer get excited about a first dance or a first reception of the Eucharist. Such concerns are only to be understood through the prism of historical distancing. What child of the 1980s and 1990s attaches significance to a first anything? Experience swarms around us today; we hardly realize that that was our first rock concert, brassière, marriage, funeral. We get over our firsts quickly.

So we go home after the post-interment brunch and take up our dizzying round of other firsts, nothing too final. In a week we've forgotten the family plot and we never wonder whose funeral will be Andrea's second. She's still only a child; she's got her whole life ahead of her.

By the end of April I was coming out of the shocking veil of hilarity I'd cast over the events of that post-Easter week. Linnet. Dead. Isabelle Archambault Goderich. Dead. My two beloved women gone in the week following Easter. When I was a child I'd have noted that the Sunday after Easter was traditionally called Low Sunday because of its position in the liturgical calendar. After the shock of resurrection, what might follow? Nobody thinks about such things now. Low Sunday is a Sunday like all the others, low, middling, high, who cares? I was unable to put a name to my feelings about the events of that dreadful week for a long while afterwards, and if I can't name them, I can't feel them. How can you tell that what you're feeling is love if you can't call it love? If love had another name, anger, say, it wouldn't be love, you wouldn't be able to say what you were feeling. The words open the way for the feelings. I started to feel a bit less numb only when I could say, about Linnet, why these are the pangs of loss.

When my chest contracted and I almost sobbed, one night at the end of that awful April, I said to myself, that's a loss-pang, and then I knew what I was feeling. If I'd been keeping a journal I could have written in it: Tonight at one A.M. I felt a pang of loss. Not a hunger pang or a muscle spasm, but an honest-to-goodness pang of loss.

Layers of emotional tone began to roll away from the top of my mind. No, that's not right. They weren't layers, and they didn't lie on top of one another like geological strata. They were all wound around each other like a horribly tangled ball of string viewed from inside. I'd be thinking about Linnet and how much I'd loved her, and all the time I'd be remembering Edie in another corner of my mind. Awareness seems to be divisible into a large number of areas and functions. How could I go on loving Linnet, knowing that she was dead, that I would never hold her again, and simultaneously *suspect* Edie, or have feelings about her? There doesn't seem to be any way to describe this. Nothing else is like awareness, or consciousness. It is the one element in life that is incomparable. Figures of speech are useless in trying to talk about it. What are you doing when you're mourning two women who never met, whom you never saw in the same room, who didn't look like one another yet resembled each other in an infinitely obscure way? I found myself thinking like this as soon as the pangs of loss started up.

How does a pang of loss feel? The thing that surprised me

about them was that they were physical, like a birth contraction or a heavy reflex reaction towards possible wounding. A pang of loss hurts in your middle, just below the rib cage. It doubles you up and you start to sob; you might make some half-articulated noise. How can you think and feel about your dead mother, your dead lover and your estranged wife all at the same time? I had dreams about Ishy and Linnet and Edie, where they were all confused together. I might see Linnet wearing a dress that I was sure had belonged to Edie, though I'd never seen her in it. In this dream Linnet was in the dress but it was Edie's dress and at the same time it couldn't have been because it was in the style of 1980, not 1973. When I woke up in the middle of these images (I was undergoing strong feelings of sexual excitement in the dream), I found that my cheek was wet and salty and that I was physically aroused. My mother didn't appear explicitly in the dream, but I believe she was behind it, as a wash of presence, the emotional underpinning of the story.

In the story of this dream we were out west somewhere; it might have been Arizona. A hot sunlit place, flat and arid, with distant mountains just rising on the horizon. There were crevices in the floor of the desert around me. A young woman wearing a new dress stood against a wooden fence in a posture of invitation. There was the bony skull of a sizable dead animal at her feet, with shocking empty eye sockets. It was very warm. I began to struggle to wake up when I felt how excessively warm it was. I was aware in the dream that I must wake up at once. I tasted the salt at the corner of my mouth. Raising a hand to my face, I could feel wetness. I was reluctant to go back to sleep. Although the setting and properties of the dream narrative had been innocent enough, there had been something dreadful about its tone. I had many such dreams in the course of that month.

Then the spring deepened and deferred condolences drifted in, letters from London and Leeds and Sherman Oats, California. I heard from Tony first.

28 Heath Hurst Road
Hampstead, London

I don't know how to address you, Matt. Should I say "Dear Matthew" or some other harmless phrase? I've never written to a brother whose wife I've stolen. You see, I start off with a defensive gesture, but I have to write to you because after all she was my mother too. Very jumbled phrasing. I've been in touch with Amanda Louise and (you won't like this) with Andrea too. I talked to Andrea on the phone as soon as I heard, the day she died. She said you were coming back as soon as you could for the funeral and that I needn't bother to come over myself. She was very blunt. I expect she doesn't like me very well.

This is all preliminary throat-clearing. I have no idea what to say to you. Matt, you were always her favourite. She always thought more of you than she did of Amanda Louise or me. Amanda Louise never fought with her, but wasn't behindhand to marry a New Yorker and move there permanently.

Oh God, I don't know what Amanda Louise thought about Ishy. I've tried to write about mother-daughter antics now and then. I'm starting to get hints of a possible novel on the subject. Mothers and Daughters. An obvious title but not much used apparently, a basically comic approach. I see that good old Barbara Pym has just died, otherwise she might have had a go at it. Or perhaps one of the women around Virago.

I can feel myself hedging, dear brother. I know you've got me cast in the part of the wicked little brother, Claudius to your Hamlet the elder. Can'st move i'the earth so fast, old mole? I think Claudius was subject to pressures of which the two Hamlets knew nothing. Wretched queen, adieu! The most moving speech the old boy ever conceived. I don't know what to tell you, Matt, except that I'm sorry I ate the tires off your Dinky Toys.

I don't expect that we'll meet soon. Perhaps not at all. I'll be forty-seven next birthday, and thank God I've got lots of money, otherwise I'd have serious problems. I think my luck started to change when Linnet and I split up. I haven't had a big success for over a decade. Or did I run out of luck when I went to Toronto for Dad's funeral? Maybe that's why I stayed away this time. I like the <u>Mothers and Daughters</u> idea, it might bring back my luck. Makes me think of Edie's Mum, who had her good points too.

I'll just say it and shut up. I wish I'd been able to be there, but I would have had to confront you and Andrea and I'm not ready for that, maybe in a while. Meantime I know what you must be suffering, and I'm as sorry as can be. I know what else I should say, but should me no shoulds, for a while yet anyway. I really am most awfully sorry, Matt.

Take anything that's going, chum.

Big T.

Looking through this handwritten communication I thought, what a piece of denial, what a compendium of evasions and half-truths, which my brother had the temerity to point out as though I couldn't see them for myself. If Tony wasn't ready to see me or Andrea, whom after all he'd beguiled into following him to London, then I certainly wasn't ready to have anything to do with him. I took the letter in both hands as if to rip it across and dispose of it in the garbage. It was the very first message I'd had from Tony since he relieved me of my wife and children. But something stayed my hand. I knew that the froth of anger that impelled this reaction was a superficial one. There is superficial hatred as well as superficial affection. It isn't always the violent wicked motives that lurk in the depths. Perhaps anger, hate, envy are more often on the surface than we imagine.

Why shouldn't love be the repressed emotion? Hate shows up better than love and is a much more popular story in the papers. The more I thought about Tony's letter, which I've kept in my files for closer study, the more I smelt love. Ever since he ran off with Edie and the children I've been troubled more by my inability to hate them than by anything else. There's something missing in my nature. I can't stay angry for more than a few hours, and I can't manage to hate the people who have injured me. Perhaps what Tony and Edie did was a true injury, perhaps it was good fortune in disguise. I'd never have known Linnet, never had those feelings about her, if Edie hadn't gone off. Linnet was the most important person in my life. I loved Linnet.

Studying Tony's letter, I got the impression that he would be glad to effect a reconciliation among the three survivors. Linnet was his friend long before I knew her, just as Edie was married to me for twenty years before she defected to Tony and life in the U.K. Four of us in a neat little square like the basic plot of some awful artificial comedy. How can you love two people at the same time? How can I have felt what I did about Linnet — oh God — and simultaneously have been unable to forget Edie? How can two terribly strong attractions, for two totally different people, remain vivid, prominent in one's consciousness, swimming around inside each other for years, even after one has died and the other removed herself permanently, or so it seems, from one's life? All feelings are mixed feelings. The more I think about this, the more I see that I have no hope of straightening out the mess. Tony's letter of condolence — if that's what it was meant to be — was crammed with pleas for forgiveness, stories that failed to hang together, and mere writer's gestures. At the same time it exuded a strong wish for reconciliation and mutual forgiveness. This made me wonder whether I had done things that might deserve Tony's forgiveness. I was partly responsible for Linnet's accident. If I'd been in Venice on the night she went for her last walk, she certainly wouldn't have died in the way she did. I'd have been beside her, to protect her, help her out of the water, summon help. But I hadn't been there, and she had drowned. Would Tony be able to forget that? He had loved her first, and felt that she was the pure source of his luck.

Sometime afterwards I received the letter I'd been dreading.

32-A Beauchamp Place
Knightsbridge

Matt: how are you surviving? I know what you must be going through, and I don't want you to have to endure more pain than you can take. Are you all right? I feel such a little bitch writing to you. You don't want to hear from somebody like me, but it's a long time ago and I can't be silent about this. I know how you felt about Ishy, Matt. Do I ever know how you felt about her, gosh, did I ever! Your mother worked her way into more people's lives than I'd ever have believed possible. I used to believe that poor old May-Beth Codrington was the queen of the managing mothers, but when I think!

Now Matt, I realize I can't go on like this to you and I know you must be feeling like you'd been left for dead on some lonely coast. I know that. I had twenty years of you and your mother, and I remember that when you thought about women you thought of her first. Lots of men are like that. I can't complain about that, it would be like complaining about the rain and the wind. Every woman knows that she's competing with men's mothers, and every man has a mother, and some mothers are more mother than other people's mothers. That last expression makes sense. Read it again, Matt. All the time we were married, your mother came first with you. I don't mean that you

*were the conventional mama's boy like Adam Sinclair. I
mean that your idea of what a woman could do, how she
might think, they were all Ishy. I can't compete with that,
nobody can. The last summer we were together, you spent
your time in Toronto, taking care of your mother. So did
your uncle. What a strange bunch we are. You and Uncle
Philip and Tony, and even the great man himself, all
revolved around Isabelle like planets of different sizes
around a giant star. The great man went halfway around
the world to end his life running up the steps to the top of
the Great Wall of China. What a strange way to go!*

*I'm sorry to do this to you, Matt, but I'm in pain. I'm
in worse pain than you can possibly be, because I know
what your mother meant to you and I can feel it at a
distance. Do you know something, I can feel it in our boys,
can you believe it? When we heard that Ishy had died,
Anthony cried. I don't see how the impact can have been
transmitted to him, but I saw the tears start in his eyes
when I said "Your grandmother has died." He hardly knew
her, Matt, and yet he was sensing her through you. John
was different; he was bright-eyed, and started to ink in a
genealogical chart showing how our relations all worked
out. He knows more about my mother of course. He may
have them slightly mixed up. But his chart was bang on,
and I know he thinks about them. How does a physicist
experience and feel about death?*

*What about Andrea, Matt? When are you going
to send her back to me? A young woman needs her mother
beside her, surely you can see that? Andrea will be twenty-
one soon. She spent her late teens nursing your mother if
I understand matters rightly. This has to end somewhere.
Couldn't you arrange for her to visit us?*

*I'm all right. I'm painting every day, mostly semi-
abstract expressions of feeling about colour. I've never
been much of an expressionist though, the work may be*

radically bad. The public will judge; it always does. This is a first letter and is not meant to be well written. I do know what you're feeling and it doubles my pain. It hurts, doesn't it?

Edie

I don't know London intimately, I've only passed through it from time to time, but I do know that Knightsbridge and Hampstead aren't terribly close to each other. I pondered this. Edie had enclosed a short note from our son John, which pleased me and brought back bits of the middle-distant past, trips to Expo 67 and things like that.

Dear Daddy:

I'm so sorry to hear about grandmother. You must be grieving in a way that I can't imagine. I wish I could help you. When I heard about it, I tried to chart all the different ways that people in families are linked. It turned out to be a very peculiar set because of the way the links repeat themselves, with different values depending on the possible varieties of priority. I used coloured inks for the chart and the whole thing made an elegant design. Uncle Tony says that only a theoretical physicist could have drawn it up. Hawking probably thinks with similar images, at least it seems likely; the assignment of values is the key.

I think about you every day and wish that we could meet. I'm working extremely hard at the moment, special coaching for the entry examination. I believe that with very good luck on my side I may get a place at Cambridge, we shall see. Meanwhile don't take it amiss if I mention that I pray for you and for grandmother, and for young Emily Underwood.

With much love,
John Sleaford Goderich

Trying to imagine a theoretical physicist's understanding of love and loss made me dizzy; this note was the most moving I'd received until then. By the time it arrived, in early fall, I'd passed from acute bereavement into chronic grief. I still couldn't talk much about these matters to anybody except Andrea. We used to get phone calls from New York, often instigated by Emily regardless of expense, during which she would chatter to us about everything on earth except my mother. She seemed, for whatever reason, to be specially interested in news of John. I mentioned his remarks about family ties and she seemed to grasp at once what he was thinking about.

"That's fascinating. I can do math, you know. I wonder what his chart looks like. Did he use more than four colours? It must look like a circuitry diagram. I'll have to put Mark to work on this."

I think of her brother, Mark, as a baby. "Is he old enough to be into that sort of thing?"

"Uncle Matthew, he's a veteran hacker. Computer literacy is his thing. Our apartment is crammed with Mark's junk. He has teachers from school over here every night, playing with programming. My mother says that she thinks they're into something highly illegal but she can't tell what. None of Mark's teachers is over twenty-five."

"I can see how that might be," I admitted. I started to say something else, but Emily was off again, bounding along ahead of me miles down the track of the conversation. She's a remarkably quick thinker. She reminds me of my brother.

". . . and I remember John from when I was a very small girl. We met when my grandfather died."

It took me a moment to realize that she was talking about my father; of course he's her grandfather, but it isn't a close association in my mind. I'm so used to thinking of him as my father and nobody else's.

"I'd love to see John. Has he any plans to come over here? He sounds just my type."

"Everybody's your type," I said, and she giggled. She's a charming child. "Do you remember Anthony as well as John? I've just had a long letter, a very helpful letter, from him. You'd like him too."

"I like most people," said Emily. I could hear her mother begging her to get off the phone, but there's no holding Emily Underwood when she's in full flood.

"Certainly I know about Anthony," she said. "No, Mamma, I'm not finished. I'll give you money for the call out of my allowance."

I could hear Amanda Louise scoffing at this remark, the teenager's invariable response to parental harassment.

"When I was a little girl at the funeral in Toronto, I thought Anthony was a grownup, not like John at all, tall and serious. He's the one who's a literary critic, isn't he? I want to get to know him too. I love having cousins. In New York nobody has any, you'd think they were disgraceful or something. Andrea's about my favourite person alive."

At this point Amanda Louise wrenched the phone from her child's iron grasp and came on the line to say goodbye. "I'm not sure how she comes to be so gabby," she said. Emily protested in the background.

"She gets it from me," I said.

"God, I hope not. What would Tommy think?"

"Tommy's equal to anything. You're lucky to have him."

"I know we are," said my sister, then she hung up.

I thought about Emily's view of cousinship. Only fourteen. Lives in Manhattan in a midtown apartment. How could she have any notion of the possibilities of extended family life? Why should she feel solidarity with her cousins? I made a mental note to ask Andrea about this at some quiet moment. I remembered the quiet, gentle tone of Anthony's last letter to me. I wanted to see him, and I went and fished his letter out of my files. It was very long and detailed. I won't quote it at length because it says things about Linnet that hurt me. He seems to have loved Linnet almost the way that Tony and I loved her.

Two brothers and a son/nephew in love with the same women, Edie and Linnet, and all three numbed and aching, unable to accept such a loss. And all this layered over the loss of an adored mother or grandmother. As I thought of these whirling strands of connection I suddenly saw why John would picture them to himself as coloured circuit diagrams of breathtaking complexity. I'd never imagined these matters in this way before. I hope John makes better sense of them than I do. Thinking about how Anthony must have felt about Linnet — how my son felt about my only great love — made me feel dizzy. I refused to let my mind dwell on the exact nature of the relations between them, but I knew that they were terribly close. Aunt/nephew? Sister/brother?

Family ties are never — I say again never — emotionally innocent, though they may be free of criminal contact within the meaning of the law. In the 1980s quasi-incestuous family ties became a hot story, constantly on the front pages, revelatory of many forms of family life that never got talked about in public before.

Of course I loved my mother sexually. I see that now, though I could not have said so prior to 1980, and wouldn't want it proclaimed from the housetops at this moment. I loved Edie. I loved Linnet. And my brother was my ally, my twin, in each of these relationships. As a consequence, he and I can't live in the same hemisphere. If I were to visit Britain or Tony were to return to Canada, the sky would fall. So when I learned from Anthony's letter that he was thinking of coming to Canada to live, perhaps with a graduate degree and a career connected in some way with writing, I sensed a heavy new swell, an oceanic current of new experience. I cannot and will not compete with my elder son for the love of the dead Linnet or the living Edie. Why are these matters so infernally complex?

What if one member of the set — only one — has untypical sexual and emotional biases? Assume the presence of a dozen people knotted together in the way I'm describing: Tony, Anthony, John, me, Amanda Louise, Emily, Mark, Tommy Underwood, Uncle Philip, my father Andrew, Andrea, Linnet, Edie, Ishy. Makes thirteen. No, wait, fourteen, thank goodness. And then blend in the ineffable presence of Adam Sinclair and what do you get? I don't like to contemplate it, and yet the last letter of condolence that I got came from Adam in the week after Christmas 1980. Imagine the possibilities! Adam had known me closely since we were very young children, almost infants. He had ties to Amanda Louise and to Tony from day one of our history. He knew Linnet in London and Edie from Stratford, Ontario, days. He was known to Andrea in the flesh, and to Emily and Mark by his reputation and appearances in films and on TV. He and Uncle Philip were the irregular wandering moons or meteorites in the constellation. Between them they offered a catalogue of the varieties of erotic need. Mother troubles, father troubles, childlessness, fraternal envy, entrapment in fantasy. If I hadn't known that they were separate persons I'd have insisted that they were the same man. Damn it, for every practical purpose they *were* the same man, the man who gets locked into a prison of the emotions very early in life, probably in infancy. This may be the specific characteristic of the actor's inner nature, that harbouring of unactable wishes that issues in eternal role-playing.

Just at the turn of the year I had news from Adam, in his latest role of luxuriating Californian. This made me wonder whether orbiting meteors sometimes followed each other around. Could Uncle Philip have gone like Adam to California, or to some destination similar in imaginative structuring? I knew that Adam lived in a perpetual confusion of fantasy and live action. Uncle Philip must have lived in the same unalterable state. You can't give headroom to an unactable need for sixty years without mixing fantasy, desire, frustration and a good deal of anger into your actions. Uncle Philip must have gone like Adam to a California of feeling.

2174 Hidalgo Boulevard
Sherman Oaks, Calif.

Happy New Year, Matthew. Can I say that now? And see where I am. Would you believe it? I suppose you know that Sadie is queening it out here as the cult-object of millions. She's only just begun to appear on your home screen as the resident Dragon Lady of the Oklahoma oil industry, in that dire series — which I feel certain you have not watched — called simply and overwhelmingly, <u>Fate</u>. A good name for a nighttime serial. The thing is really only a tarted-up soap, not as well written by any manner of means as <u>Bed Sitters</u>, or <u>Out by Midnight</u> but the network execs are sold on it, absolutely raving, and Sadie Schatzenberg MacNamara is on her way to becoming the richest woman of our time. She owns a large piece of the action. <u>Fate</u> indeed! It is to laugh! Still and all the old girl's earned it, keeps her weight down, files for divorce every six months and then declines to proceed. Perhaps I shouldn't go on about that. <u>Fate</u> has made the woman independent for life and she was independent enough when she was poor. What is going to happen to all of us, Matt?

I was devastated to hear about your mother. I remember her from when we were toddlers. I used to play in your backyard and I suspect your mother thought I was a bad influence on you and your tiny wee brother. Perhaps not. When I search my memory I remember your mother vividly and behind her a looming female presence, could that have been your grandmother? Your Mamma had the sweetest nose, not small but delicately formed, and somehow I always imagined her as French. Not French-Canadian but French as in the movies. Not Michèle Morgan exactly, more Danielle Darrieux. That's it, she was a Darrieux type. I can offer no higher praise. Darrieux was a consummate professional and enjoyed a very long career. I met her once

at Cannes. If you remember her at all, you will know what
I felt about your mother. Cool, alert, beautifully rounded
features, charming forehead, knew how to be silent when
the situation called for it. Neat contrast with your quite
terrifying father.

You know I mean well, Matthew, don't you?

That MacNamara woman keeps angling with me to
make some sort of cameo appearance on her nighttime
soap. Can I have come to this? I might get trapped in a
serial that could run for years. Then I'd never get an
important lead again. I might become Adam West instead
of Adam Sinclair. Disaster!

I adored your mother, Matt, and I think of you both
all the time.

Be a good boy.

Adam

With Adam on the record the period of condolence and recovery wound down to its end. I wasn't quite leading an untroubled
emotional life but I stopped having confused dreams that made
me wake up with salt on my cheek. By New Year's 1981 Andrea
and I had shaken down into a contented life together. Sometimes I
felt as if I'd arrived in my final harbour like the last of the wooden-
hulled windjammers, some Conradian vessel tied up at wharf-
side in Timor or Surabaya and left to settle lower and lower as
the hold fills with leakage and the timbers rot from neglect.

The comparison alarmed me, and I sometimes begged Andrea
to warn me whenever our harbour threatened to become too
snug. I might be a bit leaky in the timbers below the waterline,
but careening for caulking should make the hull sound once
more; then I'd be fit to proceed to sea. Meanwhile I would
wait for a change of owners, new rigging, an unforeseeable
destination.

All this time, Uncle Philip remained invisible, though traces of
his movements were constant. Mail came in for him that had to

be looked after. Andrea and I divided the responsibility. Deposit of the steady flow of pension cheques, dividend cheques, windfalls from brokers. I found myself making frequent visits to the bank used by both Philip and myself. I believe that Andrea ran a small account there too. She seemed to know all the people in the branch, by appearance if not by name. Sometimes she looked after Uncle Philip's banking affairs; sometimes I did it.

Philip Bentinck Russell Goderich was clearly a valued and familiar customer of this particular branch. The staff never made any difficulties about accepting deposits from us on his behalf but were slow to reveal information about his affairs that might have been convenient for us. He made regular withdrawals from his accounts there. He had at least three accounts, one for payments currently due, another for savings, and one he seems to have used as a sinking fund not to be touched except for major investments or purchases. Statements for each account would turn up at month-ending. Andrea filed them in a set of shoeboxes or gift cartons, leaving them in Uncle Philip's room for him to examine should he choose to return. There was never any doubt in our minds that he intended to come back. He was a living presence to us, somebody who just happens to be away for a while. I never checked through his bank statements; that was none of my business. I did throw out his junk mail and I noticed that, financial matters apart, he received almost no first-class mail, personal letters or cards. He had left the city about two weeks before Ishy died, in obvious emotional distress.

"You remember that time just before I got back from London," said Andrea, "when Uncle Philip was taking her to the eye doctor's, and she went into cardiac arrest? He never got over that. When she reached the very last stage he wouldn't come to the nursing home. Once or twice he said things that showed what he was thinking. He could remember when Aunt Amanda was born, and the first family Christmas after that. In 1927, I think it was. He could go on about that for hours, just the two of us alone in the apartment and a March wind blowing down the ravine outside. It wasn't the most enjoyable time I've had. We both knew that there wasn't much further to go, and you were in Ottawa, or on your way back to Venice. It was hard to word that telegram." She was referring to the telegram I got in Venice, after I'd read the newspaper account of Linnet's accident. They were the two worst bits of news I've ever received, and they came two minutes apart.

"It must have been right around the first of April that he left. I came home from Saint Raphael's very late on a Monday night, the last day of March, cold blowy weather. When I came up past the subway station I saw that the apartment was completely dark. You never forget these events. The entrance hall was dark and cavernous. I wondered where Uncle Philip was. I let myself in. There wasn't a sound, just that long dark hall and a faint smell of dust and airlessness. Superior Home Services would be around next morning, I thought. Meanwhile the place smelled stale, not dirty, but closed up, silent, I wished you were with me."

This comment made me simultaneously happy and sorrowful. I can count on the fingers of one thumb the times I've heard Andrea admit to fright or depression, she's one courageous young woman. She shouldn't have to manage things like funerals by herself, with nobody to support her. I thought about Edie's letter and could recognize a certain justice in her claims. A woman at twenty needs her mother beside her to help her over the bumps and lumps. What should I do about this? Send her back to London? That couldn't be the solution.

"When I got the lights on in the living room I saw that it looked different somehow, something was missing. I went down the hall to my own room; it was just as usual. Then I put my head into Uncle Philip's room; it was plain that he'd gone away. That big old calfskin case of his was missing, and his shaving kit, and his little alarm clock. There was a note propped up against the lamp on his bedside table. I haven't kept it, but it said something like, 'Gone away to think things over, Andrea dear. Will be in touch shortly.' It was very brief, almost impolite, and that isn't like him."

"No," I admitted, "he's never inconsiderate. He must have been feeling awful. He'd known her for over fifty years. I know it did things to me, and I didn't have to watch." I'd left the watching to Andrea. The seldom-seen Matt Goderich.

"That's nine months ago, Daddy," she said.

"What do you think we ought to do? If he was in trouble or sick we'd have heard by now. I know he has plenty of money. What's he up to?"

She's such a wise person. She said, "If I know Uncle Philip he's somewhere, riding around on trains."

I saw at once that she'd picked up a lead. Uncle Philip had put in a full generation as an Express employee. He'd risen very slowly to a middle-management position in the claims department. I suppose any forwarding company has an ongoing comical series of claims against its service. Lost animals, damaged steamer-trunks. He used to bring home stories about unusual claims. There was one about a stuffed bear travelling from Union Station to Yarker. Where is Yarker? I should know that. A rail centre anyway. The bear had shoebutton eyes of semiprecious stones upon departure from Toronto. But when it got to Yarker it had been blinded: the gemstone eyes were missing. They might have fetched a hundred dollars in some equivocal jeweller's back room. The exchange of correspondence over that claim dragged on for many years, staying in Uncle Philip's files as he rose slowly through the ranks of management. The Express finally paid the claim in full and the insurer took the small loss.

Thirty years of this had earned Uncle Philip a comprehensive free-pass entitlement on our major railways. He used his pass recreationally, ordinarily within the boundaries of Ontario, sometimes venturing farther afield. I'd had communications from him, though not recently, from most provinces.

When Andrea mentioned it, I grasped at once that the most characteristic reaction my uncle would have to bereavement would be a retreat action, a disappearance into the coiling shelter offered by thousands of miles of northern Ontario railways. He'd spent much time in mid-northern Ontario in the late 1930s, usually acting in allied capacities, geologist, surveyor, camp manager, in some program of topographical survey. What we might now call land-use evaluation.

It is amazing to recall how mysterious, remote, underpopulated and poorly documented the Ontario northland seemed to us southerners, as late as the period of World War II. Now most of us are aware of the immense development that has gone on in the North, for good or ill. As far as I knew at that time, Uncle Philip's northern travels were amateurish and unadventuresome. As I remember observing at the time, "he never visited the Far North." I didn't have any idea where the Far North started. Fort Albany? Resolute Bay?

Andrea and I suspected that Uncle Philip was up there somewhere: Kenora, Sioux Lookout, Pickle Crow, moving around, keeping silent, making a good recovery.

One day in the early spring of the next year, 1981, almost a year to the day since my mother had died, I was sitting in the big living room of the Crescent Road apartment, thinking about nothing and riffling through the mail, when all at once I came upon that unmistakable object, a letter from a high-powered lawyer's office. The usual stiff expensive paper with an embossed address. The very firm in which my grandfather had found house room upon his arrival in Toronto in the late 1920s. It was appropriate that Uncle Philip and I should communicate with each other through the medium of these now very prestigious partners. My grandfather, I recalled, had never been offered a partnership, even though he had brought some Nova Scotian business connections to the firm, as well as one or two inconspicuous links of minor importance to the Liberal Party of Canada. These good folk had had prepared both the Squire's and Uncle Philip's wills. I seemed to remember that I was one of Uncle Philip's executors, in association with a member of the law firm in question. Until now I had given no thought to the administration of my uncle's property. He was alive and in good health so far as I knew. I tried to remember the exact date of his birth. I reckoned that 1912 was correct, after consulting some family reference sources. Just short of seventy. Perhaps some attention to estate matters was now seasonable. As I tore open the thick paper I hoped this wasn't an announcement of my uncle's death. Coming up to seventy, I thought, right on schedule.

It wasn't a death notice, though it concerned testament. It was a brief, rather curt announcement that I was no longer one of the two executors of the estate of Philip Bentinck Russell Goderich, "because of the infrequency of your reciprocal communications, and your consequent imperfect understanding of testamentary intention."

Beneath the ornamental linguistic surface, this letter was simple and, I guess, honest enough. All it said was that Uncle Philip did not expect to spend most of his time in Toronto, that he and I would no longer be in very close contact, and that he therefore wished to name another person as his executor, at the same time thanking me for having served in that capacity until the present. The new executor was rather surprisingly a woman, a Miss, or Ms., Jeanne Magill, also known as Jeannie Magill, resident in Toronto at an address in the Annex, well within walking distance of Crescent Road.

The letter gave as the reason for this change "her long and close association with your uncle." This, now, was a genuine surprise, even a rather disturbing development. Jeanne or Jeannie Magill, who could that be? Uncle Philip had no ties to any unmarried woman that I knew about. And what sort of an address was this? I looked at the letter again, a Huron Street address, probably two or three blocks north of Bloor Street. Weren't those mostly rooming-houses in poorish repair?

It sounded from the wording of the lawyers' letter that its writer didn't think too highly of such an address; there was something in the tone that conveyed mild disapproval. Still, there it was. I was freed of a considerable responsibility, thank goodness. As the man on the spot I'd been encumbered with heavy responsibilities for various bequests and inheritances. I was the principal administrator of my parents' estates, and was still lumbered with the management of most of Edie's property in Canada.

These matters involved sizable sums of money and the upkeep of some valuable property, particularly in Stoverville and Montreal. Our house at 620 Belmont Avenue in Westmount, although rented on a long-term lease to a highly acceptable tenant, still required regular maintenance. The business in Stoverville, a sensational money-maker, had to be overseen and reported on quarterly to Edie.

Perhaps I should have resented this but really I didn't because it gave me an occupation. I had only just managed to discharge my final responsibilities at Venice in 1980 by delegating my powers to junior arts officers on site. The Canadian pavilion got rave notices from the international art press in 1980 and I came in for much praise for its lively conception, but I was out of things by early April. At present I was unemployed, perhaps temporarily unemployable. I pondered this, waving the lawyers' communication in my hand. Maybe it was just as well that I had no pressing employment on my schedule. This affair of Uncle Philip and Jeanne or Jeannie Magill might require intervention. There might be some question of undue influence, though I certainly hoped not. Uncle Philip could have no reason to involve himself with an unknown and apparently unmarried woman. Magill, what Magill? I checked the phone book and there were plenty of McGills, a few MacGills, and yes, a number of Magills, including a J. Magill at the Huron Street address.

Obviously the thing to do was to go over there on some pleasant spring evening and take a look round. I decided to think this matter through very cagily. After more than a year the loss of Linnet and my mother was still affecting my judgment. I wasn't sure I could cope with new problems, like the disappearance from the scene of an uncle.

The lawyers' letter was signed by one of the very senior partners, Sylvain Ginestier, QC. A familiar name, turning up now and then in the *Globe and Mail* in some political context; might it be fund-raising? I suspected that my uncle's continuing executor was a bagman for one of the provincial political parties. I had no idea why my uncle might choose such an adviser. It might be pure coincidence. At the same time I decided not to indicate any unseemly curiosity. I wrote a polite acknowledgment of the letter and sent it off to Sylvain Ginestier, QC, or rather to his legal secretary, a very intelligent woman named Margot Châtellerault with whom I had dealt in the past. Uncle Philip's lawyers had once or twice acted for me in local matters. My own lawyers were Stogdale and Klein, of Stoverville. Wilfrid Stogdale, now the senior partner, took care of the legal affairs of Edie's family connection in her old home town, especially anything having to do with the management of *Codrington Hardware and Builders' Supplies. Since 1867.* I don't know how well Stogdale and Klein were doing out of the company's legal work; they were certainly doing a great job for us. The company's annual earnings continued to increase like the seed sown on good ground. Divorce from Edie seemed more and more unlikely, given my commitment to the management of the company and my dependence on the reasonable income I derived from it. I could have gone ahead with a divorce, I suppose, but Edie never intimated that she required one; she just went on living with Tony. Or did she? Knightsbridge, I remembered, was not Hampstead. If cohabitation was out, what could be the nature of their relationship?

Brothers' wives. Trouble! Uncle Philip and my brother Tony had this in common: a brother's wife had been the focal point of their emotional lives. The older man had never spoken his love; the younger had simply gone off with the girl. People of my generation might take husband-wife-brother links less seriously than our parents and grandparents had. I had an alarming, almost exhilarating, feeling that the incest barriers were crumbling. What one generation called child molestation might by the next be considered a legitimate sexual tie between father and daughter or brother and sister, uncle and niece. An act scorned and regarded with repulsion by all of humanity in 1960 might twenty-five years later be widely regarded as normal, desirable, even praiseworthy. Nobody outside my immediate family and two lawyers with a professional interest in the matter had ever mentioned to me the curious fact that my wife was living openly with my brother in another country, in another hemisphere, without even the legal formality of divorce. It's amazing what people can overlook or ignore. When our separation began in the summer of 1973, I felt pilloried, the object of public contempt. But nobody took the slightest notice of what had happened, family apart.

So your brother has your wife? So what else is new? And there goes *Hamlet*.

Now in 1981 and 1982 they're no longer cohabiting. This made me feel my neck. Suppose they were to part; where would that leave me? Would I want her back? Would I take her back? Perhaps it wasn't really a question of wanting or taking her back. Legally she'd never been away. We were husband and wife, and certain legal regulations as to the ownership of joint property applied. It was imperative that I find out something about Uncle Philip's new executor, Jeanne or Jeannie Magill of Huron Street. I hoped that she was a business associate and not a much younger woman friend, some questionable association.

I rang up Margot Châtellerault. I felt free to question her about the identity and lifestyle of this Jeannie Magill. I was starting to think of her as Jeannie. Somewhere at the back of my head lurked a previous reference to a Jeannie in my uncle's life; there couldn't be two of them.

"I can't tell you much about her; she's never been into the office," said Ms. Châtellerault. Margot has an enchanting telephone voice. I might almost qualify it as seductive if she wasn't a paralegal charged with heavy administrative duties. We've lunched together now and then, never with Sylvain Ginestier, QC, in attendance. Impressive in person, Margot comes across even more impressively on the phone.

"I have an idea that Ms. Magill comes and goes frequently. In and out of the city, if you follow me. Sometimes she replies to letters immediately, sometimes not for weeks or months. We've never met. In our work you have to do a lot by correspondence. It's better that way. More binding."

"The Squire used to urge my father never to put anything in writing, and then he went and wrote those books," I said. "I guess the equivalent today is never to say anything on or near a cellular phone."

Margot became brisk. "This is not a cellular connection and my line has been swept. Anyway, I've nothing confidential to communicate. Ms. Magill has replied to our letters in due form. She has a Toronto residence, for which I've given you the number. The nomination as executrix — to use a sexist term — is perfectly in order and you're off the hook. Let's have lunch together soon."

"Good idea," I said, and we shared sandwiches a few weeks afterwards, in the downstairs coffee shop of the Royal York, a place where you could comfortably remain unnoticed, now long since transformed into a noisy deli. Margot Châtellerault is keen on remaining unnoticed. Meanwhile, I thought I'd just stroll over to Huron Street to have a look-see. I might notice something, might even be able to identify Ms. Magill by sight, without committing myself to an encounter. I had no business with her, and no claim on her of any kind.

On the evening of May 20th, 1981, I sauntered off about six forty-five, across Yonge Street and through Ramsden Park. I crossed Davenport and walked south to Bernard, and that peaceful region inhabited, I remembered, by at least two of my former girlfriends. The sun was still shining in the tops of the trees as I came along Bernard and crossed St. George. Not far off there stood the enormous red-brick structure in which the Squire and Uncle Philip had shared an extensive flat at the end of the 1930s. My uncle's tenancy had been interrupted at that period by long absences and fits of willed obscurity.

A few steps brought me to Huron, and a sequence of sizable brick buildings, not exactly mansions but still massive and in certain ways intimidating. It amused me to think that these had been single-family dwellings as late as the 1930s. Then the war finished them off as such; one by one they had been turned into rooming-houses or groups of smallish apartments, three or four to a building. I had the street number written down on a slip of paper, which I consulted as I wandered quietly down Huron Street. I didn't want to look like some busybody checking on Ms. Magill without her knowledge. I might bump into her on the sidewalk or be spotted by her from a window. Her apartment was number two in the building, most likely a ground-floor location. I kept my eyes peeled.

Halfway down the block I came in sight of the house. As I'd expected, it was a sizable three-storey structure with a side door and a front entrance protected by a roomy portico. There were a few red sandstone carvings in evidence here and there. The building had been conceived with some style, perhaps in the 1890s.

I walked around a short, curving driveway and in under the portico. Some piles of newspapers lightly tied with brown twine lay beside the front steps; there was a well-filled green garbage bag a few yards off, beside a struggling shrub. The house's glory days were well behind it. I stood peaceably at the top of the steps and tried to see into the front hall. The large brass or copper house numbers typical of half-hearted renovations a decade earlier were loosely attached above and to the right of the door. One of those buildings that a succession of hopeful owners had tried to render profitable at no very great outlay. I swung the heavy door open and passed into the hall. There was an apartment-style row of mailboxes with the occupants' names in little slots above the individual boxes. One or two of these names appeared to be those of small business partnerships, which seemed inappropriate for this residential district. Two apartments were temporarily unoccupied. There were six of them in all, besides a dwelling without a number that was probably the building super's basement residence. His address card gave a German name.

There was a neatly handwritten label in the slot for apartment number two, bearing the name of J. Magill. The door to this unit was just past the mailboxes on the north side of the building; a small brass knocker hung on the door. It was formed in the image of some dwarf or elf or other folkloric being of the upper Rhine, with a grimacing little face and stocking cap. I heard nothing from inside the apartment, so I went outside to a narrow porch that ran around the front of the house. I edged along to a point where I had a view through the wide front window of J. Magill's apartment. I was now in a position to inspect this person's living room, clearly visible in the early evening light. The room was certainly being lived in, probably intermittently. It was very comfortably furnished, in a mixture of styles. The furnishings had evidently been well cared-for. There were no magazines or newspapers on the tables or shelves and no ashtrays in use, no plants or flowers that might have been watered recently. A trained investigator might have deduced much from this view. There were books in the bookshelves, neatly standing side by side in colourful dust jackets, but none lying open anywhere.

The place had certainly been at one time the permanent home of one or two people. It looked big enough to have two bedrooms as well as the spacious living room, and certainly a bathroom and kitchen located towards the rear of the building where there might also be a rear entrance. There was an open fireplace, without any clutter of ashes or firewood, the flue and chimney rising up the north side of the building. A hallway ran out of the room on the inner side of the house, but nothing much was to be seen in its shadowy recesses. On the wall facing me hung a painting or watercolour about three feet by two. As I stared at it I thought that it looked familiar. I think it was an early work by my wife, executed in the first years of our marriage, sometime in the mid-1950s.

It caused me surprisingly mixed feelings to see this work, in which turquoise, sea-green and indigo predominated, hanging in the living room of a total stranger. The picture, which I didn't recall clearly, was undeniably a link among several of us, Edie, me, the tenant and certainly Uncle Philip. I remembered that he had helped us out occasionally at that early stage of life by making purchases from Edie that she had not placed in a gallery, at rather low prices, fifty dollars, seventy-five dollars, which had nonetheless been extremely welcome at the time. I wondered if perhaps this apartment housed a modest collection of early Edie Codrington Goderiches. Could J. Magill have consented at some indefinite period to provide hanging space for other works by this artist? Might some of them be lurking in that shadowy hall or in invisible bedrooms?

"Can I help you at all?" said somebody behind me. I gave a jump and turned around. Here plainly stood the building super, a man in his late forties speaking Canadian English with a slight middle-European inflection. Somebody who had been in Canada for quite a long time, perhaps since the early 1960s. German, or perhaps Austrian, if the distinction still means anything. There was a liquid, flowing quality to this gentleman's speech that suggested the South.

"I was wondering whether Ms. Magill is still living at this address. I'm the friend of a friend of hers, a lawyer actually, who asked me to drop in on her if I happened to be passing. I live in the Annex too. Well, not actually in the Annex, more on the edge of it." I should have prepared a cover story. But my incoherence aroused no mistrust in the super's mind.

"Ah, ah, J. Magill, tenant in number two, yes. I have not seen her lately, but her lease is always attended to in good order, so the manager tells me. Her belongings are all in place. I have the master key for these locks, you understand, and she allows me to enter sometimes when she is not here, to see that everything is in order. Also I receive her mail when she is away and I dispose of the useless advertisements, the junk mail."

He seemed proud of his command of idiom.

"She has lived here for a long time, but not so regularly recently. She comes and goes, you know? I could not say when I saw her last. I expect she will be here one of these days. I had a telephone number for her but I have been unable to find it. I remember that it had the area code 705."

This didn't tell me a whole lot. I asked him to describe the woman and give an account of her movements.

"She was living here when I took over this property," he said. "That is fifteen years ago, in the middle 1960s, when I arrived in the city. I brought my family with me. Now the children are grown up and departed and I really do not need so much room, but what is there to do? We have a splendid home, and the work pays something additional."

I think my expression may have suggested indifference.

"But that is of no interest to you. You want to know about Madame Magill, or Miz Magill. I don't know whether she is Madame or Miz, and it is none of my affair. I call her Miz. She had the apartment number two that you can see through the windows when I first came here. I don't think she had been in Toronto long before that. She had her friend, *natürlich*, the man who helped her to furnish her place from auctions and second-hand shops."

"What sort of work did she do?"

"I could not say for certain, but I think she may have been a manageress or hostess in some restaurant or hotel or club. She was out at different hours but never early in the morning. I expect that she worked nearby. She has no car. We have no garage spaces here, and most of our tenants have no car. That means nothing. We are almost next to the subway station, is it not?"

Food service, I thought. Hostess, perhaps a superior barmaid, a club manager, hotel receptionist or assistant manager. "About how old?" I asked.

"Perhaps she seems younger than she is. I think now she would be past fifty, but not yet sixty. When I came here she seemed like a young woman, but that is fifteen years gone by. She would then have seemed less than forty."

"Could you describe her?"

"Oh, certainly. I know her very well. She has a dark complexion, but not like a Latin person, not Spanish or Italian or Romansch. There is a different colour to her skin, bronze or red. Copper-coloured. Long dark hair, almost black. She has plump cheeks, but is not an obese person. She stands very straight. She may seem taller than she is. She has a very individual way of walking."

He didn't seem to mean sexy or indecent. "What kind of walk?"

"Long-striding, like a person in the sports field, a runner or jumper."

"Still, in her fifties?"

"Oh, yes. I think Ms. Magill is in very good health. She is a fine-looking woman, strong and healthy, you know."

Then he seemed to think that he was talking too freely. I thought of asking about the lady's friend. Was there only one, or a series of them? But the question might frighten him.

The interesting image of the person he'd described rose vividly in my imagination as I walked home. A 705 area code. Lives in the city and is absent for extended periods. Must work in some business or trade or profession that allows for free-lancing, or intermittent stretches of leisure and employment. God knows, she could have been anything.

Had he described an actor or singer? I didn't think so. She was into her mid-fifties. Not many entertainers go on that long. The distinctive walk suggested conscious attention to her appearance, especially when in motion. Doesn't need to drive to work but might use the subway daily. Doesn't keep office hours. A handsome woman rather than a pretty one, copper-complexioned. Is most likely meeting the public in her work, and doesn't do whatever it is she does before midmorning. Television hostess? Physiotherapist?

When I got back home I got out the phone book and checked for code 705. It covers central Ontario north of the Toronto region and all the eastern half of Northern Ontario. Barrie, North Bay, Sudbury, Sault Ste. Marie and most places west of the Quebec border and east of the Lakehead. She could have sprung from anywhere. What I needed was a phone number to go with the area code.

Over the next months, my information began to coalesce into a picture of Ms. Jeanne Magill. I started, idly and with no specific purpose, to keep a little file of notes about her, like somebody in one of Raymond Chandler's books. Soon I had compiled a credible profile. A respectable person with an unimpaired reputation. Known to the police? I never checked this out. I had no idea whether the police are receptive to inquiries about innocent private citizens. I was not about to engage the services of a private agent. Does anybody ever actually hire a detective in real life? I would not have known what to say to a private eye. I once had a friend whose father was a private detective, and this friend never at any time suggested to me that his dad prowled Toronto in snap-brim fedora and trench coat, dodging bullets and leaping out of the way of speeding cars in parking garages. There was no way I could rent a cop, so to speak. I didn't feel justified in approaching the Missing Persons Bureau — if indeed Toronto boasts such an agency.

At the same time I could feel the fascination that attaches to researches of this kind. I could feel a growing awareness of the existence, somewhere in the immensities of Northern Ontario and perhaps in Toronto (I never went back to Huron Street to see if she was around), of some perfectly real woman of around fifty-five who was now acting as my uncle's executor and who had known him for at least fifteen years and maybe longer. The puzzle began to occupy my mind very fully. Andrea used to remonstrate with me about this; she thought that I was spending too much time thinking about the matter, and not enough actually doing something about it. But what could I do? The protracted disappearance of Uncle Philip and the mysterious comings and goings of Ms. Magill were not police concerns. There was no question of violence or foul play, no unexplained death. Uncle Philip seemed to be in contact with his bankers and lawyers and what he said to them was none of my business. He was nearly twenty years older than me, a member of an earlier generation. It wasn't my place to take his affairs in hand.

When I caught myself thinking along these lines, I would say to myself that Matthew Goderich, the seldom-seen, was up to his usual evasions and refusals to take responsibility. You can't alter the mental habits of a lifetime because somebody — even an adored daughter — instructs you to. I didn't mind being told what to do by Andrea; what I minded was having to do it. I let some months drift along as I thought over what I'd seen through Ms. Magill's windows, bits of furniture that I might have seen somewhere else. That painting or gouache, which I'd almost been able to identify specifically. It was almost certainly one of Edie's works from the mid-1950s. I grew sure that the male companion mentioned by the superintendent could only be my uncle.

There was no question of my uncle's having cohabited with this lady for more than fifteen years. I could document his movements since the late 1960s, especially after my father's death in 1970, during the family's tenancy of the apartment on Crescent Road. I could remember the precise date on which we had taken my mother to the nursing home where she was to spend her last years, November 15th, 1976. That was a date of some mini-importance in another context of Canadian life, and a benchmark for me as a means of putting a finger on Uncle Philip's movements.

It had been more than two years after that, as far as I could judge, that he began to absent himself from our apartment for longer or shorter periods. Days, then weeks at a time. That would have been towards the end of 1978 or early in 1979. Now, as we headed into 1982, it struck me that my uncle could perfectly well have been seeing Ms. Magill, as friend and counsellor, for many more years than I'd imagined.

On the evidence my uncle was about fifteen years older than his mysterious woman friend. She'd have been born somewhere around 1924 and was therefore only about six years older than me. That 705 area code suggested that he had met her some-where in Northern Ontario. Their acquaintance might go back to before the war, to the time when Philip Goderich was circulating around the northern part of the province in the service of the government. Pickle Crow, I thought. Sioux Lookout. Hearst. Gogama. I didn't know where Gogama was, but the name echoed in my ears. In my childhood it had acquired mytho-logical status as one of the known points on my uncle's obscure pathways. We don't pay enough attention to uncledom these days. I don't think we even use the word.

The relationship has often been represented in tragic drama. We think immediately of Creon, Claudius, Uncle Vanya, to instance three widely varying styles of uncledom. Had I ever, for example, seen my uncle as a potential rival for my mother's affections or erotic responses? I had now and then felt that my brother was sharply jealous of Uncle Philip. He, Big T., might even have evolved into the seducer of his brother's wife — my wife — by following a path first trodden in our family by our uncle. In family narrative, younger brothers are traditionally regarded with suspicion. Loose cannons. Dangerous rivals of the father or the elder brother in the eternal contest for possession of the affections of wives, mothers, sisters, daughters.

A horrid phrase began to trouble the back of my mind. *Transporting women for immoral purposes.* I knew that there were federal laws on the books in the United States, under the Mann Act, to deal with such trafficking. What did the Criminal Code of Canada have to say on the subject? I was in no position to ask anybody about this.

Jeannie, Jeanne? Long ago I'd known a Jeanne, my indomitable grandmother. Somebody in the fairly recent past had spoken to me about a Jeannie. I had been preoccupied with my mother's final illness and had paid little attention. I had thought of an aural pun on the name, equating it with "genie" and imagining this person rising like smoke from a little uncorked bottle. Now, thinking about the Mann Act, I reconceived these suggestions of turbaned magical figures in transparent flasks. Who had spoken to me about a Jeannie?

Somebody in a bank. Our bank. I suddenly remembered who it was, Patrizia Lemmo, a vivid dark woman, the senior assistant accountant at our branch. Ms. Lemmo, sure! As a Ms., she could legitimately be invited to lunch without prejudice, an invitation that I risked the next time I was in the bank, about March of 1982.

I was standing at the counter buying a bank draft in sterling when I noticed Ms. Lemmo smiling at me. Not exactly staring but the next thing to it. I returned the smile and gave that sort of nod that signals the wish to start a conversation. She moved towards the counter and stood there while a junior staff member prepared copies of my draft and took my signature.

"Can I talk to you?" Ms. Lemmo said.

This approach startled me. I wasn't sure that we had something to discuss. But when my draft was ready and I was sticking it into an envelope and licking the flap I moved along the counter out of the way of other customers and waited for further proposals from this arresting woman. I knew that her approach was not directed at me personally. It must have something to do with Uncle Philip.

"When do you go for lunch?" I said to her in a hushed undertone. I don't know why I pitched my voice so low. Canadians are always getting up to mischief in branch banks. I was acting like a character in a TV serial, perhaps the one starring Sadie MacNamara, was it called *Fate*? I thought that this was a marvellous title for such a series.

"I can go any time now," said Ms. Lemmo. It was just past noon, and I felt that I could cope with a sandwich. I waited while she picked up her coat and an interesting-looking satchel. I took her to the place on Yorkville where we'd lunched — or brunched — after my mother's funeral a couple of years earlier. There was no necessary connection between the two occasions. Coincidence is sometimes just what it seems.

When we were seated and chewing on outsized sandwiches (tuna for her, pastrami for me) we went into her reasons for speaking to me. The branch she worked in was flourishing under a new manager. Stuffy, close-mouthed old Mr. Schneller had been bumped sideways in a complete reorganization of staff in the Toronto district of the bank.

"You don't astonish me," I said. "I'm surprised they didn't simply get rid of him." The dislike and disapproval in my voice must have startled Ms. Lemmo. She gave me a sharp inquiring look. "I don't dislike many of my casual business acquaintances," I said, "but I did dislike this fellow Schneller. I used to ask him for important information and he wouldn't say a word. Some nonsense about confidentiality, when I had a perfect right to know where my uncle might be. Never got a peep out of him.

"I hate that play-it-close-to-the-vest attitude that minor bank officials adopt. Half-smart, and the wrong half at that! The banks are due for a rude shock one of these days. That man insulted me. He made me feel as though I were spying on Uncle Philip, when all I wanted to do was let him know that my mother was very sick. Talk about human sympathy! All the banks in this country have ever done for their customers is to hold on to their money at low interest rates and lend it back at high interest rates. They'd better wake up, and soon." My anger surprised and alarmed me. At my age I should be past spontaneous outbursts of that kind.

"I wouldn't want to be quoted on this," Ms. Lemmo said, "but I'm one hundred percent in your corner. We're beginning to change though. We've got rid of your friend Schneller."

"No friend of mine," I grumbled.

"And we've got a new branch manager, a woman. Have you

peeked into the manager's office lately? She's the very slender person about my age, shoulder-length brown hair. Smiles a lot."

"I know who you mean," I said, "but I didn't realize that she's now the manager. I thought she might be with the auditors or something. What's her name?"

"Irene Eagleson. She's one of the new breed." This was said with a trace of envy. Perhaps Ms. Lemmo had just missed out on a wave of promotion opportunities and would not rise higher in the organization. Perhaps she felt the need to conciliate her new boss.

"She has her eye on you," she said. "She asked me to talk to you."

I found this alarming. I like to think of myself as invisible. To go unnoticed in the crowd is one of my dearest wishes. I didn't want Irene Eagleson to know things about me before I knew things about her. There was nothing about me that could be of interest to strangers.

"What's to discuss?" I asked.

Ms. Lemmo seemed prepared to sit with me over coffee for as long as it took to get what she wanted from me. "It was two years ago by now," she said. "You were in the bank talking to Mr. Schneller about your uncle. I happened to be outside the manager's door, and I overheard some of your conversation quite accidentally. I spoke to you on your way out of the buildings. I believe I mentioned Jeannie."

"So it was you," I said. This cue opened up new avenues of investigation. "I've been trying for months to remember who mentioned Jeannie first. It was you, of course. You said something about Jeannie. And you said that you'd seen her around for years, am I right?"

"I may have said that. She's been coming into the branch for as long as I've been there. She's a close friend of your uncle's, and has been for at least twenty years, if I'm any judge. We all know her."

"You said something about her living in the Avenue Road–Bloor district."

"Did I give you an address?"

"No, but I've got it from another source, from my uncle's lawyers. I went over to see her but she wasn't in."

"She gets around," said Ms. Lemmo dryly. "She's had a series of positions."

I wondered if a satiric intention lurked behind this economy of phrase. "What exactly does she do?"

"Hotel and restaurant work. She's a hostess."

Aha, I thought. I got that bit right.

"She might help to organize a conference or a big banquet, or supervise service in a good middle-bracket restaurant. She's worked in this neighbourhood for years. You've probably passed her on the street."

I thought for a minute. "I suppose the bank wouldn't have a photo."

"No, we don't make our customers submit a picture, not yet anyway."

"It'll come to that," I said, "probably quite soon."

"We haven't mounted visual surveillance yet," said Ms. Lemmo soberly, "but we do keep track of the people who use our services. For instance, I think you have a key to your uncle's safety-deposit box, isn't that so?"

It looked as if the time had come for Ms. Lemmo to come to the point. "Is that what you wanted to see me about? I'd have been glad to discuss it with you on the bank's time."

"I've enjoyed the lunch," she said. "I'm not here on orders, but we'd be glad to recover that key if you have no further use for it. The box has been changed for a larger one. Could you drop the key in the mail to us? We won't bother sending you a reminder."

"I'll do better. I'll hand it to you right here. It's on my key ring with a lot of others I should get rid of. Let me take a look." Sure enough, it was snapped into one of the middle hooks on my ring, next to a brass key I'd been carrying around for decades, on the off-chance that someday I'd remember what it was for. The hook holding these keys was very tight and it was hard to extricate the bank's key. It was a flat object with the number of the box stamped on one side, and the words "Chubb Mosler and Taylor Canada" on the other. It was Patrizia who finally wrestled it off the hook. She then handed it to me.

"I thought you wanted it back."

"It would be better if you handed it to the manager. Would you mind coming back with me?"

"This all seems very mysterious."

"We want to open the box and transfer its contents to the new one. This seemed the easiest way to approach the matter."

I got a strong feeling that Ms. Lemmo was more than a senior assistant accountant. Might she be some sort of security agent, or troubleshooter? She escorted me back to the bank, rather than the other way around. At a crossing she took me tactfully by the elbow. We got back to the office at two-thirty and Ms. Eagleson was waiting for us. She smiled approvingly at my escort when we came in and dismissed her authoritatively. "Thanks, Pat, that'll be all right now."

"What's this all about?" I said. Do banks always make a fuss about closing a safety-deposit box? I had no idea. I'd never seen it done before. Ms. Eagleson stood up, shook hands with me and glanced at the key I was holding in my left hand. "You've got it there. Do you always carry it? I wish more people did that. You'd be amazed the trouble we have over lost keys and the problem of replacement."

"But surely the bank has access to duplicates."

"Of course."

"Then why the fuss about recovering this one, or any one?"

Before she answered me I got it. They were simply trying to spare me the embarrassment of being asked to turn in the key in favour of the new box holder. I'd been dealing with this branch for a long time, and might continue to bring them business; they didn't want to offend me. I handed the key to the manager perfectly willingly. I'd never had any reason to use it, and I'd been carrying it around for almost a decade.

"Now we'll go and empty the small box. I'd like you to witness this, if you don't mind, although it isn't strictly obligatory."

We went back into the range of safety-deposit boxes in that little room like a confessional, where you and the bank officer fumble with keys and sign entries of date and time in the record-book. Patrizia Lemmo suddenly reappeared and stood behind us as I slid the box out of its narrow slot in the numbered ranks. When I opened it I was amazed at its bulging lid and the mass of papers inside. I didn't particularly care to know what the box contained, but I couldn't help noticing stock certificates, bonds, insurance policies, and even some cash in bills of large denominations.

"Hmmmn," I said. "Cash!"

"Do you want to examine the contents?" asked Ms. Eagleson.

"No. I can see that the box is now empty, and that's really all I need to know."

I'd swear that Ms. Eagleson and Ms. Lemmo exchanged glances of relief. Yet why should they have had any such feeling? Were they simply defending a fellow-woman's rights and interests?

"Now we'll transfer these materials to the new box," said Ms. Eagleson. "You needn't bother to witness this unless you want to."

I couldn't make out what all the mystery was about. It wasn't as if Uncle Philip was an eccentric millionaire or somebody suspected of running a money laundry. He could have nothing to conceal. Did they want me to witness this transfer or not? I decided to hang around, more out of curiosity than anything, and I think their attitude was one of relieved approval. They opened a much larger box at the bottom of the rank. It might have been three times the size of the one we'd just rifled. Perhaps "rifled" isn't the correct word. The whole proceeding was carried out with scrupulous legality and openness.

They opened the big new box in front of me — and again I was obscurely aware that they wanted me there as an observer

— and I was amazed to see that it was already partly full of documents of one kind or another. I spotted the logo of an Alberta-based oil-exploration company that had recently received massive funding from the federal government. I spotted some bank stock too, and a couple of City of Detroit eight-percent municipal bonds. Not that I was prying. I just noticed them as the two bankers deposited the rest of the paper. They closed the big box and returned it to its place.

"There we go," Ms. Eagleson said with relief. "Held jointly by Philip Bentinck Russell Goderich . . . that's correct, isn't it?"

I nodded agreement.

". . . and Jeanne or Jeannie Three Streams Magill."

"What's that again?" I said.

"Jeanne, or Jeannie, Three Streams Magill."

This was the bit of information that I'd been waiting for so stupidly. Once it arrives, naturally, everything that you've been thinking and learning comes together in a significant pattern. Height, complexion, hair colour, manner of walking, place of origin, surprising name, this must be one of our native people.

"An Indian," I said unthinkingly, and then wished I could recall the phrase. This was 1982, after all, and the place of our native peoples in Canadian society had been much modified since the 1930s, when it seemed perfectly all right to refer to the Ojibway or Cree of Ontario as the Indians. "Our native peoples" was now the accepted description and, yes indeed, it contained in three terse words an enormous body of special theory and political decision.

When you used to speak of the Indians, the Ojibway from Georgina Island on Lake Simcoe, for example, you were thinking of odd-job men, almost unemployable, who might do a bit of guiding on the lake, or wash dishes in the misted-up kitchen at a summer camp. The young women might do some waitressing or bedmaking at the camp or in neighbouring restaurants; they wouldn't be very good at it, you thought. They would seldom rise to responsible positions because they hadn't the schooling and were undependable. Many — perhaps most — people thought that way about the Indians; it was the reflex unthinking prejudice characteristic of the times. There is nothing to be said for it.

My father, to the contrary, had continually on his lips the sentence, "These are good people who haven't been treated right." He encouraged Romola Kechechemaun to stay in school as long as she could and he enjoyed her father's companionship, and used to spend hours listening to him and his son Timmy, during long slack afternoons at the Lazy Bay Grill. Paternalist condescension, you say, as though nobody in the 1930s could be as free of racism as you are today. But I think my father was as free of racism as anybody I've ever known. And you will counter that this is in itself a prejudiced attitude, that race prejudice is found in us all, at all times.

All this went through my head as I reacted to the unexpected surname, Three Streams. Lovely, poetic, evocative, and certainly an Indian name. Was it prejudicial to say "an Indian name"? I had an uneasy feeling that it was. A name like any other? Three Streams, how elegant! What did Kechechemaun mean? I suspected that it was rendered in English as "Big Canoe." I wouldn't swear to that. I remembered that Romola Kechechemaun (Big Canoe?) and her husband, also named Kechechemaun, had come down from Georgina Island for my father's funeral in 1970. She had never made a career for herself away from the reservation and had married a close relative. Nothing wrong with that. I had an idea that women who married away from their extended family amongst "the Indians" were then subject to certain penalties and loss of status within their native group.

Anyway, Romola had remained close to home, and after our family left the Lake Simcoe district in 1939 I hadn't seen her for more than thirty years. She turned up unexpectedly in Mount Hope Cemetery at my father's graveside, visibly much troubled by his death. Like many of us around the family plot that morning she had shed quiet tears. Romola Kechechemaun. Why had our lives followed such divergent paths? The answers to that conundrum lay deep in our common past. Where the lively, intelligent, dominating Marianne Keogh would proceed to a university and finally rise to an exalted position in the federal civil service at the deputy-ministerial level, Romola married a first cousin and remained on the reservation. She had acquired a home-nursing qualification of some kind and did good work for the health and social services on Georgina Island, whereas Marianne Keogh had had a rather public career. Her M.A. in history from the University of Toronto qualified her eminently for a life in the public service, for a long time as my father's executive assistant, and then for a dizzying decade after his death in a series of highly visible appointments, first in the Secretary of State's office, then with the Commissioner of Official Languages, and now with the Human Rights Commissioner, at the top. These appointments had more or less been willed to her by my father, who seems to have called in a few IOUs posthumously.

Powerful friends were not behindhand to promote Marianne Keogh's interests and advancement. Now in 1982, just past sixty, she was rumoured to be about to accept the most senior appointment of all. I couldn't see how this might be possible; she had no consort, unless I was in some degree a kind of ethical consort, and I was a little too young to be Marianne Keogh's partner. She was more like a combination of mother and big sister to me.

Romola and Marianne had started out as summer waitresses at the Lazy Bay Grill in 1939, and look what had become of them. It was just within the limits of possibility that Marianne Keogh could be the next Governor-General, in which capacity she might later be found investing Romola Kechechemaun with the Order of Canada for her exemplary work in health service among the Ojibway. That seems to be the way life in Canada goes. Is it correct to say of Jeannie Three Streams that she's probably an Indian? Is the phrase inadmissible? One of our native peoples, an aboriginal, an Ojibway, one of the Dene?

"Certainly she's an Indian. Didn't you know that?" Ms. Eagleson said brusquely.

"No, I didn't. I don't believe I've ever seen her." I noticed that Ms. Eagleson didn't mind saying "an Indian." I wish I knew the most acceptable form. "Where is she now?" I asked.

"She's lived in different places in Northern Ontario but until recently she's been more or less a full-time Torontonian. I don't know where she was born. We've had letters from her from Hearst, from North Bay and I think from Sudbury. This is over a period of years, you understand. And now we've finished our business, Mr. Goderich, if you'll excuse me . . ." Ms. Eagleson had other fish to fry and didn't try to conceal it. Female or male, a banker is a banker, just as Ms. Thatcher was a woman a long way after she was prime minister.

I came out of the safety-deposit room into the light, saying goodbye to Patrizia Lemmo as I passed her.

"I don't need to know anything more about these papers, I'm no longer my uncle's executor, but I'll keep the information on file in case I can be helpful at any time." The only time I might be helpful, I thought as I left the bank, would be in the event of my uncle's illness or death, neither of which seemed imminent. What exactly could be the relationship between him and Jeannie Three Streams? I no longer thought of her as Ms. Magill. I found out much later that Magill was a surname of considerable historical importance in her native district, and that she'd been brought up by a Magill family as a foster child. Her name from birth was the mellifluous, poetic Three Streams. That's how I remember her.

Sometime after this meeting in the bank I got around to discussing the mysterious lady and her role in Uncle Philip's life with Andrea. She was not nearly as surprised as I had been to find that a woman not my mother had figured large in Uncle Philip's life.

"You're a terrible reactionary in these matters, do you know it?" she told me. "Did you expect him to go all these years without female companionship? He's not young, but he's a very nice man, what I'd call an attractive man."

"But Andrea, he's nearly twenty years older than I am."

"You're as old as you feel," she said sententiously, "or as young."

I could feel the conversation sliding towards comedy. I don't know why it is, but whenever I talk to Andrea I feel buoyant and optimistic. Is this because she has such a fine life ahead of her? I don't know anybody who doesn't feel better for an hour spent with my daughter. Sometimes I thought of asking her if she wouldn't perhaps like to go back to Britain to be with her mother, but I never got up the courage to put the question. If Edie wanted her back, let her raise the question herself. Andrea was beginning to form a network of links to Toronto life. Another five years and she'd be locked into the city, married perhaps, or living in some studio flat near Queen and Ossington. Her boyfriend at this time, Josh Greenwald, might be her partner for life. Who could predict how her life would develop? Did she need the constant advice and encouragement that a mother could supply?

I had the feeling that some great change was impending in our lives. Our term of occupancy of the Crescent Road apartment might be coming to its end. My father and mother had first leased the place in mid-1966, sixteen years before. It had sheltered various family members during that whole period. At the present time I was the lessee, having taken on the tenancy after my mother's death. I considered the place as the home of at least three people, me, Andrea and Uncle Philip, as well as an office for myself and the storehouse for a great many family archives. I could never persuade Amanda Louise to bunk in with us on her trips to Toronto. Almost always accompanied by Emily, she preferred the comfort and centrality of a small suite in the Park Plaza. She would often visit me in the apartment. I don't know that she ever passed a night there.

Emily treated the place as a haunted house and repository of family legends and ghosts.

And the apartment was the place Andrea had headed for

when she made her epic flight across the Atlantic in 1976, disguised as her own mother. When Andrea left, there would be little point in my staying on alone. And yet I suspected that the place might still have certain family uses. As I wandered around it at night, or dickered with Superior Home Services for a break on a renewal of contract, I had an obscure sense that family responsibilities of which nothing was yet known could still attract new persons and new actions to my unreasonably large dwelling.

For example, Andrea wanted Uncle Philip back. She was very fond of him, and missed him, and she was a tireless celebrant of family ties. She kept bringing Josh Greenwald to the apartment for meals, to see me, as she said. I didn't mind this too much. I liked Josh and considered him a very suitable companion for Andrea. He had something of her idealism and at the same time seemed to be able to earn money. Three of his architectural conceptions had won prizes in international competitions for architects under thirty, models of low-cost housing units, comprehensive school buildings for erection in northern climates, designs for inner-city storefront synagogues and churches. He didn't consider public places of worship anachronistic. He believed that they should be active centres for human traffic, in malls, subway systems, the emerging underground networks in places like Montreal, Toronto, Calgary. I remember telling him about the multi-faith chapel in the railway station in Florence, Santa Maria Novelle, and it made a big impression on him.

"I've always found it a refreshing place in which to pass a quiet fifteen minutes in meditation," I told him.

"I'd like to see that. I'll have to go there the next time I'm in Italy. There's more to religious life than preserving old churches on an antiquarian impulse, and more to architecture too. Why shouldn't a synagogue or a chapel be in the mall, and brand new?"

What an intelligent man, I told myself. I decided to encourage his friendship with Andrea. Josh was far too young to think of beginning practice on his own; he still had to complete his professional internship by working in the offices of a famous partnership as a draughtsman and as a builder of beautiful, highly ingenious sculptural models of his projects. He did fine delicate work in cardboard, Plasticine, masking tape, watercolour, producing dozens of maquettes of town centres, fast-food restaurants in shopping centres, model houses on stilts for construction over permafrost, with solar traps on their roofs and siding, designed to maximize the thermal yield of long sunny northern days. He was very interested in designing for northern sites, and in the allied social problems they implied. The first time he and Andrea and I shared a meal at the apartment we spent most of the night talking about garbage and waste disposal in tundra locations.

"You can't put a cellar, a basement apartment, any sort of excavation or footing, down into frozen bog. It's uneven, shifty, and if you heat it, then your building is footed in mush. So you site your building on stilts, as in early lake cultures. The air under the floor keeps the bog from softening. Of course the floor insulation has to be highly effective or you've got cold feet all the time."

"I hate cold feet," said Andrea, looking over Josh's shoulder at some of his sketches. They reminded me of Hokusai, elegant and formal, but immediately readable.

"You could mount a holding tank between the floor and the ground level. There's no reason why northern dwellers should be made subject to disease because they live in an exacting climate. If Canadians are going to develop the North in a planned and rational way, without harming the environment, we're going to have to solve the tough problems at the start: waste disposal, proper sanitation, adequate heating and lighting and proper transport, and medical services. I'm off to Yukon on my next vacation —"

"Now you hush, Josh. Daddy doesn't want to hear all that over a takeaway. Lighten up and pass the rice."

"No, really, Andrea, I'm fascinated," I said. "I think Josh is in on the ground floor of something. I've never been farther north than Sturgeon Falls and I'd like to know a lot more about it. Like mathematics and physics or computer science." I was only half trying to be polite. I really did feel interested; there's an immense space up there. Somewhere in it, a pair of dots on an enormous map, were Jeannie Three Streams and Philip Bentinck Russell Goderich. When I tried to guess their whereabouts they seemed like doomed survivors of the final Franklin expedition. I didn't know where to look. I know nothing about the North. Do geographers divide the huge space into Near North, Middle North, Far North? I suspected that I might find myself making use of the distinction before much more time had passed.

"Whitehorse," Josh said, his word half-covered by shushings from Andrea, who seemed to want to show him in a good light. There were signs of an intimate shared affection, perhaps the first signs of love. I thought, oh-oh, now it begins.

This acquaintance with Josh began towards the middle of 1982. I had heard about him for some time before this, about how brave he was, and how independent. How he worked all night in a busy restaurant in order to keep himself in school. How promising he was thought to be and how well the partners in his firm thought of him.

"When he won this last competition, they gave him a cash bonus of a thousand dollars."

"That's very encouraging," I said.

"He's using it to fly to Whitehorse on his holidays. The bonus will just about cover his airfare and the hotel."

"What kind of hotels would they have in Whitehorse? I imagine him staying with the Mounties or in the Hudson's Bay trading post."

"I don't think you've got the right idea, Daddy. Whitehorse isn't like that. It's no further north than the Orkneys. It's about sixty-one degrees north, hardly the great white frozen wasteland that you're thinking about. Josh has a whole file of travel posters."

"Travel folders from Whitehorse?" Vistas opened before me.

"The hotel is part of the Westmark chain with services through-out the Alaska/Yukon region." She was evidently quoting a travel brochure of some sort. "I don't suppose you'd consider . . ."

I got in ahead of her. "Paying your expenses to go along on the trip. Sure. Why not?" Like the rest of her generation, Andrea has been content to move from one ill-paid job, on or off contract, to another, without tying into the permanent location that leads to the gold watch and the pension after forty years. I highly approve of this; at the same time it often means that one's backlog of savings remains low. Andrea will inherit money at some point, probably a one-third share of our equity in *Codrington Hardware and Builders' Supplies. Since 1867.* This will in the end provide her with a considerable fortune. Already she received small quarterly payments from Stogdale and Klein, as did her brothers. But she never paid much attention to money matters, and generally had little to spare.

"When are you going, and how long will you be away?"

"Josh has two weeks in early July. Apparently it gets really hot in Whitehorse then."

I wondered what "really hot in Whitehorse" would be like. They made reservations at the Westmark by phone, something I'd never conceived possible, though any sensible person could have told me it had been possible for decades. Area code 403. I've even got the hotel's phone number around here somewhere on a sample bar of soap. 668-4700. Matt Goderich, storehouse of information. They flew off to Vancouver, where they changed planes and went on to Whitehorse. I'd envisaged a trek across tundra, ice-floe, glacier. Mukluks. Pemmican. At fifty-two I was a superbly ignorant man. They spent two weeks in Whitehorse and came back raving about the city and its services.

"You wouldn't believe the quality of the hotel coffee shop. It's as good as you'll find anywhere. We ate most of our meals there." This was Andrea on her first night back. "When you drive in from the airport you come down a big sweeping escarpment.

The airport is up above the city, and as you come down Two Mile Hill, the first thing you see is the golden arches."

"You're kidding!" My preconceptions about our great empty romantic northland were being shattered.

"It's just at the side of the mall," Andrea said.

"No, it isn't, Andy. It's more out towards Fourth Avenue. It faces Fourth Avenue."

They looked fondly at one another.

"If you say so," Andrea said, grinning. "But it's just this side of the mall as you drive into town."

"The mall," I said, in a disabused voice. "I suppose Colonel Sanders is just down the way?"

"Not that we noticed, but there's a very handy Dairy Queen on Second Avenue, quite near the Westmark. And banks. Lots of banks. The Commerce, Royal, Toronto-Dominion. Why would they have so many banks? They're all down near the hotel. And they've got the most magnificent territorial government buildings, and there's a legislative chamber — we peeked in while it was in session — with a very handsome interior. We were impressed."

"I couldn't believe the housing, and the lawns," Josh said. He was especially impressed with the septic tank systems that perhaps fed those green lawns, remarkable in a country with such a short growing season. "The whole time we were up there I kept comparing the daily temperatures with those in Toronto. It was warmer in Whitehorse than in Toronto every day."

"There's a very charming Catholic cathedral in Whitehorse," Andrea added. "Small and unpretentious, elegant and airy inside, said to be comfortable in deep winter."

"It's a major city," Josh said, "population of twenty thousand."

"As big as Stoverville," I said, and Andrea took me up on this immediately.

"Same number of people but it's much more spread out than Stoverville. It has a better airport and it has the legislature. Whitehorse receives much more federal government spending than Stoverville. The fact is, Whitehorse is the future, Daddy, and Stoverville is stuck in the past."

"That makes me feel my neck."

"Poor Papa, have I hurt its feelings?"

Josh grinned. "Isn't she awful?"

Poor Josh, I thought. If he only knew.

"It's when you get out of Whitehorse that the problems start," he said. "I'm almost sure that raw sewage is going into the river upstream and down. The person who solves the problem of garbage and waste disposal will hold the future of the northland in his hands."

"Or her hands," Andrea said. They spent the rest of the evening discussing the piles of garbage bags, frozen solid, that clot the estuaries and shoreline flats of so many of our great northern rivers. They reminded me of a couple of characters in some serious-minded novel by Margaret Drabble.

"The problem of the disposal of garbage and human waste is to the North what industrial pollution is to Buffalo and the whole Love Canal syndrome in the Great Lakes region," Andrea said.

It was clear that she was repeating something Josh had said to her. Perhaps this is the true post-modernism, I thought. When I was young I looked instinctively towards the cave paintings of Lascaux and elsewhere for instruction in the meaning of human culture. The post-modernist, despairing of the past, looks to the empty North and to space exploration and sees his or her chance to escape from the past and the errors of humankind into a boundless and so far meaningless future, wholly uninscribed, without privilege. Was the Arctic truly a land without a history?

Whitehorse wasn't the Arctic, and on Andrea and Josh's showing was simply an extension of the vast North American parking lot. You could drive from Edmonton to Whitehorse on the Alaska Highway if you didn't care about the undercoating of your vehicle; you could even cross to the Mackenzie Delta via the Dempster highway. Farther north than that you would require air transport to the regions where the edges of the great parking lot have not appeared. Could Uncle Philip have travelled past the edge of asphalt?

It's really remarkable how often some apparently trivial incident can be predictive of dramatic new developments in one's life. I had thought little about Josh and Andrea's Yukon junket, supposing that a single visit might exhaust their interest in the place. I should have known better. When they came back, their excited accounts of the sheer accessibility and livability of Yukon should have warned me that some new aspect of my life was about to descend on me from nor'ard, though not from as far up as Whitehorse. It intruded in my life about three months after Andrea and Josh came back south. I received a series of telephone appeals — messages left on the answering service in an unfamiliar voice, asking me to return the call to a 705 number. I found this request on the record on three evenings about a week apart in mid-October 1982. I wasn't in a hurry to reply to the recorded appeal because I had a pretty good idea who the speaker was, even though I'd never heard her voice before.

You can always tell, can't you, when somebody wants something. There is just that little nuance of hesitation, of slowness to utter, that makes it clear to you that a favour is about to be asked. I guess we were into November before contact was finally established. And what a contact! I knew it, I reflected. I just knew that it meant trouble. Uncle Philip was the member of the family around whom trouble just naturally clustered. Early baldness, for example. And not even what you or I would think of as drastic baldness. Just an idiosyncratic thinning along the parting and at the crown, implying long discussions of the possibility of new hair growth, various restorative practices. This was already going on when he was in his early thirties. The last time I'd seen him, more than two years earlier, Uncle Philip had retained as much cranial hair as any man his age had any right to expect, and an agreeable mouse-gray it was too, clean and sometimes almost wavy.

This time it wasn't hair loss that was at issue, or unrealizable attraction to a brother's wife. This time it was marriage! He'd gone and gotten married. At very nearly seventy-one, his first marriage. To one of our native peoples, and joy and happiness to them both. To Jeannie Three Streams! How could this relationship, which I only now understood to be serious and permanent, have grown up, matured, deepened, been consummated, over a period of at least twenty years, without any of the family even suspecting its existence?

Patrizia Lemmo had known about it. Margot Châtellerault must have known about it, and Sylvain Ginestier, QC, and perhaps old Schneller, and certainly Irene Eagleson. Yet none of the dozen members of our little family compact had guessed it. Had we created a myth of Uncle Philip the adorer of Isabelle, the incestuous younger brother figure, and imposed it on the poor man so thoroughly that in the end we simply couldn't see him? Yes. That's exactly what we'd done. I blame myself. And the others too, of course.

JEANNE THREE STREAMS' STORY

I first met your uncle Phil at Moose River in the summer of 1939, when he was twenty-seven, and still very boyish looking. I was fifteen, feeling very sorry for myself. My mother was nothing more than an all-purpose house servant for the Magill family, without any contact with the band authorities at the Moose Factory reserve on the island in the mouth of the river. I never knew who my father was, or where he disappeared to. There was the name, Three Streams, and the things my mother remembered and wouldn't tell me about. Henry Three Streams was my father's name. I don't think I ever saw him. My mother moved up the river after he left or disappeared or was drowned. She was an energetic creature, poor soul, and even with me dragging behind her, holding her back by the wide folds of her skirts, she found her way to the mine site sometime in the 1920s. Mrs. Magill, the manager's wife, was in poor health. I think she'd had a bad pregnancy and a miscarriage, and never recovered her good spirits and her vitality. Mr. Magill, the manager, hired my mother as a house servant who could do a little bit of almost everything, get meals, wash, clean the manager's quarters, nurse his poor wife, and do anything else that had to be done. For all that she got room and maintenance for herself and me and a few dollars once a month. I lived near the mine workings for the next twelve years. I was there, just a child, when the accident happened down the mine. I think I was ten or eleven years old when it occurred. There was a long rescue attempt, and I think two men were saved from the disaster, but I can't say for sure. There were troops of strangers around the mine for the whole of that time; they frightened me and I learned to distrust people from down south; they made such a fuss about everything, and they made Mrs. Magill cry. Every time they came over to the office or to the family's quarters they made a disturbance. Some of them asked to sleep on the floors in the front rooms, or even in the dining room. They were terrible people. I remember that well. They speeded up Mrs. Magill's death. The mine was shut. Most of the people went away, and all the children. There had never been more than eight or ten children in the place, and nothing like a real school. A one-room shack that was so cold you couldn't learn anything in it. I was nine or ten before I really learned to read and write and do the times tables.

Mrs. Magill stayed in Moose River because she had no idea where to go. She was a sick woman; she'd had a terrible shock. My mother was there to help her, and after a while they both came to depend on me for a strong back and a willing pair of legs. It was then that the few people who passed through began to call me Jeanne Magill. I was never adopted by the family; for many years I wasn't sure what my right name was. I'm Cree on both sides, and I've proved out my parentage with the band authorities. I've earned full statute rights and now I know where I belong and where I came from. But when I was a small girl I just called myself Jeannie Magill because everybody else did.

Phil must have thought of me first as little Miss Magill. I was never really that little. At fifteen I looked almost grown up, within an inch or two of my full height. I first saw him at a distance sometime about the middle of June 1939, when a Lands and Forests crew came through to make records about the regional topography. They were supposed to be trying to find the best way to manage development of the district. I think they made some kind of estimate of regional resources and population movement, in co-operation with the Ministry of Mines and the federal Department of Transport. The railway was always in need of additional financing for track maintenance. Nowadays that's taken for granted but it had to be fought over in the 1930s.

So anyway there was Phil, looking like nothing on earth, like a cowboy or some wild man from Australia. I thought he'd dressed himself up to be in a movie. He had on a wide-brimmed canvas hat with the brim turned down all the way around, I suppose to protect against sunburn. A red flannel plaid shirt, much too heavy for late June, trousers that were stained all different colours, and boots that looked two sizes too big. He always wore two pairs of socks with those boots.

I thought he was about the funniest thing I'd ever seen and I started to laugh when I saw how he moved. He was the picture of somebody who couldn't keep his mind on what he was doing. He had hold of a little hammer, and he was chipping away at a chunk of light-coloured stone he'd picked up down by the water. He didn't seem very sure of what he was supposed to be doing. I think he heard me giggling, which was very rude of me, because he dropped his bit of rock and came up to me. He seemed to me like a person who had grown up but didn't feel sure of it. I could see right away that he was unhappy about something. He asked me what I was doing there, and whether I liked it, and had I been able to go to school much. He was pleased when I told him that I'd be serving dinner that night. They were to eat in the manager's quarters. Sure enough that night I waited on him and the four other men in the survey party. I did my best, and didn't drop anything, but I had to run into the kitchen twice, to find

things I'd forgotten to lay on the table. I don't know what he can
have thought of me.

But we must have made a strong impression on each other
because he came in and helped with the dishes after supper, and
took me for a walk along the riverside afterwards. He was lonely
and acted like he'd been driven away from his home. He told me
that he'd had a disagreement with his father, who had a new
girlfriend. Phil seemed to think that his father was too old to be
bothered with new girlfriends. I think his father — he always
called him the Squire — was getting close to seventy. Like father,
like son. Phil is seventy, but I'm not a new girlfriend. I've known
him and loved him for over forty years. I think I've got some rights.

I told him all about myself, that my father was gone away, that
I was just a servant and not really a Magill. This didn't seem
to bother him, but it was a long time before he advised me to
change my name back to what it really should have been. He
was my big adventure. He might take me away from the mine
and the river. Maybe he would be my friend, somebody I could
go to for help when I went down south. I followed him downriver when the party moved on, to Moosonee, where I got a job
as a dishwasher and cleaning girl at the restaurant. My mother
let me go. By this time there was nothing left for us at Moose
River; going down to Moosonee was like moving to the big city.
I hoped that maybe Phil would stay there for a while, but by
autumn his work was finished, and he decided to go south to
Kapuskasing or Cochrane, to look for a wartime job. He didn't
seem ready to go back to Toronto, and as it was the first year of
the war there were jobs opening up all over the place. Naturally
he couldn't take me with him. That would have been illegal and
dangerous, and I don't think he loved me then, but he promised
to write to me, which he did, very regularly and honourably. He
always began, "Dear Jeannie" and ended "with love."

But you know how it is in these matters. Not being together
makes all the difference, and besides that, he'd never seen me
after I grew up. I was just about sixteen when he went south

permanently and I was almost full-grown, but I wasn't what you'd call a grownup. I was a child in a young woman's body. I don't want people to feel sorry for me. Phil never made me any promises, and he never fooled around with me. He was a decent modest man. I never had any complaints about that. If anything he made life hard by spoiling other men for me. There was nobody like him in Moosonee or Moose Factory. There were the band councilmen, and the managers of the Bay, and railway officials and priests and police officers. And there were guides with boats of their own, and fishermen and trappers. And in the district along the shore three thousand Cree, a people without many prospects.

After a while I got a letter from Phil to say that he was going back to Toronto; he was sure he could get a permanent job there, something he could stick to, and perhaps I could join him later. He seemed to think that I might eventually join him in Toronto. I don't think he was looking further forward than that. He had heart trouble, if you remember, and it kept him out of action while his brother was doing the spy work, or whatever it was that made him famous. Here was Phil, a clerk in the claims department, while his brother was heading for the big prize. Quite a difference!

Then after another interval he wrote to me that he'd moved in with his brother's family and that he was trying to keep an eye on his sister-in-law and her kids. He talked a lot about the kids, but less about their mother. This was just before the end of the war; there was the problem of keeping them in school without too much money around. I believe that quite a good part of Phil's pay went into helping his brother's family, especially at the time when the war was just over, and his brother had to stay in I think it was Switzerland.

When one person in a family makes a big name for himself, somebody else in the family has to pay for it. Phil talked in some of his letters about his niece, Amanda, wasn't it? He was very fond of her and proud of her record in school and college. Then there was the middle child, Matthew or Matt, and Phil never said much about him. I suspect they were a lot alike. The third child, a little boy called Tony, was a bit of a scamp. Phil may have disapproved of him somewhat, but he always mentioned how bright he was. Phil found himself helping to put the children through school, and he couldn't do much to help me. He wrote once or twice a year to different places that I worked in up north. He often suggested things for me to read. He sent me a free copy of his brother's book about the Jews and the Holocaust; I could not finish it, too much like being Cree. You never know when some authority is going to take a dislike to you and then you find that you don't have the same rights as everybody else. I understand the book pretty well, and it certainly made the name of Goderich famous. I don't know whether that was so good for Phil; he never seemed ready or able to connect himself with people.

Then I read in the papers that his brother had won this big award. I was sure that when the money came into the family Phil could go out on his own. He'd been in the same job for five or six years by then, perhaps longer. People don't seem to understand that he would have been good at anything he took on, without making a big show of himself. When I finally caught up with him a long time afterwards I found that he was very respected at the Express. He was very good at tracing lost shipments; he knew every forwarding agent and stationmaster in Canada by name. I don't think the Goderiches ever understood that. Some of us get to win the big prizes and some of us do other things, and do them just as well. Phil was an extraordinary man, just as much as his brother. He was generous and kind and loyal and faithful. I guess I loved him all right, even when I could see what everybody could see. He couldn't tear himself away from the family, especially from his brother's wife.

The last letters I had from him at that time — they came about eight months apart — told me that his father had died. He used to call him the Squire; he was kind of under the Squire's thumb. They lived together in Toronto at different times until the old man died at a great age. I thought then that I might go down to the city and look Phil up to see if he really remembered me, but something held me back. I saw that even his father's death wouldn't make him independent. His brother got into Parliament, and used to leave his wife in Toronto all week while he was up in Ottawa. Phil used to have to be company for his sister-in-law, Isabelle. He used to visit her in the evenings and keep her occupied. It was about this time that his letters stopped coming. Before that, I always knew pretty well how he was and what he was doing. Now he seemed to close in on himself and the letters stopped. That was in the early 1950s. And though we'd only been together for a very short time years before I'd always believed that we'd get in touch again.

He might decide to come back north or I'd go down there. If you can read well and put your thoughts down in writing you've got the necessary equipment to go on with your life. I never had any trouble finding work. I decided early on to make a point of keeping myself very clean and fresh and smart. I kept up with my reading. I never lived in a town where I didn't join the public library. Hearst, Cochrane, Kapuskasing, North Bay. They all have excellent libraries and don't cost much to join. Reading has made me able to talk. I don't make many mistakes in my speech any more, and I've had many jobs where I had to meet the public.

I do hotel and restaurant work, and small convention management, and I've learned the business from the bottom up. I've worked in bars and taverns, but not lately. I never thought that working in a bar or a tavern was degrading, or not up to my standards. The people who go there are entitled to good service, the same as anybody. I've learned how to handle customers from tavern work, but gradually I worked myself up. Lounge hostess. I've been the hostess in some very high quality rooms. I've worked on the reception desk in several major hotels and I've remembered what I've seen and learnt. I'm a self-taught professional. Phil and I, we've both made something of our lives from small beginnings. I'm proud of this, but when I was learning the business I never asked him for help, and I never tried to embarrass him or make him feel that I had a claim on him. I don't like to use the word, and it's really nobody's business, but I never felt that I'd been his lover. I didn't owe him anything and I never made any claims on him but I always remembered him. During the dead years when I was moving from place to place I used to send off letters to the last address I had for him, but I didn't get any answers. I don't know exactly why; we were still young enough to get together.

I had something like a beat, a home turf, that I covered regularly. I never worked west of Hearst, or east of Kirkland Lake. I never got into Québec province. I was afraid to move south of, say, Cobalt. I felt I'd get lost down south. Hearst, Kapuskasing, Cochrane, Iroquois Falls, Timmins, Kirkland Lake, that was my beat. I started off waitressing for a few months in Fraserdale and from there I moved to the Country Kitchen outside of Cochrane. I was there two years, doing everything you can think of, bedmaking, dishwashing, laundering, night clerk and eventually assistant manager. I never got the job title. I mean nobody ever actually called me the assistant manager but I did everything an assistant manager might do. Ordering. Preparing bills. Taught myself how to touch-type, using a manual somebody left in one of the rooms. I was my own trainee.

After my first stint in the Cochrane district I moved south as far as Timmins. Well, really South Porcupine. I was there, and then in downtown Timmins, for close to eight years in the mid-1950s, watching the town grow up. I was the principal hostess in the dining room of the golf club. People said that we had the best dining service in town. I think so myself. We had the waitresses in smart blue uniforms, and we must have had the cleanest kitchen in the northland. I'm a stickler for that; you never know when the health inspectors are going to turn up, and you want to have the reputation of being ready for them at any time. After that I worked at a big new hotel-motel complex on Riverside Drive right beside the Mattagami. I liked that because the river runs all the way down north to the bay. It joins Ground-hog River and the Kapuskasing, and a couple of others, and then they all turn into the Moose River and there you are, back home at tidewater. I always liked to look out from the cigar counter and cash desk and see the river flowing past me to the north. I used to think that when the rivers flowed south they were headed for a country of sickness and death. People don't understand how far south the watershed is. In places it isn't much more than sixty-five miles north of Georgian Bay or Lake Superior. On the other side of the main-line tracks, all the rivers flow north to the Arctic. People in Toronto and Ottawa don't seem to know that. It's amazing.

It took me close to twenty years to work up the courage to cross the height of land and go south. I still don't like to see rivers flowing the wrong way; it makes me lose contact with the people and things that are important to me. It was in the early 1960s that I decided to move south. I knew that Phil was alive and well. I used to read about his brother in the newspapers, two to three times a year. I was sure that if anything happened to Phil the papers would write it up, because of his brother. So when I went to Toronto in 1964, no, in early 1965, I thought that I might see Phil on the street sometime, and I wondered if we'd recognize each other after twenty-five years.

Well now, Toronto is a big place, and you might think I'd have no chance to meet him on the street, but I've been around enough smaller places to know that big or small they're just collections of little neighbourhoods. Probably Phil would have a neighbourhood of his own, that he wouldn't stray from very often. I recalled a few addresses he'd used in the old letters, like St. George Street. It certainly wasn't hard to find. I figured he might live somewhere around there. I didn't exactly go to the city to look for him. I thought that I could get hotel and restaurant work there, and I had big plans. I wanted to show everybody that an uneducated Cree woman from the reservation could make a success of her life in Toronto. I never tried to pass myself off as anything but what I am, and I didn't meet with much prejudice in Toronto. Nobody ever refused to rent me a room because my skin is dark and my hair straight black. I called myself Jeanne Magill at first.

By this time I was forty, and I'd been around the block a few times. I knew enough about food service and hotel/motel operation to do a good job in many different situations, and I only had myself to look after, so I could save money. I'd had boyfriends. I'm no nun. But I never got pregnant and I had no dependents. I had good recommendations and good jobs, and I minded my own business and spent my money on good clothes and my appearance. And I read a lot of newspapers and books. I watched and listened and learned how people behaved in a great modern city. It was different from Moose River and Timmins in many ways but not in the most important ways; people are much the same anywhere. I felt sure, knowing what I did, that some time or other I'd meet up with Phil. I didn't try to track him down, but I did look him up in the phone book. I saw that he, and his brother and sister-in-law, shared an address in the mid-town area. I did two or three things that maybe I shouldn't have done. I took jobs that located me in the Bay and Avenue Road district. I usually roomed near there. I might walk up Yonge Street in the evening, as far as Crescent Road or even the Summerhill subway stop. At least twice I dialled their phone number and when somebody answered I found that I couldn't speak up. It was a woman's voice. I guessed it was his sister-in-law's voice, and if his brother was in Ottawa, sitting in Parliament, then Phil was sharing living space with the wife. I didn't know what to think about that, but I didn't believe it was any too healthy.

At that time Phil was in his early fifties, not old, but not a boy. I wondered what kind of a life he'd had, was he all right, happy, working? And then I met him!

I knew I would, sooner or later. It was in the summer of 1966, and he was walking along Bloor Street, just about three on the

Friday afternoon, July 8th. I recall the date so well; he was on his vacation. I believe he was entitled to three weeks by then, and with the July 1st holiday tacked on at the beginning he got most of July off. I remember that the first thing he told me was that he had plenty of vacation time, and accrued sick leave, coming to him, so that we could be together often. I think he'd just come out of his bank because he was sliding a passbook into his pocket. I saw him coming before he recognized me. I thought I was going to faint. Twenty-five years! He was stouter and he had less hair, but he was the same chap who had befriended an ignorant little camp girl.

"Phil," I said as we met, "do you know me?"

He stood there and squinted; the sun was in his eyes. I walked around him slowly, and he turned to see me better. The sidewalk was crowded. We had to shift from side to side to be able to stand still. It was noisy. I could hear pigeons.

"It's me. Do you recognize me?"

By circling around him I'd clarified his vision and blurred my own; now I was facing west into the afternoon light. It was hard to read his face. I put out my hands, my arms, like a blind woman and reached for him. I felt my hands grasped, pulled together in his so that our four hands were together in a single clutch. I was eased sideways to my right, through passing pedestrian traffic towards a storefront and a shady entry. Now I could see his face. He wasn't old. That was the nicest thing; he wasn't all lined and blotched. Something had preserved him for me. There would be time for us.

"I'd have known you anywhere, anytime, for the last twenty-five years."

I wanted to say his name over and over. "Oh, Phil, Phil."

Twenty-five years melted away in a moment, I thought. If I look down I'll be wearing a flannel shirt and boots with fish-scales on them. But that was only an illusion.

"I'm on summer holidays," he said stupidly, as though he'd been hit on the head. "I've got plenty of time. Where can we go to talk?"

"I've got a room on Berryman," I said, "and they let me sit in the garden. We'll go there; it's not far. They have nice little iron benches. It's cute."

"I may know the house," he said. "Sometimes I walk around there. It's all changing."

I'm a good walker, and Phil had a good stride. In ten minutes we were sitting in the shade of some huge old plants that ran along the back of the garden; it was a crazy place. I only stayed there because the owner's wife knew some of my family in Moosonee, may even have been a relation.

"I'm looking for something a little roomier," I told Phil. We were starting to be able to talk. I wondered if I should offer to show him my room. I was supposed to work that night, four to twelve, and I thought I'd have to call in sick. I said something about it.

"No, go to work," he said, "and I'll come and get you at midnight. We'll talk more then. I'm on vacation. I don't have to be in the office at nine. We might stay up all night. I want you to show me your room. Could you do that now?"

I led him into the ramshackle old cottage and showed him where I slept, at the back of the second storey, looking down on the tomato plants. I wasn't ashamed of my room; it was clean as clean.

"We can do better than this," Phil said, and from then on he kept me looking for a better place to live. He came to get me that night, and we closed one of the neighbourhood bars, not drinking much, just talking. Next day he showed up at Berryman before noon, with the early edition of the *Star* folded open at the want-ads. "What you want is a real flat or an apartment close to your work, with a proper living room, a real kitchen and bathroom, and two bedrooms. You can always use a guest room, in case you have a visitor." He didn't smile or snicker when he said that. Phil has never never tried to take advantage of me. When he got me apartment hunting it wasn't to set me up in a hideaway where we could be lovers. It was to make me more comfortable; he wanted me to stay in the city permanently. Now that we'd found each other again, it looked like that might happen. He helped me find my place on Huron Street and he helped me to move in. I was so proud of my apartment. It made me feel dignified, like a real citizen.

When we located the place on Huron Street, Phil was so pleased! He kept on telling me that he and his father had lived right near there before he went north, before he ever met me. "You'll be in the best part of Toronto," he would say, "and I can come and see you whenever I like."

He helped me to buy furniture; he was wonderful at finding secondhand bargains. He bought me a coffee table right after I moved in that was the most solid piece of furniture that I've ever owned. Heavy, good-quality stuff. It's still in the apartment. And he brought over one of his niece's pictures. At first I thought it might be hard to live with, but after a while I felt like it had always been there; it's funny how a picture will grow on you.

He used to bring cans of cleanser and work on the sink and the bathtub and basin and that. He was a funny man.

And finally, I have to say, he helped me with the rent. I guess he was kind of keeping me, and then we got to be lovers and I felt that my place was his home. Not his second home. His true home.

He did so much for me. He helped me to get better positions. He got me turned on to conference organizing. The hotels are always looking for occupancy. If you put a deal to them right you can often line up accommodation at unbelievable prices. I began to move into conference management, where I could help to schedule events, choose the right size rooms for meetings, arrange snack services for the conference breaks and lunches, and usually a closing dinner. There's a knack to visualizing how much accommodation you require, for what dates. Then you offer the package to the midtown hotels, looking for the best rate. I was good at that, and Phil was just wonderful. He was always full of ideas. He had useful contacts at the Express and the railway management. We've been together like that, ever since I met him on Bloor Street.

He never told his family about me, I don't know why. His brother was this big gun, member of Parliament, prizewinner, author, name in the papers three or four times a year, sometimes more. Went to China for years, I never understood why. When his brother was in China, Phil was left with his brother's wife on his hands. I never met her. I was never asked to their apartment on Crescent Road.

"You're ashamed of me. I'm just your damn squaw or something," I cried once or twice. Now I wish I hadn't said that, he looked so woebegone. He didn't try to answer. I couldn't get him to talk about his folks. I knew what it was, all right. He was very jealous of his brother, and that got turned into lusting after his brother's wife. If you asked me whether he was in love with her too, all I could say would be that she felt like a rival to me. Phil would never take me on full-time while she was there. Then the brother died, and there was this great fuss over his funeral. They brought him back from China; it was all over the papers for a week. Once or twice that week Phil got away from them for a few hours, and then he would come and lay his head in my lap.

"Don't you grieve too much, Phil," I said. "He had a very good run."

They were twelve years apart in age.

"He was always like my father," Phil said, "and Isabelle was like my father's second wife, not like my mother."

I wish he hadn't gone on staying with her after that, but I could never have invited him to move in with me. It just wasn't possible. Not then, and not for ten years afterwards. He'd come around in the evenings and we'd watch TV or play two-handed bridge or euchre, a good game for two players. I was better at euchre than Phil, quicker to take advantage of the fall of the cards, but I tried not to take advantage of him in other ways. He had a strange kind of innocence. He might just as well have stayed a boy, like he never had to look out for himself at all. First his father took care of him, and then his brother and the brother's wife, and finally his nephew. I think in this last few years he'd been in danger of being taken over by one of his nephew's kids. He's never come right up against life. You felt that there was something missing in him as far as sex went. It was the longest time before he'd even put his arm around me, and this was when he was in his sixties. It makes me want to cry to think that a full-grown adult could have lived a whole life without any true emotional satisfaction. All his life he'd been slowly putting on weight, a pound or two a year, just from eating a little too much and staying tied to a desk job. About the last time he ever got any regular exercise was when I met him in Moose River. At that time he was almost slender, certainly not heavy. He hadn't filled out.

After that he just started to gain weight so slowly that nobody noticed it for a long time. When I met him again on Bloor Street he'd filled out for real; he weighed at least thirty pounds more than before. Stout, that's how I thought of him. When we got the Huron Street place organized I tried to get him to eat with me. I'm not much at cooking, but I do know how to keep weight off, by keeping portions small and staying away from second helpings or big desserts. In my work I've had to stay trim and take care of my appearance. Phil always had to have somebody do it for him. I wondered if he was really in love with his brother's wife, or perhaps had some awful illusion about her. His mother died when he was in his late teens, not long after the family moved to Toronto. He used to talk about it; he seemed to have his mother and sister-in-law all mixed up together. And I do know that he was longing to have a relationship with a woman; any woman who knew him well could see that.

But he wouldn't fool around with me for the longest time. I had the apartment all set up, in beautiful shape, for a good three years and more before he got into the habit of passing his evenings there. That was when his brother died and there was this big funeral in the Catholic cemetery in North Toronto. I went to that funeral and stood at the back of the crowd. It was the first time I'd ever seen all his family together, and all those famous politicians, Trudeau and the others. It was so crowded that I could easily keep out of sight. I saw Mrs. Goderich being helped away by Phil and his other nephew, the one who lives in England. I could tell that Mrs. Goderich was almost blind, from the way the two men were helping her along. It was an interesting occasion. I saw at least two Indians there, right close up to the front, and I saw the other nephew turn and speak to them, and take them by the hands. I don't know who they were. They weren't Cree from the north country, and they were older than me.

I felt like I'd been a spy at the time of the funeral, and I decided not to see much of Phil for a while. I don't know whether he'd spotted me in the crowd, but I felt I had to tell him I'd been there, the next time he phoned me.

"I know I wasn't invited, but I hoped you wouldn't mind."

He cleared his throat noisily. "I won't tell you what that means to me," he said. And after that, far from staying apart, we spent much more time together. It was then, while his sister-in-law was going downhill, that we became lovers. All these happenings had some deep meaning for Phil; he always kept me on the outside of his feelings about his family. I was inside our feelings about each other. That was enough. He was the gentlest, kindest, most polite man I've ever had anything to do with. As I told you, I'm no nun, but I've never been a pushover. I've got a good reputation; at the same time I've had certain experience and I can make comparisons. I was lucky to have Phil and I knew what he felt about me. He came round to see me one night and practically hid in my arms. He'd been in a taxi taking his sister-in-law for an eye checkup, and she'd had a blackout in the cab, she practically died in his arms. Well, you can imagine how that would leave you. He was in a terrible state.

Not very long after that the poor woman went into a nursing home. She needed round-the-clock care that Phil and the family just couldn't manage by themselves. I've walked by that nursing home. It's in a very good location and it looks bright and clean, but still and all . . .

I was terribly frightened for Phil. I thought, what's going to happen when Mrs. Goderich dies? Apparently she could have gone at any moment of her last few years. It was towards the end of that time that we really began to be together as much as possible. When Mrs. Goderich was dying, right at the end, Phil was distracted, frightened, as full of sorrow as anybody I've ever seen. I wasn't sure he'd survive her. He just couldn't stick it out; in the last few weeks he kept begging me to come away with him. He told me that he felt like a coward and a deserter, leaving his nephew's girl — is it Andrea? — to look after things but he simply couldn't stand to see the end.

I got him to come away with me, back home. We went up on the Northland towards the end of February 1980, when one of his nephews was in London and the other off in Venice. I never understood exactly what he was doing in Venice. And their sister was living in New York. They really don't seem like Toronto people to me. London. Venice. New York. And they weren't around at the end and neither was Phil. We stayed for a week at the Polar Bear Lodge; then we moved over to Moose Factory, to be closer to the Number 1 Reserve. I've been back to Toronto several times to wind up my affairs, and I've kept the apartment on, so as to have a place to stay when I'm there. I don't expect to keep it on much longer though. Phil says we've been living like the Squire and Nancy Carroll. I'm not sure what that means, but it was Nancy Carroll's affair with the Squire that first sent Phil north, so some good came of it anyway. The Squire never married his Nancy Carroll, so we've gone them one better. We decided to get married just when Phil turned seventy. It's about time. We had a nice private wedding at Our Lady of Perpetual Help church six months ago.

That was the story communicated to me in a series of letters and phone calls over the fall and winter of 1982/83. I was confused at first by the references to Perpetual Help church, because that was the name of the parish church on St. Clair Avenue at Clifton Road that we all went to in the 1930s. For some time I thought she was telling me that she and Uncle Philip had been married in the heart of midtown Toronto, twenty minutes' walk from where I lived. That was a false impression. The Catholic church on Moose Factory Island is also dedicated to Our Lady of Perpetual Help. I've been in that church. I went looking for it as soon as I got there. It stands on a sizable plot, catty-cornered from the big gift shop.

Right to the end I expected to see him at least once more. I thought that a couple of years in the Near North might refresh him and give him an incentive to come back south with his wife, if only to show her off to us, to prove that he could handle family responsibilities as well as anybody. I don't suppose he expected to become a father because by this time Jeannie was nearing sixty. Still, you never know, he may have had hopes in that direction which he gradually gave up on. I wish he'd come back to Toronto, but Toronto wasn't his first home, had perhaps never figured as his true home. Barringford, Nova Scotia, must have seemed like home to him, and there was no prospect of his ever getting back there. At the end of his life he turned away from home, and started off for uncharted realms of silver.

I think I've given a pretty accurate account of the matters Jeanne communicated to me. I've tried not to present her as in any sense a "character," a quaint, faintly comic person unworthy of serious attention. She was nothing like that at all. On the phone she sounded much younger than she really was; she had a low voice, not the voice of an ignorant or unlettered person. We should get rid of these foolish expectations about people whom we don't know. There was no reason why Jeanne Three Streams Goderich shouldn't speak as educated English as anybody else. Residual racism can clot and sting and take root in surprisingly small crevices. Sometimes I almost felt as though I expected to find her clad in native dress, or at least the southern Canadian's idea of native dress, buckskins, feathers, *ceinture flèchée*, postcard nonsense. Jeanne isn't remotely like that. She has a clear, low, well-modulated, engaging voice that suggests a woman in her early forties, and her appearance is in perfect tune with her pleasant voice. A voice to mitigate hard news.

She was the one who had to tell me about it. About seven P.M. on Friday, June 3rd, 1983, I got a telephone call from her, calling from the Polar Bear Lodge in Moosonee, to say that Uncle Philip had died suddenly that afternoon, from a coronary attack, while standing on the public dock at Moose Factory, waiting for the boat to bring him across to Moosonee to meet his wife. They'd been married a bit longer than eight months. Jeanne says they were the happiest times she ever had, and she thinks it may have been the same for him. There was no pain, no protracted suffering, at the end. He simply dropped to the ground and he was gone. The dock is just behind the hospital. They took him there at once, but there was nothing to be done.

"We're burying him Monday morning," she said, her speech just as even and clear as if she was discussing some utterly unimportant event. Maybe burial is an unimportant event; maybe that's why we find it so hard to keep a straight face at funerals. Another funeral, I thought. Why does it have to be so quick? Why can't they wait till I can get there? There was simply no way I could get there by Monday morning. I knew you could fly in, but I wasn't prepared to do that. I'm terrified of the approaches to small airports, and of small, propeller-driven passenger aircraft, and I might have had to cope with that. This phobia has been growing on me this last decade or so. I couldn't risk the flight then, and I won't now. Since then I've been tempted now and then to fly in, and then to dog-leg around and have a look at one of the goose camps, but I've never mustered up the nerve to do it. If I'm going to fly, I want to be seated in a sizable multi-engined jet. I don't want to have the impression that I'm piloting the plane myself.

I had to tell Jeanne that I'd make arrangements to come up by rail, and that I'd leave a message for her at the lodge, giving the time of my arrival. I couldn't get there until Tuesday, just before noon. Another family funeral planned by somebody else, who wasn't exactly a member of the family. And yet, when you thought about it, she was. She was my aunt-in-law, if there is such a term. Certainly the relationship exists, and it can be close and functional. Here was I at fifty-three, with a new aunt; it was like being a child again, like being introduced to somebody in the family you've been too young to meet until now.

I thought about the surrogate fatherhood of the uncle in the family. If your parents had many brothers the relationship might not be very close. But if there's only one uncle around, the tie can be almost as close, and as poignant, as the tie to mother or father. What had Uncle Philip meant to me?

A paler version of Dad. A weak copy, for my mother, of her husband. A sexual nullity? Almost a wastrel? Certainly the last of the older generation. To be resented for leaving me alone, without available counsel from my parents' generation. Because of his relative youth, a mediator between that generation and mine. Utterly irreplaceable! The last iceberg to break away from the pack and drift into unknown waters. An action in some sense final, the end of a mode of life I'd enjoyed for more than fifty years.

As I thought this over a huge form began to rise up in my imagination, shining, silver-grey-indigo. A pure North.

I had a terrible time getting accommodation on the Ontario Northland rail service to Moosonee from Toronto, on the Monday. I got a return ticket on the Northlander service by the skin of my teeth; confirmation of the booking came through late Sunday afternoon; there had been a cancellation, and I got the last available space. It had me departing from Toronto at noon on Monday, getting into Iroquois Falls, a place I'd never been, just before ten that night.

After an overnight stay there and a bus ride to Cochrane early next morning, I caught the connecting service, Cochrane to

Moosonee, for the hundred-and-eighty-six-mile run down to the estuary of the river complex, and tidewater at James Bay. It's a fascinating ride, like sliding down a flume that gathers in an enormous river system. It gradually brings together the Missinaibi, the Mattagami and its tributaries and the Abitibi, to say nothing of a dozen lesser, sometimes nameless, streams that swell the confluence of the three major systems and carve out the deep wide estuary of the Moose, where it flows into the great mass of James and Hudson Bay. This is one of the greatest watercourses of Canada; it didn't surprise me to find the train so crowded. Even at the beginning of June, with the exhilarating holiday season still three weeks off, you could sense an air of expectancy and excitement in the train crew and among the people on the platforms at infrequent stops. It reminded me of pre-season preparations at the Lazy Bay Grill in the summer of 1939. Nothing in our country is quite like the simmering expectation of summer pleasure that permeates resort country about the first of June.

The train arrived at the end of steel, Moosonee, just before noon. The station platform was crowded with welcoming parties come to seek out travellers; the sun was high and very bright. The river lay a few blocks away, down First Street, past the public school and the local centre for higher education, and the OPP headquarters. Then, on one side of First Street, Christ the King church, and on the other side CHMO, "the voice of James Bay." Two ways of spreading the good news. Over everything I could see in the bright sunshine hung that air of expectation and futurity, and the gleaming vibrant light and air of a townsite next to a grand watercourse. I've noticed the same shine in the air in Stoverville and sometimes in Montreal. In Moosonee the fact of this great rush of water down to the tidal basin is present all the time, unignorable and gorgeous; you spend most of your time contriving boat trips. At least Jeanne and I did.

She met the train, an action of surpassing graciousness and warmth. Philip had been buried only the day before. Only a very few intimates had been present at the funeral. It had been an almost invisible, uncelebrated departure from life, more an escape than a formal leavetaking. Here before me stood Jeanne Three Streams Goderich, my new aunt. Unbowed, composed, able to smile at me as we picked each other out of the crowd. I'd have known her anywhere. She was exactly as she'd been described to me by various accurate reporters.

She came up to me hands outstretched. Not a very tall woman, about five feet five or six, but upstanding and erect. I noticed her athletic stride at once; she walked with a long, even swing of the leg from the hip, like a distance runner. Though she was nearing sixty her hair, a shiny dark brown, showed no trace of greying or loss of colour or tone. It was long and smooth, hanging almost to her shoulders. It had been much combed out and brushed, but not by a stylist, probably by Jeanne herself. Her face was a pleasing compromise between width and length, neither too broad nor too long for harmony of proportion. She had full round curving cheeks and a rounded chin, and very good teeth. I was six years her junior, but I felt old beside her.

She wore a bright red sports jersey top with a zip-front, something like a jogging suit, and white sports trousers. Looking closely, I saw an ornamental clip fastened to her jersey top, the white plastic image of a polar bear. This made her look like a tour guide. There was no hint of a mourning costume, of sadness or any fear of having been left alone.

"I can see that you're Matthew," she said. "I knew I'd recognize you." This was a disarming opening. It made me wonder what she knew about me, how I had ranked in Philip's esteem. I had never been able to guess what he thought of me. He might have told her anything.

"We could easily walk to the lodge," she said, "but I've got a taxi, if you'd sooner have that. Where are your other bags?"

"I've only got the one," I said, a little embarrassed. "I won't be here that long, unless there's business . . ."

"Nothing much to keep you here," she said. "If that's all you've got we might walk down to the hotel. We can do it in ten minutes. I'll just go and tell Bob."

She spoke a few words to a cab driver who sat in his vehicle by the taxi-stand. While I stood there, I observed that several passers-by, young women, strongly resembled her in colouring and hairstyle. I realized that she was living among her own people and I was the outsider. I wondered how Phil had handled this.

"Come along," she said, "and give me something to carry."

"There really isn't anything."

"Well, give me that attaché case, or whatever it is, just for fun."

I really don't know why I'd brought the attaché case. It had nothing special in it. I think I'd expected that there would be documents to take back to Toronto, but I was beginning to understand that everything would be taken care of at this end; this was no weeping widow in need of a shoulder to cry on. She led me down First Street towards the shore, past the post office and a crafts shop, to the corner of Révillon Road. Here the full, shining view of the river was overwhelming. It was flat calm this noon, and although the current must have been moving strongly below the surface there was no impression of motion. The vast expanse of oily turquoise, taking its colour in reflection from the sky and the land along the shores, looked like a still northern lake, as fresh and clear as though it were the only element of the scene. A few outboard canoes buzzed about on the motionless surface, barely audible at this distance.

We must have been ten miles upriver from James Bay but there was an unmistakable air of wide, almost oceanic coast hereabouts. The estuary is tidal, with a rise and fall of from four to five feet. I could make out what appeared to be a few sand-bars, which might be covered at high tide. Ontario tidewater: what a paradox. I think of life in Ontario as very far inland, far from coastal turbulence or oceanic power. But here we were, half an hour's travel from open sea, with the smell and sound and light of the sea moving over us. Révillon, I thought, where have I seen the name Révillon? I remembered the neat, delicate script on shop windows in New York and Paris. "Is that for Révillon Frères, the fur people?" I asked, pointing to a street sign.

"They founded the town," Jeanne said, "at the turn of the century. It was a fur trader's paradise, all around here. I don't think they have any land rights now; it's an Ontario town like all the others."

I spotted the docks and the hotel, the Polar Bear Lodge, and took a second look at the big bear clipped to her jersey. "What about these polar bears? Is that your local symbol?"

"We use it for advertising, to give the place an identity. And there's the *Polar Princess* down at her dock." She pointed to a trim excursion vessel with a spacious maindeck, wheelhouse above it forward, and an upper deck extending aft above the wheelhouse. There were life rafts fastened to the roof of the upper deck. The whole craft was white picked out with red the colour of Jeanne's jersey top. Crew members came and went aboard the *Polar Princess* in their shirtsleeves! There was an unlooked-for mildness in the scene, a persuasive softness and springlike ease. One young man stood on the foredeck of the excursion boat, attending to her mooring lines; he wore a T-shirt, shorts and jogging shoes. Ten miles from James Bay.

We went into the Polar Bear Lodge and Jeanne led me to the reception desk; she displayed total familiarity with hotel procedures. The woman on the desk obviously knew and liked her. I'd been pre-registered and was able to go straight to my room, a big double on the second floor with wide windows looking down on the docks and the water. The view was like an enormous animated mural, and the room was eerily like motel rooms I'd stayed in all over North America; there was very little in the furnishings to suggest the vast openness spreading out just north of us. The bedspreads and curtains were in a blue-and-white striped pattern, with little golden flower motifs distributed along the white stripes. The walls were covered in some nubbly off-white adhesive paper. Writing table, bedside tables, breakfast table. I might as well have been in Stoverville at the other end of

Ontario. But this wasn't a Stoverville happening. We sat down at the breakfast table.

"It isn't the Royal York, but they can make you very comfortable here and you won't be cold at night," she said. "It can get quite cool after dark, even in June. Poor old Phil. He hated to be cold at night."

I liked her, and felt terribly sorry for her, but there was nothing much I could do for her. I think she'd wanted to have a child with him, for years and years, and now it was too late. She never talked about this, but it seemed plain enough. After more than forty years of admiring him and wishing to be close to him, after more than fifteen years of close association ending in marriage, she'd been left alone. At least, I thought, she's in her native place and not in Toronto. I realized with a shock that I liked the place and felt at home here. I considered the possibility of getting to know the farther North. Moosonee seemed like an extension of Ontario cottage country, but it was also a gateway to infinity. Who could tell what might lie out in the big bay beyond and the mysterious white islands above. I was starting to feel some of Uncle Philip's fascination with the place.

"He knew he'd come to the end, when once he got here to stay. He'd never have gone back to the city. He used to tell me that his brother — your father — had dreamed all his life of where he wanted to die, and when the time came he found he was there, just where he'd imagined. Wasn't it on the Great Wall of China?"

"That's certainly where my father died," I said, surprised at this revelation. Had my father gone to China to look for his death?

"Phil knew he didn't have very long," she said. She stood up and went to the window to gaze downriver. She kept her back to me. "And then when your mother was so sick he found he couldn't wait. He had to get here, and he brought me with him. I'd have gone much further north to be with him. You don't know what he was like. He had no Peace Prize and no headlines and no seat in Parliament, but he helped me in ways you couldn't imagine. He made it possible for me to have dignity, and a life of my own. Everybody here loved him. As soon as we settled in for good, two years ago, he made friends with the Bay manager at Moose Factory, Allan MacKinnon. He helped us to settle in Moose Factory as soon as he knew that we wanted to be there. He rented rooms to Phil in the Bay Staff accommodation. I don't think he'd have done that for anybody else. It didn't hurt that your family is well known, but Allan is pretty independent and does what he thinks he should. They were comfortable rooms, a sitting room and a small bedroom, with a little kitchenette and bath attached. Nobody made any fuss about this. I had access through a side entrance. There isn't the prejudice there used to be, and everybody knew we were going to be married as soon as we could get the church formalities straightened out; the priests won't marry just anybody, you know. That was last fall; we had eight months together as man and wife. It doesn't seem much out of forty years."

I didn't want to cause her to turn towards me. I put a casual question. "Were you looking for a more permanent place?"

"We were and we weren't. There are complications for a native woman married to a non-native. Problems with residence rights and property rights and band membership rights. I don't know yet where I'm going; it was all so fast. He only died last Friday, and it's Tuesday and he's in the ground."

I admired her steadfastness, and had no idea what else to say. There might have been some physical reason for the rapid burial, but I wasn't going to ask about that. At least there were no questions about her inheritance; she must have seen his will. Maybe I could discuss that with her, but she would have to open the subject. We ordered sandwiches and coffee, and began to talk about estate matters while we ate.

"I'm sure you've got a copy of his will," I said.

"Oh, yes, I've had one for nearly two years. Have you read it?"

"As a matter of fact I haven't, but I assume everything goes to you."

"It does, you know, except for a few small items he wanted you to have, personal things. Then there are cash bequests to you and your sister, Amanda Louise, I think it is. Am I right?"

"That's it. She lives in New York."

"And she has a small daughter, correct?"

I paused to pour out coffee refills. I noticed that Jeanne drank off her coffee thirstily, with an air of real pleasure. I also noticed that she didn't smoke. I've never known her to drink anything with alcohol in it. She drinks water with her meals, and plenty of coffee.

"I wouldn't call her a small daughter," I said thoughtfully. "She's seventeen, and quite tall; she's a bit of a heartbreaker, I'm afraid, young Emily Underwood. Why do you ask?"

"There's a little cash gift comes to her, and to your daughter, Andrea, for being around when needed. The will says that in more formal language. The cash bequests only amount to a few thousand dollars. Ten thousand, divided in four equal shares, as remembrances, the will states." She looked me squarely in the eye without embarrassment. "The rest — and it's quite a lot — goes to me."

"And so it should," I said. "I can't tell you how glad I am to hear this."

She began to pace around the room with her handsome long stride. Then she stopped, over by the big window, and looked down towards the widening estuary; her shoulders relaxed. I liked and admired her, and was glad to see the barriers beginning to come down. I thought again with amazement that this woman whom I'd just met was my aunt. By marriage no doubt, but authentic family. I spoke to her back. "Would you like me to call you Jeannie or Jeanne, or do you prefer Mrs. Goderich? Or what?"

"Phil always called me Jeanne," she said in a muffled voice. After that I always called her Jeanne. Diminutives are almost always used as put-downs after all. I'd sooner be called Matthew than Matt.

I said, "Jeanne, when I got that letter nominating you as

executor in my place, it was like taking a great weight off my shoulders. I've got my mother and father's estate matters to deal with. My wife and I are all balled up in community property tangles. I don't know where they'll end; we don't live together, but I look after her business affairs in Canada. Just as long as you don't feel you've been lumbered with a responsibility you don't want to deal with, that's just fine."

"We talked it over," she said, "and he wanted me to handle things. He said he wanted to be sure I was looked after. The thing is, it's quite a big estate. It runs well into six figures."

"Well, I'm delighted for you," I said. I didn't care to know the exact amount. I'd seen that large, well-filled safety-deposit box with those City of Detroits and the cash in large denominations. Never keep cash around, I thought. You're losing interest every day. But I didn't offer Jeanne any advice; the matter lay in her hands. I never did find out the size of the estate, but I did some mean-spirited little calculations on my own initiative when I got back to the city. Uncle Philip had stayed with the same employer for well over thirty years, quite long enough to build up a sizable equity in a pension plan. He had spent virtually nothing on himself; his clothes were always modest and inconspicuous, and he always seemed to have plenty of money to buy our children lavish presents when he came to visit us.

I would not have been surprised to find that the amount that went to his residual legatee was close to half a million. Not surprised at all. I could see what he'd had in mind. He owed Jeanne a life, forty years of personal devotion that he'd been unable to reciprocate. He'd only felt free to turn to her when my mother was dying. Then he'd made his turn. Sitting there in the sunny hotel bedroom, I found myself faced with one of the fundamental puzzles of existence. I had no doubt that my uncle had in some profound sense loved my mother and deeply envied my father's marriage to her. And yet he had kept silence and maintained, on the whole, an admirable independence of feeling. He had never competed with Andrew for Isabelle's love. This had continued from 1927, when Philip arrived in Toronto, until 1970, when his brother had died. And after that there had been no attempt to persuade Isabelle to love him. A brother's wife.

In the late 1960s Jeanne had reappeared in his life like a phantom possibility from the distant past. Not perhaps the great passion of his life, but a liberating love. He could do things for her — find her an apartment, help her out with money when she was between jobs, give her family paintings, or at least one painting. Then when he was free to go home with her and marry her at last, towards the end of a full human life, past seventy, he'd been united to her. I wished with all my heart that he'd been able to have a child with her, but it was too late.

I noticed that three of the small bequests were made to Amanda, Andrea and Emily, three women of whom he had deeply approved. The fourth to me. I wished that I could find out from Jeanne what he'd thought of me, but the question didn't come up just then.

"Can we go over to Moose Factory tomorrow?" she asked. "I've got my copy of the will there. I want you to go over it. If you'd care to have a copy we can have one made at the Bay office. Perhaps we can have copies made for Amanda, Andrea and Emily. Have I got them right?"

"Perfectly right," I said. I was starting to be aware of a strong family resemblance among those four women. Amanda Louise, Andrea, Emily all seemed quite suddenly to be more like Jeanne than like my mother. There was the same moral persistence, the same spontaneity, a kind of gaiety, and there was great strength. My mother, the centre of the universe for anybody who came near her, in some ways almost an object of worship, lovely, untouched, had been the focal point around whom we all orbited, a being vested with an extraordinary spiritual endowment, as her last weeks on earth had testified. In those weeks, according to Andrea, who had helped her through them, who had lived her death with her, my mother had seemed to be already in eternity, still in this world in the body, but gone away into eternal presence. This was not the kind or quality of existence of my sister, my daughter, my niece. Their endurance and energy and gaiety were much of this world, in a strange cousinship with Jeanne's. Uncle Philip had left nothing to my brother, I saw. And I knew why. "O! my offence is rank, it smells to Heaven," says Claudius. The Bard understood these things. I didn't see how Tony could ever come home.

We sat there for a bit, finishing our sandwiches. We let our first serious conversation dwindle into a lazy, companionable silence. The huge light hanging over the estuary and the bay shore flooded the room as the sun moved overhead. Two weeks until the longest day of the year, when the daylight would seem interminable. Already tonight the darkness would be postponed until very late. We had a long afternoon to get through while trying to get to know each other as comfortably as possible. Where would she go? Would she return south and invest her money, living off the interest and waiting for the Old Age Pension to kick in? Would I see anything of her in Toronto? This seemed very unlikely, but time would tell. I got to my feet. The sunlight in the room was overpowering: you could watch individual pinpoints of dust swimming in the beams. There was a constant light motion in the air of the room, not a cold draft, just a sort of steady breathing. Motes of dust wavered on it, gleaming in the broad beams.

Thoughts of mortality somehow intervened here. This poor woman had buried her husband of eight months yesterday. It would have been insolent of me to offer comfort. We were total strangers and yet I felt that I'd known her for a long time. I made a sudden guess.

"While you were living in Toronto, did Phil ever point me out to you?"

"Oh, yes. I've often seen you at a distance."

"Did we ever pass each other by? Could I have seen you before?"

"Once, not long after your father died and they brought him

back for that big funeral. Maybe six weeks later. We were on the same subway car, on the northbound Yonge Street line. I was sitting facing you and we kept making eye contact. You wouldn't remember because you didn't know who I was, but I knew who you were. You got off at Rosedale, so I guessed you were going to the family apartment."

I found this deeply disquieting. The religious believer grows used to the notion that his or her movements, innermost secrets, lie open before the all-seeing wisdom of the Creator. And the watchings of lesser invisible beings, angels, the saints in glory, seem equally normal, the rule of existence when once the presence of the omniscient Almighty is recognized, but we do not expect our movements and thoughts to be monitored by ordinary beings like ourselves. Was Jeanne Goderich a being of some special kind, an agent of divine knowledge, sent to watch over my infirm strivings towards a more perfect justice? Property, gain, money, City of Detroit tax exempts had nothing to do with the question. But I had, just this hour, been able to tell Jeanne that an inheritance of half a million belonged by right to her, without a stirring of jealousy. I felt no need, no wish to share in it. My meeting with her had allowed me to escape from the need to possess, if only temporarily. She seemed to be some sort of guide to virtue. I'd have followed her anywhere.

The next morning after breakfast we left the lodge, crossed Révillon Road to the docks and hired an outboard canoe to ferry us to Moose Factory Island. The boat owner was inevitably a friend and a cousin of Jeanne's, introduced to me succinctly as Henry. His boat was a square-sterned, sixteen-foot fibreglass canoe about five years old. A fifteen-horse Evinrude about the same vintage as the canoe, probably original equipment, sat on tilt at the stern. Ours was the third of a squadron of half a dozen craft moored across the dock from the *Polar Princess*. It took a couple of minutes to ease the boat out of the crowd, into the open water of the estuary. I dipped my hand into the shining clear water and found it flavoured, but not poisonously salt. We drew out into midstream, heading towards Charles Island; the crossing must measure four or five miles.

"Aren't we a little under-engined?" I asked Henry.

"Not for this size hull. I know the current and the eddies like the furniture at home. I've been making this crossing for forty years. Mind you, I won't go out in all weathers."

We drew into the Charles Island gap, along the channel towards Moose Factory docks. We did the trip, taking our time, in under an hour. It was close on noon when we landed at the public dock. We arranged for return passage for me, then said goodbye to Henry and caught the little local bus for the run up the road to the Bay staff quarters, where Jeanne and Philip had shared their eight months of married life. It might have been a ride of about a mile. I know I walked back down to the dock that evening, to pick up my return boatride.

Behind the Bay headquarters ran a series of lodgings shaped like a small motel, erected on cement-block piers over a low air-space. It looked to me as if the floor surfaces would be very chilly, but Jeanne said no. On the contrary, their quarters were almost oppressively warm in winter, being lined with state-of-the-art insulating materials. She led me into their apartment, freshly dusted and neat, and showed me their bedroom, where some of my uncle's clothes and other personal belongings were spread out on the twin beds. Then she left me alone and went into the next room. I sat on the bed nearest the window and considered my options. I saw that a familiar large old brown calf-skin bag, with sturdy buckles and straps, lay open between the beds, presumably for me to pack up and take away.

I'd seen that bag in one room or another, under a bed or at the back of a closet, in half a dozen dwellings we'd shared with Uncle Philip: at the Lakeview Hotel, Centre Island; in an apartment much like this one on Lakeshore Road at the island in wintery conditions in the depths of the war years; on Moore Avenue; on Crescent Road; in two or three other places shared and quarrelled over by the Squire and his second son. I could smell the calfskin. It had precisely the same odour as in 1939 or 1942. Somebody had scoured it free of dust quite recently and rubbed up the external parts with brown shoe polish. What did Jeanne want me to take away, everything or nothing? I looked hesitantly at the piled clothing and the three excellent pairs of shoes, the framed photos. The same old shaving kit I'd been acquainted with for decades. I felt tears rising behind my eyes at the sight of these familiar objects. Surely there was nothing here that I could take away. At the same time it would be impolite not to go through these survivals with attention. The shoes might go to the district used-clothing bank; they were a common size and not much worn. Then there were the underwear and the socks and handkerchiefs. A use might be found for them, but there was no point in my carrying them back to Toronto to lie in a drawer. These things were all of good, but not luxury, quality; they looked to me like they might have originated with Woolco or Zellers or some similar chain. Well aired out and clean, quiet in colour, worn but not to the point of dilapidation, they seemed infinitely expressive of my uncle's nature. He had never sought luxury, or any degree of indulgence beyond adequate comfort, had never distinguished himself by bright plumage. What had he done? He had spent a quiet life harbouring inexpressible need, had saved his money, and in the end had been able to leave his wife — his closest friend — enough property to keep her in the same modest comfort he'd asked for himself. Two very quiet lives, lived on the margin of their times. At the margin. The more I thought about this, the less certain I was about the location of the margin. The place where we were at this moment could only be identified as marginal if you'd never studied a map of the northern half of the globe with the North Pole at its centre. On such a map Moose Factory is far closer to the centre than Toronto or Tokyo.

I looked over at the chest of drawers on which a number of small personal possessions were laid out for my examination. A hairbrush, not new, very clean. A pair of military brushes housed

in a neat leather case, likewise very clean. Four framed photographs, in silver frames. Two family groups, and individual portraits of the Squire and Katie the key. My grandparents. The
portraits obviously dated from the Edwardian decade, the clothes
and hairstylings of their subjects elegant and very far from
casual. I took up the portrait of my grandfather and studied the
back. A sticker bearing the name of a photographer in Yarmouth,
Nova Scotia, still adhered to the mount. The pictures showed my
grandparents at about the age of thirty-five, and for a moment I
considered asking for them. Andrea would find them interesting and important, for use in developing a family archive. But
there could be no question of removing them from Jeanne's care.
They formed part of her family records too, and should remain
with her.

I wondered again which of us was marginalized, and realized
with a slight tremor that in this part of the world I was a marginal
figure. My familiar watercourses ran south to the Great Lakes
while all the rivers hereabouts flowed into the Arctic Ocean. I
was now in the North, not the deep North but its approaches.
I could sense this all around me in the unearthly light.

The two family groups must have been taken in Toronto at the
end of the 1920s, one of them showing the Squire and my grandmother, my parents, Uncle Philip as a slender youth and
Amanda Louise in a baby dress, perhaps a year old, held tightly
on my grandmother's knee. They seemed to be sitting on the
veranda steps of a tall old Toronto house, probably the house on
Summerhill Gardens where Amanda had been born.

The other family group was one I'd often seen before; in fact
I appeared in it as an infant in a wicker go-cart, surrounded by
grandparents, parents, uncle, sister, in front of our little house on
Summerhill Avenue, a year or two before my brother was born;
that would put it at about late 1931. Sight of the two groups
made me feel the vertigo of history. The pictures expressed
simply and strongly the fashions and attitudes of the Toronto,
perhaps the English Canada, of the day. And here I was in 1983,

half a century later, in a place utterly removed in feeling, style, location, appearance, people, in every human respect, from that time and place.

And yet I was linked to that time and place by the most powerful of ties, and what I had to do now was to bring them together with the times and places that Jeanne Three Streams Goderich had lived through. I was the appointed mediator of two totally disparate kinds of life. If I was supposed to introduce Jeanne to the Goderiches, to make her feel one of us, at the same time I had to accept, gracefully and candidly, as close a link as possible to her and her story. Later that day I named each of the figures in the pictures to her, commented on their clothes and hairstyles, their expressions, the look of the two houses in the pictures. In a short time I tried to — what is the word — to *familiarize* her with all that huge collection of lumber in the attic that forms a family's life history.

I would ask her to tell me as much as she could about where she came from, about the mine site and the mine superinten- dent's folks, the people of the Cree reserve a couple of miles from where we sat. Maybe we could arrange a boatride downriver to the open bay, so that I could have a look at the widening North. I fingered the articles on the bureau, then picked up an object so familiar to me that it made me dizzy to contemplate it. It was a small silver pen-knife, engraved with the initials *PG*. At the base of the larger blade, when it was unfolded, were visible a few words in neat lettering, much smoothed by the passage of sixty years. On one side the words were LAMPLOUGH: GERMANY, and on the other OSTEREI: STAINLESS: INOX. I would not swear to OSTEREI; the lettering was almost worn away by use.

The two blades of this elegant little tool had been worn narrow and honed to extreme sharpness. I had first seen it when I was eighteen months old. It had lain around the Crescent Road apartment for most of the 1970s. I think Uncle Philip had acquired it as a child in Barringford, perhaps at the age of ten or twelve. Once again the oceanic past seemed to open underneath me. I felt about to be engulfed. That knife, insignificant and almost useless in appearance, had nevertheless served over sixty years for a multitude of purposes: to open letters, to cut string, to scratch initials on trees, to cut items out of newspapers, the texture of a life. I could not keep back a few shaming tears. I was holding Philip Bentinck Russell Goderich's life in my palm. I decided to ask for the knife, and besides that selected a heavy tweed jacket, scarcely worn and not far off my own size. In these last years I had thought of Uncle Philip as a stout man, but his jacket was none too loose on me. I took off my own jacket and put his on, and went into the next room.

"May I have this for a memento? Oh, and his little pen-knife? I don't think there's anything else. And I want to tell you all about the photographs and the people in them. I'd like you to have all the other stuff." I felt very gauche.

"That's just what he'd have wanted," she said. "I'll see that his clothes go where they're useful, and I'll keep the pictures to look at. He often used to tell me who the people in them were. I feel as if I knew all of you. But we can leave that for later. It's only about half past three. I thought we might walk along to the cemetery so you can see where he is. It's a historic site, you understand. There are some very old stones, with the names of traders and missionaries and settlers from very early times. It's still consecrated ground. We had to get special permission to dig a grave. It isn't at all the regular thing, but everybody was very kind. If we go along now I can show you some sights along the way. Centennial Park and the museum, and we can have a look around the Anglican church on our way back. You can spend the night here; there's a good fold-out couch in the living room, or I can go back across to Moosonee with you, to arrange things for the morning. I guess you go back tomorrow, isn't that right?"

"On the late afternoon train. I'm not certain of the time. It departs around five and I really should be on it. Tell you what, though. I'd really like to take the trip downriver to the bay. Would there be any chance of that?"

"The excursion season hasn't started yet," she said, "but I just happen to know that they're taking *Polar Princess* out for her shakedown run tomorrow morning, to check over the engines and the navigational marks, and the position of the channel. They'll do two or three runs before the season. You might like to go along — I'll come with you. I've already arranged it; we've got permission to be on board."

"Wonderful, just great! I suppose there'll be time to do the trip and get back for the train?"

"Plenty of time. We're going out at ten in the morning, and we'll be gone about five hours. The whole excursion tour takes closer to six hours, but we won't be doing the side trip to Moose Factory. There'll be plenty to see, and I'll have you back to the hotel by three-thirty. Plenty of time to make the train."

She's already a full-fledged Goderich, I thought. This care for times and travel arrangements reminded me powerfully of myself and everybody else in the family. At the same time it might be typical of the entire Cree people.

"Do you have many family pictures?" I asked her suddenly. She smiled very sweetly.

"I wondered if you might ask me that. I have two or three. We could look at them after we've visited the cemetery. We can have our supper here, then I'll take you back to Henry's boat later tonight."

I kept Uncle Philip's warm tweed jacket on. I thought that the intoxicating northern air might grow cool as we walked along, but I was wrong. In half a mile I'd had to take the jacket off and was holding it draped across my arm. "It's as warm as Toronto."

"It's often warmer." She may have heard my remark before. Visitors often irritate residents with their clichéd observations. I felt a bit of a fool, walking along through a landscape that was so little like what I'd expected. It was the pedestrians in shorts and shirtsleeves that surprised me most.

"Tourists expect igloos," Jeanne said succinctly, "and for igloos you'd have to go hundreds of miles north of here, maybe a thousand. Edmonton is farther north than Moose Factory."

This observation startled me. Polar Bear Express. Polar Bear Lodge. *Polar Princess*. The pole must be a long long way off! I saw that I'd got it right years before, when I'd said of Uncle Philip that "he never visited the Far North." I stood beside his freshly filled and trimmed grave at the north side of the old burial ground and wondered whether he'd gotten as far north as he'd have liked. There was nothing especially northern in the look of the cemetery. It reminded me strongly of lost little grave-yards hidden in the back townships of eastern Ontario. I knelt briefly; the ground under my knees was dry and warm. I said a few prayers for the dead as Jeanne knelt beside me. There was a brief moment of silence. Then we stood up and turned away.

On our way back to the lodging at the staff house we had time to continue along towards the Anglican church of Saint Thomas. This is a beautiful small building, white woodwork under a red roof and a graceful steeple. In bright sunshine the paintwork gleams with invitation. We had time to go inside and admire the stained glass with the bright light shining through it; it was like being inside an illuminated jewel box. The church is a hundred and thirty years old, full of memorial plaques and local artifacts, an intensely civilized site. More imaginings overthrown. I saw that I'd come here with completely unrealistic expectations. Ignorance, reader, pure ignorance. It was the same that evening over supper, as we sat handing snapshots and framed photos back and forth with the coffee cups. I'd thought of Jeanne as a person without any recorded history. Of course she had a history as long as mine or longer, and she had ties of cousinship and ancestry as richly complex as those of any European noble house.

"Do you recognize him? That's Henry, the man who brought us across this morning when he was a little boy. That's his father, my first cousin. They're standing in front of an old Chevrolet of Mr. MacKinnon's. I remember that car; he had it before I left the district."

"I hadn't been prepared for cars."

"No, you were prepared for kayaks and snowshoes and sleds."

This woman was no fool; she kept me looking at local scenes and Three Streams notabilities until I started to feel kinship with them. After all, I now had an aunt who was a Three Streams by birth. It wasn't until it was time to go down to the dock that I managed to get in a few words about the Goderiches and their origins. The only documentation to hand was the quartet of photos that Uncle Philip had preserved. When I'd commented on the clothes and hairstyles and the look of the houses in the pictures I hadn't much more to show; in fact, I stood on infirm and unfamiliar territory. Jeanne's people were at home here, and I was not. They had traditions and rights that were at this point incomprehensible to somebody like me. It would take me years, perhaps decades, to learn to read them. I wondered how much time I would need to unite Jeanne's sense of herself to my own. I already felt very close to her because of this incipient family tie, but I wasn't sure that I'd ever visit Moose Factory again. It was getting late for adventure.

It's all very well to discuss the margin and the marginalized; the trick is to tell one side of the margin from the other. I might take as one margin the great height of land two hundred miles to the south that parted the streams of water and their sources, sending some southwards to the Great Lakes and from there to the Atlantic and others northwards to the Arctic. Certainly Ontarians seemed ready to marginalize the people who lived in the North, along that line. But what I'd seen of the North — a tiny part of it — didn't seem marginal to me. My uncle had come here as towards the centre of life. Every monarchy considers itself the middle kingdom. The Greeks called every people but themselves barbarians. Poverty and lack of opportunity seem to us today to exclude whole peoples from life at the centre of things, enforcing colonial status and obscuring the achievements of ancient cultures. Mere weather conditions might marginalize;

not many choose to live on Ellesmere Island. Those who do seem to regard themselves not as marginalized but as privileged. I suspected that my uncle had regarded Moose Factory as a staging area for some closer approach to the centre of things.

A downriver excursion seemed mandatory. I recrossed the estuary that night with next day's promised voyage aboard *Polar Princess* gleaming in imagination, and went to bed feeling like a child who has been promised a wonderful birthday gift next morning. Anticipation and the temperate overnight weather kept me awake for a long while. I fell asleep after midnight; it had been a long day.

Up the next morning to wholesome coffee-shop fare. As I was squaring off with a pair of fried eggs Jeanne came in — this was about eight-thirty — and told me that she'd finalized arrangements for our morning boatride. I could see the excursion craft from where I sat. The crew members were moving about on the foredeck and afterdeck; it seemed to me as if the engines were already idling.

"We'd better go on out there. What time do they leave?"

"Regular departure time is about nine. We might go out and see. But finish up your eggs."

I did as she suggested, paid my bill, and we walked across Révillon Road to talk to Captain Marychurch, who was waiting for us at the vessel's stern. He smiled rather grimly as Jeanne approached him. I had a strong impression that people couldn't say no to my new aunt. She seemed to be able to get her way with officials, businesspeople, hotel staff, railway personnel, sea captains. Captain Marychurch was not an exception. A youngish man, perhaps in his late thirties, he seemed used to authority and at the same time able to accept suggestions, not to say commands, from Jeanne.

"This is Phil's nephew from Toronto," she told him, "the one who wants to see tidewater. What have you got to show him this morning?"

I shook hands with Captain Marychurch, and we exchanged

understanding glances. This trip was not going to be in our hands.

"Should take the usual five to six hours," said Jeanne. "We have to be back well before train time. Can you take us around your ship before we get going?" She spoke as though we'd just come aboard a transatlantic liner. I would guess that *Polar Princess* was about seventy feet overall, with a comfortably broad beam, perhaps twenty feet. I couldn't estimate her draft, but she was obviously designed for shallow water operations; the channel in the estuary can change from one season, even from one month to the next, because of wind and tide and shifting bottom. *Polar Princess* might draw six feet or so. I noticed that when in motion she sometimes didn't seem to have much water under her.

We went up a short gangway, right astern on the port side, through an opening in the rail. There was a small boat slung laterally over the stern, and a good deal of flotation gear hung from the afterdeck railings. I sniffed the air; it was crystalline, and there was a salt tang to it that delighted me. You can find anything in Ontario!

There was a closed-in maindeck with wide observation windows and seating for perhaps thirty-six; this layout reminded me strongly of the big excursion boats that ply the Venetian lagoons, carrying passengers to Burano, Torcello and the other islands in that famous place. There were lavatories towards the stern in the main cabin, and a small galley with facilities for preparing hot drinks and serving box lunches.

The afterdeck gave access by a staircase to the upper deck, open astern and shielded from spray by bright orange-red dodgers, with a smallish upper-deck cabin that might accommodate another dozen passengers. On the wheelhouse forward of this cabin stood a sharply raked radar mast, with the ship's ensign flying at its peak.

When he'd finished showing us around, Captain Marychurch spoke briefly to the engineer. I could feel the pulse of the engines below deck. At nine o'clock the two mates — one of them a young woman — took up their deck stations. In a moment we were free of our moorings, moving deliberately out towards the channel.

"During the season there'd be a team of tour guides along with us," Jeanne said. "I can act as guide, and I can tell you lots of things. This district was home to our people, the Swamp Cree, for ten thousand years before whites came; we've been here since the end of the last ice age. Europeans came here a few minutes ago. Well, in 1668, when Radisson and Groseilliers turned up. They built a little fort at Waskaganish, and a few years later the Hudson's Bay Company arrived and built Moose Port on Moose Factory Island, not far from where we were yesterday.

She meant Philip's gravesite.

"Moosonee only got started in 1903 when the Révillon people moved in to compete with the Bay. They didn't drive out the Bay, but they didn't get licked either. Now they've turned themselves into Revlon and they do business worldwide. But Moose Factory came first. When the Temiskaming and Northern Ontario arrived in the 1930s and located the railhead at Moosonee, the two settlements came to be on more or less equal terms. Nowadays people think of the area as a single place. Some of us miss the old rivalry."

"But you can't remember that, you'd have been an infant."

"I was eight years old, and I can remember the first train."

This remark triggered deep vibrations in my soul. I've spent much of my life watching trains and riding on them. There's much more to train travel than mere convenience and safety. There's the rhythm of observation permitted by the slow pace, the close look at the country it allows. I was looking forward to the ride back to Cochrane that evening. But there was plenty to see along the riverbanks; boat travel has its delights too. We were well out into the channel by now, the banks parting and widening, the sheet of water ahead broadening as we drew past Butler Island.

We stayed close to the western riverbank for some reason. In ten minutes more we came abreast of the remains of the supply ship *Eskimo*, which lie close to the mainland shore across from Big Duck Island. I could see part of the hull and the upperworks quite plainly; they were canted over and probably invisible at high tide.

"Got stuck in an early freeze twenty-five years ago, been there ever since," Jeanne said.

It must have been a very quick freeze, I thought. How much ice had to form, and to what depth, to bar the way to freedom to a modern, well-equipped motor ship? The ice must have formed in hours, and there she lay, a wreck.

"Nobody died. They just walked in, over the ice."

"Some walk!"

"Yes. They had much to look at."

She was right. We were getting out towards open water; in another half-hour we passed Little Duck Island and were approaching the group of islands that guard the gap. Middleboro, Horseshoe, to port the broad stretch of Shipsands Island, where all the birds are. It was too late in the year to see a migrating flock, something I was sorry to have missed. At the right time in the spring the flocks of ducks and geese darken the sky with their numbers, putting heart into environmentalists and bird protectionists. I've seen migrating flocks elsewhere that numbered in the tens of thousands. Jeanne told me that in due season the fliers over Shipsands may number in the hundreds of thousands. She has seen these sky-darkening flocks.

When we'd been under way for some time — it must have been around noon because the sun was high and very bright — Captain Marychurch took us well inshore by Shipsands so we could hear the birds calling; the sound was something else! The estuary was fairly calm, clear blue and shining, with some motion, enough to cause the hull to rise and fall gently, but not turbulent and noisy. You could hear sounds from miles away, tens of thousands of birds calling in their variety of tongues.

We were moving slowly, close onshore; you didn't even need glasses to spot individuals and make identifications. I'm not an enthusiastic or expert birder, but even I in my ignorance could pick out birds never seen around Stoverville, some of them rather unusual in appearance. The Hudsonian Godwit with long, impressive bill. The godwits were on the bay before Hudson came to lend them his name. I'd never seen birds like them before; they migrate halfway around the world to summer here, wandering along the shores on long thin legs, unmistakable with the flash of white on the breast.

There were myriads of other kinds; semi-palmated sandpipers and redknots, the lesser golden plover never seen in my home region. Unless I was completely mistaken there was a small flock of late Arctic terns. They seemed sluggish in flight, as well they might. The Arctic tern makes the longest migratory flight of any bird, from one pole to the other, covering in its two yearly flights the whole circumference of the earth, twenty-five thousand miles.

They aren't enormous birds or fantastically strong. To a casual eye they might resemble an unusually large gull; you can spot them by the dark cap and the cute little brown legs. These creatures fly twelve thousand five hundred miles south in the fall and the same distance north in the spring. Nobody understands how they manage this extraordinary annual voyage. I'd been congratulating myself on travelling a few hundred miles north by rail. I thought of the life of an arctic tern and shivered, a life spent in eternal migration. These poor birds can scarcely have arrived in the North, nested, reared their young, before they have to prepare to start south. They find their way, with their fledglings, along this longest-possible route by signals that we sophisticates can't yet analyze. And they always make the flight, and always get where they're going.

Jeanne and I discussed this identification for perhaps twenty minutes, and then I noticed that *Polar Princess* had altered her course; the Shipsands shore receded. We were running out into James Bay. This was one of the most momentous happenings of my life. I never thought I'd come up this way. One of the mates was carefully recording information in a notebook as we progressed, timing our progress and making observations about the depth of the channel, which was being monitored accurately by the ship's sonars.

"How long has the ice been out?" I asked her.

"It went out late this season, about three weeks ago, suddenly, in a couple of days, like a dream. Have you ever seen it go?"

"Not on a body of water like this, but I've often seen it happen on a lake, usually around the end of April. You're perfectly right. It goes fast when it goes, and on a lake it makes a funny tinkling sound like a sink full of ice cubes."

"We don't get any tinkling noises," the mate said. "We get a booming sound, like guns being fired at a distance."

I wouldn't have minded hearing that sound; everything about this northern coast was fascinating, almost hypnotic in its total unfamiliarity. Now we were moving out into the open bay. The coastline seemed to shrink away astern, and the estuary to merge into the low profile of the land. In the end we must have been ten miles offshore, far enough to give the impression of being well out at sea, the shore seeming nothing but an ambiguous ribbon of indeterminate hue, between a soft grey and blue-green. The water around us, under the noon sun, seemed transparent and totally unpolluted. Water as fine and clear as that is harder and harder to find.

Even the eastern Ontario lakes where I've spent so much of my life are unclear and algae-ridden for much of the summer. When I first went out to the lake district northwest of Stoverville the water had a scent like an exquisite perfume. I swear to God, when you surfaced after diving in, the spray around your emerging head seemed like a delicate cologne. No pollution moved in the water in those days; now everything has changed. You have to come north to find the pure crystal waters of Ontario. The dream has receded year by year to the North, drawing the clean waters behind it, funnelling them down the north slope to this fantastic coast. Around us the surface was a gently moving, rocking tissue of clear blue crystal. Not deep, not frigid, very pure.

I looked astern. It was now about one-fifteen and we were almost out of sight of land. A few shreds of cloud moved at a great height, tracing attenuated shadows on the water some distance away. They looked like dark fish lying just below the surface. Wandering birds signalled to each other; a few hardy fliers skimmed the sliding blue surface. *Polar Princess* came to slow-ahead, then seemed to float motionless, as idle as a painted ship. Coffee time.

The skipper joined us in the main saloon, leaving the other mate in charge of the wheelhouse. "We won't anchor; we'll just keep way on her," he said, accepting coffee and a croissant from the young woman who kept the log. The hull was still and inanimate. We lunched there, almost into the Mid-North, towards the top of the continent and the huge islands that lie nearer the pole, Baffin, Ellesmere. It was hot and stuffy in the saloon; this made me want to laugh.

"This is not how I'd imagined it."

"What did you expect?" Captain Marychurch asked, balancing his cup on one knee and a buttered croissant on the other.

"Chunks of the glacier, fog, spectral forms moving in opaque greyness, both mist and snow, gale-force winds, bears, elk. What one imagines about the North."

The vessel seemed at a standstill, lying on the water like a resting seabird in the middle of an exhausting migratory flight. How can they circle the globe once a year? I thought. Their lives are vested in wings, flight, motion at great heights coming to the North, then quitting it.

"To find what you're talking about," the captain said, "you have to go a thousand miles farther, to the other side of Ellesmere or the north coast of Greenland."

"I've seen the south coast of Greenland from the air," I said. "I didn't see any green."

"Well, you wouldn't, would you?" the captain said. "And all the same, on Ellesmere and Greenland they have to be careful of the fragile snow covering, so as not to damage it."

"You're joking."

"I'm perfectly serious. Why, did you know that Ellesmere gets less precipitation annually than the Sahara? Result is, the snow gets worn and rubbed and damaged and nothing replaces it. They're planning a park for the north coast of Ellesmere; it'll be open in a year or two. I just hope they don't rub the shoreline bare. They're going to bring in snow-making machines."

"That sounds as if you've been there."

"Flew in two summers ago," said Captain Marychurch, "with a survey party. I was along for the ride. It's a strange place, the farthest north in the Canadian Arctic. Would you believe it, in the first week in July on the north coast the shore is bare of snow. You'll find little clumps of purple flowers blooming there. Flowers, blossoms, saxifrage. The sun is out around the clock, and they come up, bloom and then die in a week or ten days. I don't know what they're rooted in. I don't remember seeing anything that looked like soil between the chunks of rock. There must be some sort of nourishment for them. And there's no snow cover; it's all been worn away by the wind."

"How cold was it when you touched down there?"

"In direct sunlight about twenty Celsius."

"Oh, come on!"

"No, no."

"I suppose nobody ever goes there?"

"On the contrary. This summer three Frenchmen are walking across Ellesmere from south to north. They won't walk the return trip; they've arranged to be flown out."

"But why would anybody want to go there? It's the very last place on earth —"

"Exactly," Jeanne said. "It's the last place on earth. I think plenty of people must want to get there. If not plenty, at least some. Well, a few." She looked very grave when she said that.

The captain got to his feet, drained his mug, brushed crumbs from his lips. "Time to be moving," he said. "Go out on the after-deck as we come about. You'll have a good long view to the north."

He returned to the wheelhouse; we felt the power coming to half-ahead as our small ship began to alter course a full one hundred and eighty degrees. In moments we were southward bound. That was my North, the farthest north I ever went. Jeanne and I went out on the afterdeck as the vessel completed her turn. An immensely wide unbounded prospect lay open northwards: James Bay, Hudson Bay. Iqaluit. Resolute. At the highest place on the globe the north shore of Ellesmere. Bare eroded stone with purple flowers unfolding under the endless sun. We are all migratory birds. I saw all at once that the north shore had been Uncle Philip's lifelong destination, rock without snow, at the far edge. Perhaps he was there now.

As we swung around I made the fundamental error of looking directly upward into the huge unmixed vault of the sky, for once empty of moving life. As the ship rotated on her heel, the entire enormous vault above me spun slowly in the opposite direction. I stumbled on the decking and lurched towards the rail. It was like closing my eyes in a dark room and trying to stand on one leg, something I haven't been able to do for several decades. I must suffer from some weakness in my ear-channels. I don't know when I've felt so completely disoriented as at that moment. The slow counteractive spinnings, the pull and strain in my neck muscles, and the water in my eyes. The sky seemed to go all grey, as though a fog were rolling in from the Queen Elizabeths.

Jeanne seized my arm as I tottered. It's just as well that she did because the afterdeck railings aren't very high. In my slightly confused state I might have overbalanced and tumbled into the water. And though the ice had been out for three weeks, that water would still be mighty chilly.

"Come here to me. You'll catch your death in there."

I'm not running after my death, I thought. We aren't involved in any kind of race in that direction. I remembered that the phrase "you'll catch your death" had been recurrent on the lips of my maternal grandmother, Mme. Archambault. It came to me suddenly that her name had been Jeanne. Many interconnections now flashed into place, startling me with revelations.

When a new member is added to your family by whatever accident of marriage or birth, all the previous lines of relationship are altered, sometimes subtly, sometimes with grotesque force and explicitness. I had completely forgotten, while following in the footsteps of my dead uncle, that my mother's mother had been named Jeanne. I hadn't thought much about my mother's parents for many years. They weren't figures in the foreground of memory. But during the long days in the 1930s, when we were all packed in together in our aboriginal dwelling on Summerhill Avenue, Jeanne Archambault had been a commanding presence in my life. An oracle. A demi-goddess who used to make it plain to me that Almighty God had His eye on me and would judge any wrongdoing at once, in some particular manifestation of His wrath, as well as at the last judgment at the end of the world, when my every transgression would be laid bare before the witness of the entire human family. "God punished you."

"*Dieu t'as puni.*"

Almost my earliest acquaintance with my second language came in that succinct declaration, when I'd fallen and skinned a knee, or caused some heavy object to fall on my head and stun me. That was my first Jeanne. Now here in this lost indeterminate waste of waters, the shoreline a narrow pencil mark on an increasingly indistinct horizon, here came a second Jeanne to connect accident with mortality.

"You'll catch your death." My grandmother had been accustomed to tell me that if she happened to catch me leaving the house on a rainy day without first having put my rubbers on. Parental and grandparental concerns for health and safety, in that easy epoch, were not expressed in the heavily technical terms of today's clinical practice. Grandmothers commanded us to put our rubbers on or we'd catch cold.

Aunts — even if only honorary aunts — might equally tell us that accident may predict mortality. Look up at the spinning heavens, wind your neck too tightly on its supporting discs, watch the skies whirl and you may get an unsought glimpse of the last! You'll catch your death. Don't put yourself in the running. Wear your rubbers, even your galoshes. This afternoon, seven or eight miles offshore in James Bay, I was wearing no galoshes. I was wearing very cheap running shoes that I'd bought in a Stoverville mall at a giveaway price.

I allowed Jeanne to haul me back to a safe place on the deck, well away from the railings. "You know something?" I said. "My grandmother was called Jeanne. My mother's mother." I felt I was getting into deep conversational waters, although the actual water under us wasn't deep at all. Sometimes you could see bottom; but you couldn't see or sound the depths of any conversation with Jeanne Goderich concerning her late sister-in-law's family. No, that was the wrong name for the relation. My mother had not lived long enough to be counted as this lady's sister-in-law. Logic, emotion, family history and chronology had made that an unrealizable state. My mother and Jeanne Three Streams could never have been allied elements in a close family system. I don't think that my uncle could ever have proposed any such connection.

"Of course, Phil used to talk to me about Mme. Archambault. That's her, am I right? I knew there was another Jeanne in his life."

This remark astonished me.

"Ishy's mother. He used to say that they looked alike."

I felt like a boxer who, at the two-minute mark in one of the late rounds, is sent to the canvas by a series of heavy blows and on rising at the count of nine finds that he has almost a minute of the round left. He has to hang on and clutch and grab until his head clears, and then he has to try his legs and see whether they'll see him out of danger. I thought to shield my head from these jolting hooks and jabs, but I could not refrain from putting the obvious question.

"Did he ever mention the other Jeanne to you?"

"Oh, sure, from the very first times I met him, before the war. He talked about all of you, Ishy and her mother most of all, and Papa Archambault, who shot all the cats. Am I right? I think Phil noticed me first because my name was Jeanne."

Stick and move. Clutch and hang on. Clinch!

"He told me once that Ishy and her mother were like sisters in many ways. Would you be insulted if I said that he thought I was like them?"

I got a few words out. "Why insulted?" I could feel the deck wheeling to starboard underneath me, carrying me into a new circle of perception. I saw something I'd never understood before. Another human being — or maybe numberless others — can be living as close to you as your parents, or your uncle or your grandmother, without your being aware of them. Such people can live in the weave, as it were, of the fabric of your life for forty years, then at a certain moment step forward and reveal their cousinship or sisterhood, and what is more, *show that they know all about you.* If ordinary human beings can survey us in this way, what do you suppose angels get up to?

We can take it as axiomatic that there are far more angels than humans; they take up so little space. Each of us, therefore, may very well enjoy the attentions of a guardian angel, living in the weave of time and no-time, witness to our innermost reflections, closer to us than we are to ourselves, except in the last faint core of existence. If the active arctic air was crammed with radio and television signals, perfectly audible once you invented your receiver, why mightn't it be full of even purer semiosis, sounds and sweet airs that give delight and hurt not? Your guardian angel may be further inside you than you are.

In just this way somebody like Jeanne may haunt us, live

further inside us than ourselves, yet never make herself known to us until very late in the game, when her close knowledge of our lives and motives may open wide new prospects on futurity, but even more on the past. Everything in my life shifted to one side when I found that Uncle Philip had been ready to compare the two Jeannes, my grandmother and my new aunt, in 1930 or 1940. Here was an intellectual problem of the very subtlest kind. What did he see as their common qualities? Strength? Candour? Undeviating pursuit of their goals? Independence of mind, upright carriage, brimming health, readiness to invoke the terrible engine of Divine Wrath? Dreadful new avenues of investigation now lay bare as *Polar Princess* turned right round and pointed her bows at an invisible coast. I hadn't realized that we'd come so far out in the bay. We were almost, not quite, out of sight of land, and the sky continued unmarred, evenly coloured and greying, spread over us like an invisible bowl.

It was getting on for two-fifteen. I had about three hours until train time. Jeanne knew this. I saw her go forward to check with the captain about our time of arrival at the dock. I went up on the upper deck as she did so, to try to spot the mouth of the river. I felt the engine begin to turn over at a higher rate of RPMS; a creamy blue-grey-silver wake foamed astern as we closed onshore. I noticed an alteration in the quality of the light. Not a haze exactly, some nearly invisible presence hung in the sky, a softening of outline, the faintest imaginable blur. A change in the weather impended. It started to seem cooler along one's arms and legs; a very faint breeze got up. I watched the line of the shore and the islands in the estuary grow definite and distinct.

The continental land mass rose up to engulf us. *Polar Princess* was moving faster now, heading into the current, as if to make up for time lost. Channel markers came into view in their regular and correct sequence. The ground swell began to make itself felt; the excursion vessel rose and fell like a cantering horse heading for the barn. In another half-hour we entered the estuary, Shipsands once more abeam, this time to starboard. The birds made their noises and their curvettings; the light somehow thickened and now we were in sight of the docks and the hotels. The mates took up their positions forward and astern to pass lines ashore. I was impressed with the dexterity and assurance of the woman who had been logging the outing. She stood on the foredeck, balancing herself gracefully against the slight motion of the vessel, mooring line held loosely in her hands as she prepared to pass it to the docker standing onshore. The craft was swinging round, coming in towards the dock at slow speed, so as to be positioned for departure, bows pointing downriver with the dock to port. Closer, closer in, here she comes, stop engines.

Polar Princess completed her turn and swung up beside the dock with no impact, the hull coming to rest just before making contact, a most seamanly manoeuvre. I was impressed. And I watched eagerly as the mates took in their spring lines and made them fast. Captain Marychurch joined us on the afterdeck, shook hands, and bade me a formal farewell.

"Didn't show you very much today?"

"Not at all, Captain. You showed me an awful lot. An opening to the north, if nothing else. If James Bay widens out into a space like that, what can Hudson Bay be like? Like the ocean, I guess."

"Well, sir, it *is* the ocean, it's like a big arm of the Arctic Ocean. It's very tricky for navigators. Have you ever been in Churchill?"

"No, but I know there's oceanic navigation out of the port there."

"About a ten-week season. It could be longer if the government would get behind it and mount an adequate ice-control service. But they don't seem to care; they say they've put enough money into Churchill already, more than the possible returns could justify. Hudson Bay is certainly tricky, and we haven't got the votes here to put pressure on anybody. We need a northern oceanic navigational service in this country. It's our longest coast, from Ungava to the Mackenzie Delta and beyond."

"Franklin's Land," I said. "I think folks are afraid of Sir John's ghost."

"You're a long way south of Franklin's Land. I don't think Sir John will trouble your sleep tonight."

"I'm sure he won't." We shook hands and said goodbye. I asked about the fee for the trip, but they wouldn't accept anything.

"Glad to have had you aboard," said Captain Marychurch. "This one's on the *Princess*." We crossed the road to the hotel. I went to my room to check for forgotten articles. I don't often leave anything behind. I had some trouble cramming the jacket I'd worn north into my luggage, but I wanted to wear Uncle Philip's jacket on our way up to the station. It was made of very good tweed. I stroked it proudly when I put it on. I'd never wear it out, not at my age. Perhaps I'd have it on the next time I came this way.

As we left the hotel Jeanne nodded to her left, at a small building with a display plaque beside the door. "Want to look through the museum?" she asked. "We've got forty-five minutes to spare."

"What museum is that?"

"The Révillon Frères Museum. Relics of the fur trade, and I do mean relics; the fur trade is very unpopular, you know. A terrible blow to our people. This country was opened up by the fur trade. Furs for fashionable ladies in Paris before the revolution."

"What do the Cree people think of all that?"

"I can't speak for my people. I've spent too long in Toronto." I was struck by the bitterness of her tone.

"What's in there exactly? I'm not much for stuffed animals."

"Old photographs. A few handsome skins, cured and mounted. Maps of the trappers' routes, a trap or two. A set of photographs of Colonel Lindbergh and his wife."

"Who?"

"Lindbergh. The Lone Eagle. Perhaps you don't remember about him. Said to have been the first person to fly the Atlantic solo, and may have been at that. Lucky Lindy. Married a millionaire's daughter, and then there was that awful kidnapping case."

I remembered Lindbergh all right, but had never associated him with the Canadian North. "What was he doing here? Why should he be in the museum next door?"

"A year or two after that awful kidnapping, maybe three years, he and his wife flew the great circle route to the Far East, by way of the Far North. Something to do with establishing the best commercial flight path to China. I don't think the route was developed — the war got in the way — but in 1933 it was a going proposition. Colonel Lindbergh flew through here in a float plane. His wife acted as navigator and wireless operator; the trip was partly financed by the Morrow interests. Commercial aviation was going to have a hot future. They refuelled here. They docked their seaplane right in front of where we're standing, moored where *Polar Princess* ties up. The Révillon people made a big thing of it. They presented the couple with furs and housed them overnight. They were putting the Bay people's noses out of joint, I guess. Anyway, there are more than a dozen shots of Colonel and Mrs. Lindbergh, their plane and the Révillon staff, grouped right here. She must have been a pretty woman, from her pictures. She wrote a book about the trip afterwards. They made other stops at Baker Lake and Aklavik. They were looking for potential bases, and they got all the way to the Far East. I've seen the book. *North to the Orient.*"

"That's a very good title," I said, with the rapid judgment of somebody who works with books. "It's a good idea for east–west travel and communication. Or for invasion by air. The war would have blocked this particular arc of the great circle completely. The Aleutians, the Pacific coastline of the U.S.S.R., Korea, Japan, they'd all have been forbidden territory. And Lindbergh discredited himself completely during the war."

"A strange life."

"Plucky Lucky Lindy," I said.

"What's that?"

"A song out of the remote past. There was a month or two when Lindbergh was the most admired and celebrated person alive."

"Downhill all the way afterwards," Jeanne said. She is certainly able to look directly at harsh reality.

This chit-chat about Lindbergh made me uneasy. "He had no luck at all after he got to Paris."

"That's the worst of getting where you've always wanted to go," Jeanne said.

The Lindbergh story has always discomforted me. I was afraid that Jeanne would go on to draw a parallel between Lucky Lindy and Uncle Philip. If nothing fails like success, it can equally well be noted that nothing succeeds like failure; we live in contrastive states. I'd sooner have lived Uncle Philip's life than Lucky Lindy's, but there were certainly parallels between the two men. My uncle, as a very young man in 1927, the year of Lindbergh's epochal flight, had had a distinct physical resemblance to the celebrated aviator, the spindly gauntness and hollow cheeks, the shock of hair and a general air of alarmed surprise. That year the Squire and his lady and Uncle Philip had arrived in Toronto fresh from long residence in Barringford, Nova Scotia, a flight almost as epochal, on a personal scale, as an Atlantic crossing made solo. I had seen pictures of Uncle Philip at fifteen or sixteen that made him look as solitary as any pilot alone over the Atlantic.

"North to the Orient, eh?" I was nagged by suggestion. "It seems an inspired choice of route, to go east by flying north. I'm about to move in the reverse direction, south to the occident, a weird dog-leg, like the knight's move in chess."

But Jeanne disclaimed all knowledge of complex board games. "We'll bypass the museum, then?"

"Yes, let's."

"I don't mind. And it isn't so long until train time." She took me by the arm, smoothing the excellent tweed of my new jacket. "I'm very glad you're taking this along. I'll enjoy thinking about you, wearing it in some stroll along Bloor Street."

"It might be a little warm for Bloor Street tomorrow. But I'll wear it when he'd have worn it. Think of me sporting it on Huron

Street in October, or visiting that bank we all seem so fond of, or strolling down Crescent Road to the subway stop."

She was close to tears; we shouldn't direct memory towards corrupt nostalgia.

"Will you keep on your apartment?"

"I don't know. I just can't say. Phil wanted me to keep it on, but now he's gone I'll never use it. I'd better write and tell them I won't be renewing the lease. I'll have to arrange to have my stuff sold or stored or sent back here."

I couldn't fight my impulses. "I could help you with that. I might find you a sub-lease, just in case you might like to come back south sometime."

"I won't close it up without thinking it over, but I have no plans to leave here. I can easily find something to do. I might work at the lodge. I might do some tour guiding, or work for the band council. I don't belong anywhere else."

We strolled towards the station in a companionable silence. I couldn't believe how close to somebody you could come in a few days. I felt as though I'd known Jeanne for forty years, and that seemed to me now to be the point of my northern excursion. Not my uncle's funeral. Not a property settlement nor examination of a will or decision about certain legal questions, not a division of the spoils. Uncle Philip had achieved an exemplary death, quitting life without giving any trouble to anybody. This was in its way as good a death as anybody's. "Gave no trouble. Went quietly."

"If you want me to oversee storage, or ship your things north . . ."

"I'll arrange that myself. Why should you be bothered?"

"I might at least arrange to see a dealer about that picture."

"Which picture?"

"The one on your living-room wall. It's by my wife."

She laughed; she must have known all about Edie. "You don't miss much," she said. I felt obscurely flattered. I'm no detective, but I could identify any of Edie's pictures anywhere.

"I like that picture. I think I'll have it shipped north." She smiled at me teasingly. Almost sixty, I thought, and still a charmer.

We came near the train platform, where the locomotive and the cars were making those tentative goose-like hissing noises that precede departures; there didn't seem to be many travellers about. The summer season was still two weeks off. I half-expected Jeanne to board the train with me to help me settle down, wish me a formal goodbye. It might be a long while before we met again, but instead she drew back, at the foot of the little wooden set of steps. There was perhaps fifteen minutes before train time. I wondered whether I'd said something to displease her, or been too offhand about the purpose of my trip. Was there some unexpected cooling of the emotional atmosphere? I couldn't tell.

We stood there looking at each other. I thought how many and how complex were the ties that had drawn us together. My mother was in Jeanne's face and posture, and my wife and daughter and sister and niece. I felt other masks overlying mine; my cheeks seemed to contort into the likeness of my uncle.

"You're so much like him," she said, reading my thoughts.

"I'm not as good as he was."

"No, I don't suppose you are. But you can keep trying."

Now she came close to me again. I sensed that an embrace was imminent. She wanted me to put my arms around her, but it wouldn't be my embrace. It would be my arms moved by ghostly intention. I damned my customary scruples and took her in my arms. She was a solid armful, unmistakably there. I looked into her eyes. "I'll never forget you," we both said, simultaneously prompted by the same impulse. I felt her right hand fumbling at the pocket of the fine tweed jacket, my inheritance from Philip.

"Don't look in your pocket until you're past Moose River Crossing," she said. "You can't miss it. It's where we met, forty-three years ago. I can't believe it."

I shrugged the jacket into a more composed position on my shoulders, took up my hand luggage and mounted the steps, turning left at the conductor's directions and finding my seat halfway down the car. There were hardly any other passengers. I peered through the shining window and waved to Jeanne. I mouthed the words, "Don't bother to wait," but she gave a determined nod, as though to indicate a wish to remain where she was; she waved tentatively. She was still standing there when the train edged its way slowly out of the small yard. Her figure seemed to diminish slowly. Then the train changed direction and I couldn't see her any more.

I found I was puffing slightly, perhaps from the exertion of wrestling my gear onto the train, perhaps from some other cause. We were moving swiftly now, well launched on the forty-miles-plus run upriver towards Moose River Crossing. I felt excitement at the thought of the mysterious communication in my pocket, my final contact with Philip and Jeanne. I fingered the object without taking it from my pocket. I waited until we were crossing the wide river on a great big bridge a couple of thousand feet long. When we were halfway across, moving rather slowly, suspended over the immense power of the flood below the train, I took Jeanne's gift out of my pocket and examined it, a small oblong package wrapped in white tissue paper and sealed with Scotch tape. I tore off the paper and uncovered a small air-blue jeweller's box in the chaste and smart style of the late 1920s. I knew what I had in my hands, of course. I flipped open the top, which was lined with excellent gold satin. In the middle of the satin lining there was imprinted a square surrounded by an ornamented ribbonlike trim, and in the middle of this tiny space some heraldic beast — possibly a lion, certainly with a mane and tail — stood on his hind legs with forepaws raised in a position of attack or defence. Below this device appeared the single word "Ryrie's."

The bottom of the box was covered in good black velvet, with a raised bracket down the middle of the space. Attached to the bracket or clip was a stem-wound Gruen wristwatch with a handsome black leather strap, virtually unworn, certainly the original equipment, and a gold and gold-plated case. The form

of the watch and the style of the numbers on the dial and the
lettering of the marker's name insistently recalled the later
1920s. I had seen this object on my uncle's dressing table a
thousand times. I took the watch out of the box and returned the
box to my pocket. I took off my own cheap Timex and stuffed it
into another pocket. I pulled back my cuff and extended a hairy
right wrist. I had to read the inscription although I didn't really
want to. It was of ancient familiarity. I had to squint to read the
tiny lettering in ornamental jeweller's script. "For Philip at 16
from Mother and Father." I set it to the correct time and wound
it carefully. I could hear an almost inaudible tick; the little
second hand in the position of the numeral six began to spin.
The piece was in mint condition. The train moved off the bridge,
down onto the east bank. In a couple of hours we reached
Fraserdale and the sight of a provincial highway. Back to
asphalt, concrete, whatever it was. The river narrowed, the
banks rose up. I began to forget what lay at my back. The big
event on the southbound run is the rise towards the divide, the
swing over the top and the reversal of the waters. The whole
continent seems to tilt. It's an eerie seesaw.

Overnight stay in Iroquois Falls; bus next morning to the
downbound train. North Bay at ten to two. Toronto at six forty-
five, Friday, June 10th. I would make a habit of winding my
watch at bedtime.

I took a cab from the station. I was tired from my trip, already
having trouble sorting out the various sights I'd seen. I would go
home, fix a TV dinner in the microwave, stare at the tube, waste
time. It wouldn't be dark for hours yet. Out by Shipsands Island
and over the bay, the birds would be up all night, no darkness,
long light. There was a small pile of mail waiting for me in the
hall, including a transcript in Andrea's handwriting of a telegram
message she'd copied for me the day before. Sent from Hidalgo
Avenue, Sherman Oaks, L.A. "Returning Toronto permanently.
Can you house me short time? Adam."

Down the hall the phone began to ring.

II

I let it ring. I'd had my excitement for the week and I wanted a hot drink and something to eat. I took another look at the text of the telegram. "House me short time." That could mean anything. The plot of the successful old comedy *The Man Who Came to Dinner* flashed into my head. Sheridan Whiteside, an awful person, a drama critic, of all the horrible things to be, who came to dinner, broke an ankle of all things to break, and couldn't be removed from the house. Remained in place for weeks, months, nightmare. I suppose we all have that dream now and then, the unwelcome guest who simply won't go away, notices no hints about business elsewhere, refuses to get out of pajamas and dressing gown, meddles in everybody's affairs and turns out to be horribly right about all of them. Let such an incubus into your dwelling and your life is irretrievably compromised. Ordinary social relations seem to be modelled on our darkest menaces. We all bear the horror of the unwelcome guest — the dark angel who has come to stay — deep in our inner awareness. Won't go. Can't get her to leave. Inescapable telephones.

Witness the strange power exerted by phones ringing in empty rooms. They seem impossible to ignore. Who is at the other end? Good tidings? Bad? Now guilt surfaces! I didn't pay that bill, answer that appeal, attend that lecture. I have sinned by omission. The damned old phone rang eleven times; some very determined caller was working up a sweat of frustration. The right time to answer a call is on the fourth ring. If you let it go past the sixth ring you've been grievously impolite. By the eleventh you have to let it go on ringing until the caller gives up, or you have to lie. You seize the receiver and gasp out, "Just caught you. I heard the phone out on the walk puff puff puff and I rushed in. Couldn't find my front-door key. Here puff puff let me put down these parcels" — you have no parcels — "There!" All this could be obviated by the installation of an answering machine. But that I refuse to do.

And then the call turns out to be a taped inquiry from the circulation department of *The Globe and Mail* about their current cut-rate subscription offer, but there isn't a living person at the other end to register your curses. The telephone directs our lives and has now become an unignorable oracle. I thought, I can ignore it. And eventually it stopped. I lost count of the number of rings but it must have been more than thirty. Had to be Adam, of course. Who else lets the phone ring thirty times? I glanced at my watch. (Should I call it *my* watch?) My handsome heirloom with the touching engraved message on the back. The dial proved unexpectedly hard to read after the flat broad statement of my cheap Timex. Just past eight-thirty. Food. Foody-food-food!

I resolved to ignore further telephone importunings. I set down my bags just inside the living room, which was wonderfully dust-free, though hot and airless. In the freezer compartment of the refrigerator lay a rich assortment of frozen stuff, chicken pies, lasagnas, desserts from McCain. I'm a sucker for TV dinners, which by 1983 had reached an advanced degree of technical sophistication in their food-mimesis. You couldn't tell them from real food unless you closed your eyes and thought hard. I chose a turkey dinner from Swansons (peas, mashed potato, apple crumble) and addressed myself to the microwave. This threatening device was a recent gift not yet six weeks old, a birthday present from Andrea and Josh accompanied by satiric backchat about my attempts to deal with modest electronic devices.

I don't allow people in my apartment to leave small appliances plugged in, toaster-ovens, heaters, the microwave. If I catch them doing it, they get the lecture. They must never detach the power cord from the wall plug by yanking on the cord. What you do is press carefully on the plate around the socket so as not to loosen it, take the plug appeasingly in your other hand, and ease it away from the contact slots. This eliminates all risk of the power cord's coming apart, leaving the plug in the wall, with current seeping out of the broken-off bit of cord that is still attached to it.

People mock me about this. I haven't arrived in the age of post-industrial communications-oriented technology, fax, e-mail, compact discs, microwaves. I'm a superstitious peasant (there are more peasants than critics) who believes that a small godling crouches inside each of these technologies and devices, eyeing me keenly in the attempt to detect uncertainty in approach. Tonight, I resolved, tonight I will master the new microwave. I found the dangling end of the power cord, a much bulkier cord than small appliances used to have (why?) with a massive three-pronged plug. I inserted it in an adjacent socket, feeling real and profound satisfaction at the tight fit, and the solid unshakable lodgement of the heavy plug in the firmly situated socket. I don't think I'd used the microwave three times at that date. I hunted out the instruction booklet. It wasn't easy to find in the half-light of the kitchen at nine P.M. You say, why didn't you turn the lights on? And I answer, I liked the half-light. I felt consumed by shadows. The booklet was in the obvious place, in the kitchen drawer beside the useful new appliance. The instructions were explicit, and not in that strange patois of computer terminology, in which the word "access" appears far too often, and of ordinary English as rendered by a Japanese translator who hasn't mastered it. Much instruction-booklet language of the 1980s seems to participate cruelly in Japanese revenge for the West's use of atomic weaponry against it, but this booklet gave no difficulties.

While the microwave was bringing my turkey dinner to the

stipulated temperature and texture, I laid the kitchen table with cutlery, glasses, salt-shaker, a small dessert. I peeled some carrots that I discovered in the crisper, fresh and firm. I love peeling carrots, it's one of the things I do best. The microwave beeped four times. I removed my dinner from the heating chamber with all due care; it was impressively hot to the touch even through a dish towel. Then I sat down to eat. I thought of leaving the phone off the hook but I knew that the telephone company would fill the receiver with injurious ululations. I ate my meal in perfect silence. It was so quiet that I could hear my new heirloom watch ticking, and its tick is usually so faint as to go undetected, even in deep silence. I could get to like the little thing very much indeed if it went on being so quiet and so clear. Like conscience.

It came to me as I sat there chewing that in many respects I truly have remained a superstitious savage who is convinced that all the objects around him are animate, telephone, microwave oven, toaster, wristwatch. The air around my head is jammed with voices that are inaudible only because I'm not tuned to the correct wavelength. Nothing is what it seems; everything is what it is, having nothing to do with me. Only listen and obey. All silences are full of voices.

I could scarcely believe that thirty hours ago I'd been out of sight of land in James Bay looking towards an empty white immensity. The shift in perspective was almost too much to bear. I could feel my head swimming with overload, the memory-circuitry flooded with signals, old codes and new mingling in a disturbing, even frightening way. Thank goodness I hadn't tackled any cookery more challenging than a TV dinner. A juicy steak would have been more than I could have managed. I was reaching the point of input-saturation. Images that at first seemed to be unconnected began to flood my consciousness, vividly, fully presented. I didn't have to shut my eyes to witness them. I was dreaming while awake. Reality *is* fantasy. I worked the last chunk of tacky apple crumble out of the depression in its plastic dish and began to chew on it thoughtfully. Water for coffee simmered near me on a back burner; in a minute I'd pour it through the filter, and as I imagined this, swivelling my eyes around the familiar comfortable room with its agreeable scent of cinnamon, coffee, quiet dust, cleaning and polishing materials, I began to see things that weren't in the room, but thousands of miles off. I was looking down a much built-over slope through screens of palm and fruit trees, across a wide depression or valley through which a vast freeway bore eternal streams of rushing traffic, a scene out of Adam's postcards and Polaroid photographs, what you see from his balcony in Sherman Oaks. The first range of mountains rose across the valley into a high limiting horizon. Scene from a thousand television cop shows and crime novels, Jim Rockford, Lew Archer, the great Marlowe himself had all examined this vista with the same close fascination I was giving it now. Not so much a place as a range of possibilities for action, an imaginative texture, the scene focussed my attention without any possibility of appeal or escape. The prowling loner, working backwards and forwards along mazy streets from Santa Barbara to San Diego, entangled in some immense conspiracy of which the murder investigation is simply the most recent complication, uncertain where the trail may lead, as ignorant as Jason, Theseus, Oedipus, suffered his alienation just as Uncle Philip or Adam Sinclair must have suffered it. I brooded on this fantasy of palms, orange trees, freeways, paranoia, until I could see it plainer than the walls of my kitchen, and smell the orange blossoms more distinctly than the steam rising from the cup of coffee that, in my state of hallucination, I now poured myself. I could not tell which was the true odour of that night, freeway exhaust and orange blossoms and palm leaves, or the clean smell of the scrubbed kitchen floor under my feet. The private investigator supplies one of the greatest — perhaps the very greatest — patterns for human experience in our present age: unknowingness, obsession, the revealing thread of one clue after another in the hand, fatigue, sleeplessness, alienation, fear of sudden attack. I was in Adam's land. Hooray for Hollywood!

And all at once, imperceptibly, like light snow beginning to fall, another imaginary state of mind began to flow into the scene, the open blankness of the true North, wide and high and cool, and the two scenes merged in imagining, their visual and moral implications running together as in a slow dissolve arrested at its midpoint. I had the middle of the great bay, the stretch towards the north shore of Ellesmere, folded fully into Sherman Oaks, the valley and the freeway, and the enclosing range of hills above and beyond, the smell of exhaust and the faintly salty, neutral tang of sea water, both in my nostrils, present and blended and at the same time distinct and identifiable like musical subjects in strict canon.

I saw that these blended scenes, which were nevertheless separate and individually visible, were the complex signs of two lives that had existed quite apart from my knowledge of them, and at the same time existed in my imagination as supplementary and almost parallel. I had been linked to Uncle Philip by the tie of blood, through my father and in another sense through my mother, as closely as human beings can be connected. We were in one another's blood.

I had been linked to Adam through another kind of bond, maybe a closer tie than that of blood, that I claimed but couldn't name. These two presences in my life were so close to me that I might as well have been entered in a three-legged race with two different runners, one on either side, in fact a six-legged race. Adam with his right leg bandaged to my left, Philip with his left leg fastened to my right. In the middle I could only swing my own legs at the instance of my companions, and my hands and arms reached out desperately on either side, reaching for the bending rocking necks of the racers. Their separate impulses bore me along in this six-legged race with no competition. Who else would conceive such an athletic feat?

What had Moose Factory and Sherman Oaks in common?

Oceanic coasts, startling scenic beauties, population largely
immigrant, barely visible native peoples, exploitation by questionable industrial undertakings. Story possibilities. Adam and
Philip, always nearly related and sometimes confused in my personal story, now seemed to be transforming themselves into a set
of almost pregnant and parallel possibilities with voluminous
implications for me and for themselves. What they had in
common was guessable though so far unknown to me, their
obscure existence "in the holes" of the texture of my own history.
They were woven into my experience in the way threads cross
other threads at right angles, over and under and over and under
so as to form the final webbed pattern. I must have existed
in reciprocal relation to them as they to me, as intermittent presences, most of whose life was lived at mysterious distances and
over long indecipherable lengths of time. I had never known
much about Jeanne Goderich until this week. She had been an
opaque distant absence/presence hinted at and full of implication but effectively unknown, a part of Uncle Philip's life, not
mine. In the same way, Adam might have gathered to himself a
platoon of surrounding presences of whom I could suspect little
or nothing. Which of us was warp and which was weft?

I had nothing mysterious to conceal in my own life, which
seemed to me perfectly open to inspection. But to Adam or to
Uncle Philip, during our long associations, I might have seemed
as hard to understand, and as mysterious in action, as any
oracle or unaccountable witch doctor. What did they know about
me and Edie, me and Linnet, me and Tony? All these people and
I myself were woven together into a fabric of which none of us
could see the pattern clearly. Adam and Philip ran across my lines
and were closely knit together in their unknowability. Jeanne was
Philip's big surprise package. Linnet might have been mine, the
element in my life whom none of my friends could have predicted.
Who was the corresponding figure in Adam's life, the concealed
surprising object of lifelong intense love?

I remembered that for long years I had judged Philip and

Adam to be obeying forbidden impulses, violating taboos. I had suspected my uncle of the sin of Claudius, connivance at the disappearance of a brother in order to possess his wife. It was not that I accused my uncle in my heart of the murder of my father. I'm not a big enough soul to rise to such a suspicion. What I suspected of my poor uncle was that he harboured conscious and unfulfilled affections towards my mother, rather than finding a lover and wife of his own. In this I had been drastically mistaken. I now began to see my uncle as a man much sinned against, and by me! I had no idea whether my sister had ever suspected Uncle Philip of half-conscious incestuous motives. On the whole, probably not. As a woman and a daughter she might take completely different views of my uncle's emotional life. She might have suspected the existence of Jeanne in the background of my uncle's life long before I did. Amanda Louise has always been a shrewder and more generous judge than I. As far as that went, my niece, Emily, seemed to know more about these matters than I did. Always the last to catch on, the traditional posture of the imperceptive male. I only excused my uncle of sin after he'd died.

Adam too had been the object of my misgivings. Until now I had usually taken a comic and satiric view of my old friend — perhaps my earliest male friend. I had summed him up all my life as sexually deviant and therefore funny. In the vulgar language of the street boy, remembered from conversation with Tom and Gerry Cawkell, Adam was to be qualified as a fucking fruit, and the contemptuous tone of this language told the hearer all he needed to know about the person so described.

Flouncing, affected, campy, not like us, unworthy of our company, somehow frightening, possibly a carrier of contagion to be avoided as soon as recognized. Fucking fruit! There were then some dozens, perhaps hundreds, of epithets to describe such people. I won't repeat them but I will say that they have almost all disappeared from the vocabulary of the ordinary civilized person. Only one or two remain in current use, one of them deeply injurious, the other accepted by those whom it describes as the least offensive of names.

The term "homosexual" seems to be falling out of use even as a neutral descriptive name, and so it should, because it groups people according to their sexual preference. Whose business is that anyway? It's none of my business what you do in private, or in public for that matter. I plan not to use the word "homosexual" any more.

There remains the single word "gay." Gay rights. Gay persons. Gay bars. I remember how on perhaps the unhappiest night of my life Adam had risen from the past like a loving ghost, put me in a cab and trundled me off to what I then referred to mentally as a gay bar. I'm in a gay bar with Adam Sinclair, I thought, and despite my anguish at having left my dear mother in a nursing home that same evening I had felt the straight male's sense of superiority to all these comical creatures, parading around in their Yonge Street sanctuary. I remember wondering what would happen next. Would I be approached by one or another of the little young men I saw in the wide room, for a clothing allowance (you could put it on your VISA card, darling) or just for twenty dollars to get him through the night? I was frightened and amused, and I began to forget momentarily that the beloved woman who had given me birth was lying alone in a room at the Saint Raphael Nursing Home, sightless and close to her end. What a terrifying blend of cruel raw experience! My mother dying and alone, Adam at the table across from me gazing with dismayed revulsion at the blurred images on the television screen, the nameless young man at my side discussing his taste in sportswear, the noise.

A gay bar. Wonderful title for some novelist, and will continue to be so for years to come, the phrase conceals so many nuances of opinion. Some of us say dismissively, "Nothing gay about it! Wait till they're old and ugly and alone, then they'll see how gay they can be!" We can't give up the need for a mean revenge, punishment for those who refuse to be like us. Kinky. Bent. Not straight. A visible minority. Stay in the closet and do as you like but don't dare to be black or yellow or red. We are going to have to give up the conception of the visible minority, the colour bar, the behaviour bar, the attention to visible differences. Who cares how Catullus walks? We are going to have to do without prejudices.

All my life I thought Uncle Philip was an insinuating harbourer of wrong wishes. I thought my earliest friend was a fucking fruit. I can't continue to live on such terms. Suspicion, rejection, the barring ford. What I had seen during my days in the Near North might best be shown by the symbol of the tilting watershed. On one side all the rivers run down to the north, and on the other to the south. When you go over the top and feel the world of waters tilt under you, everything changes. I had been wrong all my life about Uncle Philip and about Adam too. I willed the phone to ring again. It was now eleven P.M., barely eight on Sunset Boulevard or in Sherman Oaks. Surely he would try again, surely a second ringing was at hand. Adam had something to reveal, I felt certain of this. His telegram had suggested a final departure from Hollywood. Why? Were his appearances in the hugely successful nighttime soap called *Fate* becoming too much for his cherished reputation? I recalled that in a letter he had expressed the fear that the huge exposure conferred by a top-rated serial might prove corrosive to a career. Many actors had made a huge success in a single series — Hal Linden, Adam West — only to find themselves so totally identified with their character as never to succeed in another part. Carroll O'Connor, Paul Eddington, Joan Collins.

Is there life after *Fate*? That must be the question that Adam now put to himself daily. He had never been a regular on the show, preferring to make between four and six appearances in any given season. *Fate* must now, I calculated, be about to start its fourth full season on the network. Sadie had been the principal woman performer on the show since its beginnings, appearing every week, adored by her legions of fans who remembered her first American series, *Out By Midnight*, with love. That's the only word for it. She and Abe Sonnenschein had been the biggest stars on U.S. television for seven years or more, their ascendancy lasting from 1964 through 1971. Sadie, I recalled, had made feature-length films for theatre distribution while she was in *Out By Midnight*, and had maintained her immense following through the 1970s when she wasn't appearing in a series. Then *Fate* had come along at the beginning of the 1980s and now looked like running forever. Sadie, I imagined, would not achieve a third great success in a series. She must be well into her fifties, the same as me, and it looked as though she would continue to make new episodes of her current series until its popularity began to decline, perhaps three or four seasons down the line.

If Sadie were to decide to retire then, coming off a long run in a hit series, she would find herself an immensely rich woman with nothing to do but amuse herself for the rest of her life. She and Adam were still technically man and wife, none of Sadie's moves in the direction of divorce ever having continued through the final stage. I wondered about Sadie in retirement for a few minutes, then decided that no, she would never retire. When *Fate* declined in popularity (if it ever did) she would make a triumphant return to the stage somewhere or other, perhaps even at the Stratford Shakespearean Festival, where she had launched her career thirty years earlier. What parts might Sadie undertake at sixty? Goneril? Lady Macbeth? She would never be able to accept walk-ons or very youthful castings. I shivered as I thought of this. Thirty years is a long time in an actor's career. It didn't seem all that long ago, the first season in Stratford when Edie and I had been on our honeymoon and Adam had made that heavy pass at me while Edie was temporarily absent from our bedroom.

Thinking of this I felt alternate impulses of laughter and near-tears. At that time, almost exactly thirty years ago, I had judged without ambiguity that Edie's sexual acceptance of me was the thing to aim at; Adam's advances were to be as unambiguously rejected. I remembered Edie arriving back in our bedroom from some late-night working party hollering, "Damn you, Adam, I don't share my husband with anybody, do you hear me? Scat, scat!"

Then she had taken a full baseball-player's swing at him with our new broom, causing Adam to leap nude from our tangled sheets and scamper across the floor and out of our bedroom, leaving his discarded underclothes on the chair where he had deposited them before sneaking into bed behind me. Edie caught him a last solid smack across his glistening buttocks as he departed; then she shut the door and collapsed on the bed beside me roaring with laughter. We fell into the ardent newly-wedded clutch that had been interrupted some hours earlier by her departure for the workroom. Adam's sortie had been an improvised and aborted undertaking. I was incapable of responding to him, certainly not on the fourth night of my honeymoon, when I found myself incapable of determining where fantastic sexual dream left off and daylight existence began. Finding out what Edie and I could do together in bed filled the whole of my conscious and unconscious life.

The events of that week determined the subsequent course of my sexual life. I could now see how early passionate response to Edie had prepared me for Linnet, our wonderful joyful union and its terrible end. Edie had made my love for Linnet possible by marrying me and walking out on me with my brother. We are each other's moral tutors and sexual guides. But now Linnet was dead and Edie in London, still married to me but unreachable and alienated. Adam, who had seemed a zany figure of *commedia dell'arte* comic satire during our honeymoon, had nevertheless kept up his life and maintained a dignified posture, had refused to be laughed away by me or Edie or Sadie or anybody else. He was a nuisance perhaps, but not a valueless and laughable nuisance. He had lasted better than Edie, and now seemed genuinely eager to cohabit with me for some longer or shorter time. I dug out the crumpled text of his telegram and examined it critically. "Returning Toronto permanently. Can you house me short time?" I considered the varieties of meaning embedded in the innocent phrases like some great scholar of the Renaissance, Scaliger, Bentley, bent on reinstating the true meaning of some fragment of manuscript that had survived from ancient times. "Permanently." That might mean anything. All Adam's life he had been taking what he considered binding decisions only to revise them in the next moment. Permanence for Adam meant about five minutes. I needn't set much store by his hankerings for permanence. I didn't consider Adam capable of a permanent decision or state of mind. He was one with sparrows and starlings in that respect.

But the annexed proposal for short-term residence on Crescent Road was something else. In my most recent meetings with Adam, going back perhaps three years, he had hinted at a wish to move in with me on some sort of irregular basis. Intermittent, not immoral. He wanted leave to stay in the apartment now and then, as his *pied à terre* in Toronto. I had seen him in the light of a waif or stray — still a comic type — and had treated his advances lightly. It seemed impossible at that date, end of 1979, beginning of 1980, to treat his initiatives as anything but funny. Adam was a funny man, not to be taken seriously. And in any case his sexual undertakings ruled him out as a companion. I didn't want him sneaking into my bed a generation after his initial attempt. God, what a muddle!

The phone now rang, as of course it would in the midst of such meditations. I had too much in my head. I couldn't straighten it out. "House me short time?" Be careful what you concede, I told myself, and I edged towards the phone. I got to it on about the ninth ring. Just before picking up the receiver I thought, who is Adam's surprise package?

I spoke charily into the mouthpiece.

"*Well!*" (said with the emphasis and timing of the late Jack Benny).

I found myself falling into the accent and pace of radio and television comedy, as often in Adam's company. "Don't start up," I said, feeling like Allen Stuart Konigsberg. "What's to discuss?"

"I'm sitting on my balcony smelling the orange blossoms."

"Good for you."

"On Hidalgo Avenue."

"Adam, Adam, Adam, what is all this about Hidalgo Avenue. Do you know what an hidalgo is?"

"No. Should I?"

"It's a chivalric title like chevalier, or caballero or sir."

"You are a mine of information, as always."

"And you are no hidalgo. Adam, it's a word out of the Warner Brothers animation team's wildest flights of invention. Stuff for Chuck Jones and Friz Freleng to play with. I should say 'weeth.'"

"Is it nice and warm in Toronto?"

"It's the tenth of June. What do you think?"

"It's too breezy here on the balcony. I'm having trouble keeping warm."

"You wouldn't have wanted to be with me yesterday."

"Where were you, at the North Pole?"

"You're close." I expect he thought I was teasing, and anyway it's a long way from James Bay to the Pole. "But not too close."

"And now you're back to stay?"

"I'm not certain, I can't say." I had to conceal my wish to settle into one spot to stay. Best to make no firm statements.

"But you're at home now? You'll be there for a while, until I can arrange to get there?"

He was speaking in a strangely appealing tone, at least as far as I could judge. I can never understand how the human voice, translated into electrical impulses by the telephone, retains its personal appeal when unscrambled at the other end of the circuit and delivered in the receiver. A good telephone voice. I've often been told that I have a good telephone voice, and it's the one voice I will never hear on the line. Tonight the voice in the receiver was unmistakably Adam's, with his inflections and familiar professional actorish precision and beauty. I don't think

I've ever previously admitted to the beauty of Adam Sinclair's speech, on or off the stage. He always had an engaging persuasive range of vocal tone. I don't suppose you can get far into an acting career without an attractive voice.

But now there was something obscurely wrong with his voice. I detected in it some hesitation, some uncharacteristic lowering of pitch, a failure to persuade and convince, an unspoken plea delivered in wavering uncertain tones. When had I last heard that agonized tone in this particular voice? It hadn't been during a phone conversation. I was sure of that.

The words sounding in the receiver tonight were distorted and fudged by circuit noise. At least that's all I could make of it. We had a poor connection. As far as that goes we'd always had a poor connection, but tonight the thousands of miles of circuitry made understanding more unlikely than ever. I thought of saying that I'd call him back, but this would seem like rejection. Adam was presuming too much. How could I reject him when I'd never accepted him? A sound like an oceanic pulse, something like the impressions one collects from a big seashell, now began to rise and fall in my telephone ear, through which Adam's voice penetrated only intermittently. Was the phone company at fault, or was Adam himself to blame? Suddenly it seemed as though this surf-like roaring originated with my caller, not with a failure in the transmitting device. He was roaring or sobbing at intervals, only intermittently allowing his voice to show through, in a kind of solo mini-drama. The words he spoke came through these disturbances at unpredictable intervals; they were charged with emotional freight of a type that I couldn't make out. The voice, certainly Adam's, was distorted, shrunken, with curious vibrations as though the hard plastic material of the phone in his hands, or in my hands, was vibrating in sympathy with these broken utterances. His communication reached me through a shivering plastic intermediary that made him seem to be weeping and begging for help. The oceanic pulsing in my ear rose in volume. A really bad circuit. The years began to fall away from my ears; there was an apocalyptic menace trapped in the roaring sound, and now I found myself back in the Beverly theatre on Yonge Street on a Saturday afternoon in the spring of 1938. Forty-five years had been magically wiped out of existence. The roaring rose and fell like heavy surf on an imagined shore, the maddened noise of a gang of children at odds with the ushers, the theatre manager and with themselves, the boys against the girls. The wailings of Adam Sinclair rose thinly from beneath a central row of theatre seats, a posture of defence that only partially shielded the unfortunate boy from the pinchings and hair-pullings and occasional kicks of his tormentors.

The cries reached me across a yawning gulf of time, shrieking like a dentist's drill when it meets hard enamel. What is that sound, memory asks, and instantly replies to her own inquiry. That is the sound of Adam Sinclair being victimized by his peer group. I would not have expressed the notion in those words in the spring of 1938. I'd have said that the guys were picking on him. Adam was about a year and a half older than I was; it caused me a certain obscure excitement to realize that I could establish ascendancy over him though so much his junior. I've never known his exact birthdate; like many actors he guards specific information about birthdays with circumspection, but I'm certain that he is a good eighteen months older than I am, which puts his birthdate somewhere in the fall of 1928. Never a well-grown lad in early childhood, Adam wasn't much bigger than I was. I had no feelings of veneration for him such as I had for other boys his age who might be bigger or stronger, better at baseball, readier to punch and kick. I had no idea what Adam might make of his life, but I knew very clearly on those Saturday afternoons in 1938 that a dramatic, histrionic, even role-playing element had invaded his life. He had been cast as our victim, by himself as much as by his contemporaries. His cries had come to me shrunken, metallic and thin, weepy, undignified, sketching out suffering. My need to make somebody else (not me) suffer emerged out of my deepest instincts. I knew the word "victim" at that date, having often heard it in narratives concerned with the Passion of Christ. I couldn't rise to the conception of myself torturing Jesus, but I certainly could imagine myself picking on Adam Sinclair, or failing nobly to participate in such an act. I could make myself feel good and responsible, at eight years old, by saying to the other guys in the Beverly on a Saturday, "Okay, c'mon, you guys, that's enough, eh? Let him go now." For some reason they never turned on me. There were probably class lines involved, and economic status, and certain questions of physical appeal. I looked and sounded ineligible for the role in which Adam had been cast by himself, by his peers, by me, by life.

He had been part of my life since page one; long before my legs were long and sturdy enough to carry me from our house to the St. Clair–Yonge district in the later 1930s, an eon before, or about five years, Adam had manifested himself in my experience and in that of Amanda Louise, as almost our first — perhaps indeed our very first — candidate for victimhood, as we played the game my sister had invented, which we both instinctively called Executioner.

When Amanda Louise was just five and I was three and a bit, we were playing with our garden swing one lovely afternoon. We had removed the platform that linked the two facing bench seats and made them into a single swinging unit. I very incautiously placed myself between the two separated elements of the device, and Amanda, actuated by God alone knows what impulse, shoved the bench seat that I stood facing towards me with a forceful thrust. The bottom edge of the seat-assembly caught me on both shins. The blow was extremely painful, causing me to lose for a moment the muscular control of my limbs. They buckled under me, and I had to roll briskly sidewise and down to get out of the way of the hard wooden object as it approached me a second time. I put up my hand to steady it and slow it down; this diverted my attention from the acute pain in my leg bones. Golly, but they hurt! I have rarely been quick to weep, and I didn't then. I wouldn't allow anybody the satisfaction, even at the age of three, of seeing Matt Goderich crying. I can only recall one such occasion in my life. I had a pretty solidly formed conception of my social appearance at the age of three. Perhaps we all do.

The swing was now stilled, hanging straight up and down, just vibrating slightly after recent rapid oscillation. I got painfully to my feet and eyed my shrinking sister accusingly.

"You're going to tell on me," she faltered.

This was one of the crucial events of my infancy and childhood. Telling on her wouldn't take the smart away. Not telling on her would put her in my debt. I wouldn't have been able to express this at the time but I knew perfectly well what was implied.

"I'm not going to tell on you. Let's find somebody else to try it on!"

And here Adam Sinclair walked into my life. Still struggling to hold back tears, bending to reach my smarting shins and rub them, and accepting Amanda Louise's relieved embrace with appropriate dignity, I became aware that somebody was standing near us.

"Can I play?" said this figure.

"You sure can," said Amanda, and I giggled in agreement.

We had found our victim.

Everybody now knows what Adam Sinclair looks like, after seeing twenty thousand photographs of him. At that date he did not resemble himself; he hadn't found his face. Childhood likenesses of the very famous never resemble their adult appearance except in the way clever caricatures may. I could not have predicted Adam's strongly attractive adult looks from those of the small boy who confronted us, older than me but not as old as Amanda. Just the size to fit between us, a little taller than me but not as tall as my sister. The two of us should be able to handle him.

"Would you like to play Executioner?" asked Amanda in silky tones.

"I don't know. How do you play it?"

I think Amanda Louise had just invented the name of the

game. I'd never heard her use it before. "You need two executioners and a victim," she said informatively, "and an axe or something."

"What do you need an axe for?" said Adam.

"It doesn't have to be a real axe. It can be anything that you can swing easily." I had not realized that my sister was so well informed on these matters. "It's a good game," she went on. "Suppose you be the victim and I'll be the high executioner, and my little brother can be the guard. All right?"

"What does 'victim' mean?" Adam asked.

"He's the one that gets all the glory," said Amanda, with stunning half-truth. This persuaded Adam as perhaps nothing else could.

"I'll be the victim for just this once," he said. "Show me what to do." He addressed me as a conversational equal and I felt a momentary compunction. I drove it from my mind and took my new acquaintance by the elbow.

"Go with me," I said. I had to use a simple vocabulary because I was only three years old, but I was conscious of mental life behind my speeches that was far from simple. Complex motivation was never the exclusive property of grownups. I'm not sure that I knew the expression "like a lamb to the slaughter" then. I may have learned it afterwards. But that's how Adam approached our garden swing.

"Place the victim in position," said Amanda sonorously.

"Yes, my lady," I said. I have no idea where I found this phrase. I turned Adam to face my sister. "Properly speaking, you ought to have a blindfold," she told Adam. "Have you got a hankie?"

"Only a dirty one. I've got a cold."

He produced the grimy object and we looked it over. It had seen hard use.

"It'll have to do," said Amanda Louise, and she wrapped it hastily around the little boy's head, tying a big, ineffective knot at the back of the head.

"I can't see."

"You're not supposed to see."

"I'd sooner —"

"Well you can't." She hauled the bench seat away back in the air and shoved it forward and down as she had earlier with me. The results were horrendous, like the effect achieved when you shove down on a plunger and dynamite a bridge. The seat took Adam in exactly the same spot as it had me. There was quite a loud noise on impact, a *chonk* or *pock*. I can recall the precise sound fifty years later; it was alarming, and even more alarming was the victim's instantaneous and prolonged reaction.

For a mini-moment he seemed to have been struck dumb by the contact, made incapable of vocalizing. He seemed to swell alarmingly and he changed colour, or rather he turned a series of colours in rapid succession.

Normally the usual pinky-brown-grey of so-called white persons, he turned a dusky frightening red. All over, not just the face. He seemed to be moving in slow motion as he crumpled and fell heavily to the ground, like a tree felled by the wood-cutter's axe.

Terrified by the intensity of this reaction, Amanda Louise held back the seat from further motion, easing it into a stilled vertical position. Below it on the turf the silent Adam writhed and turned blue. It was as vivid witness of suffering as any I've seen, no less real for the sufferer's extreme youth. I felt awestruck. Had we broken his legs? That is, could Amanda Louise have broken them? I had a vague recollection of an Easter sermon heard days before. Christ's executioners had broken his legs towards the end. I didn't know why. I hoped devoutly that Adam's lower leg bones were intact. I stood there mentally rehearsing my story for the inquiry I knew would follow. Adam now turned almost black; it was the only time in my life so far that I've seen somebody really black in the face, right up into the scalp. A part of my mind recorded this detail quite disinterestedly, as pure aesthetic event, while the rest of consciousness flooded with admission of guilt.

Then the noise started. I have seldom heard an outcry like it, a genuine shriek of acute pain, a strangled outpouring of tears, sobs, and then the true note of agony sounding like the passion of a woman in deep labour. My sister and I, young children unable to understand the profound sources of physical pain, stood back from the agonized weeping child at our feet and trembled to see what we had done. This unknown wandering person, never previously spoken to, barely identifiable as the little boy whose family had moved in at the end of Summerhill Avenue near the very dangerous level crossing, had been changed by our spontaneous act into a blackish-purple imp like something from the pit. Amanda and I encountered deep human suffering for the first time on that day. We knew that we alone had caused it, quite unpremeditatedly and without conscious malice before the fact. We had dabbled our infant feet in a very deep pool, and did not know what to make of it.

He didn't even know our names. His mother had simply told him that other children lived halfway down the block; she had met our mother in Hollingshead's Groceries. This was sufficient introduction. Adam felt free to come up our driveway and look for us. Parents were easy about their children's range of acquaintance in those days. My mother would quite freely invite Adam's mother to send her little boy along to play with us. Nowadays much more searching cross-questioning would supervene, the new tot in question would have to produce certificates of freedom from infectious diseases, perhaps also proof of no recorded convictions. Today we don't know what contagions lurk round us.

The only element of disease that Adam had to deal with on that fateful afternoon was the old enemy that his name suggests. For in our hearts, Amanda Louise's and mine, there dwelt the same distorting element of self-love and concealed malice sited in humanity since the original Adam was formed out of the earth that gave him his name. I mean sin. Our victim was still rolling around on the worn grass between the two hanging components of our garden swing, thirty seconds after the cruel injury we'd done him. All the reflections I've just recorded in adult language ran swiftly through my head, and simultaneously — as I later learned from her — through my sister's.

One moment there stands the new playmate, quiet, eager to join the game, accommodating, if not precisely an attractive new friend at least not actively repellent in aspect. In the next instant and at our instigation he is rolling on the ground in real torment, his aspect changed almost out of recognition, his breath coming and going shortly as though he is suffocating, his eyes blind and red with tears. And then the awful howlings like the wailings of the damned. And all it had taken to bring this about was a sneaking complicity between sister and brother in entrapment and betrayal. So at the age of three I learned the terrible joy that wrongdoing promises, the shivering excitement at the sight of another's sufferings caused by me. It was exactly like shoving down the plunger and blowing up the bridge. So much consequence from such apparently small actions. It became clear to me on the instant that consequences are to small actions as the great tree to the nut, the expression of a minutely concentrated genetic code. I think of the night Hitler was conceived.

We scrambled around beside our astonishing companion, who was still emitting an extraordinary volume of noise, like the five-o'clock steam whistle at the close of a laborious working day, shrill, audible at immense distances and continuous. This noise seemed to us like a dreadful loss of blood from a severed artery. Somebody putting out such a volume of sound must surely be in danger of literally crying his heart out.

I think that we both feared that we might see this vital organ pop out of the yawning vibrating mouth, red and pulsing slimily, vomited up from among the inner organs under the unmixed impulse of grief. Is the impulse unmixed? I think Adam's grief was an uncomplicated mental state, but it may already have been tinctured with bitter resentment in the seconds following our attack. In my lifelong relationship with this friend I've never been able to free myself from recollections of our first encounter.

Never mind that my sister and I helped him to his feet, tried to put our arms around him in consolation, begged him to stop making that terrifying noise. The whole neighbourhood must know by now that we'd tried to kill him. Guilty of murder! I wouldn't swear that these exact words went through my head, but something mighty like them must have occurred to me. I saw myself a prisoner. I imagined the strokes of the hammers as men outside constructed the scaffold. Soon would come the measured footsteps in the cellblock corridor and the muttered prayers of the chaplain. Amanda Louise afterwards reported to me similar forebodings. Mind you, she had already seen a few movies, including *Public Enemy* and *Scarface* and I believe *Little Caesar*. Perhaps I heard about cellblocks and scaffolds from her. I certainly was able to imagine them, particularly the hammering sounds. Sin and guilt, crime and punishment lurk under the smooth surface of good Canadian citizenship and blameless inability to err. Present-day thinkers have banished morality and the notion of sin from polite discourse. Like most edicts of banishment, this exiling of sin contains in itself its own reversal, exile's return. If nobody is guilty of anything, then everybody is guilty of all this terrible stuff: Hiroshima, Chernobyl, Auschwitz. I first became aware, the day I helped to execute Adam, that sin is there in the heart, unmotivated, spontaneous, ever-present and powerful. The reviewer on the daily newspaper doesn't like this, or the word "moral," but there it is.

We helped him to his feet. He trembled and shook dreadfully, more perhaps from woe at unmerited malice than from pain in either shin. We supported him between us and tried to judge the extent of his bruises. Amanda Louise muttered about Mercurochrome.

Adam's outcries now began to lessen in volume. From strangled weeping he now switched to a sequence of gulpings and heavings. This suggested a need of air, which in turn meant that he intended to go on living and was not *in articulo mortis*. We considered this a welcome sign, neither of us wishing to incur the great guilt of murder or of something that Amanda pronounced as man's laughter. This mistake produced about twelve years of confusion in my mind about the degrees of guilt in capital cases. There was murder in the first degree and maybe in other degrees that we never heard about, and then there was man's laughter. I was sixteen before I got this cleared up, understanding finally that there was no connection between human mirth and the unwilled slaying of another. For more than a decade I had believed that such a deed was so called because accidental slaying was not punished by hanging or electrocution but by some lesser and more bearable exaction. You laughed because they weren't going to take you out and do something awful to you, and your laughter was richly motivated.

On execution day Amanda mumbled something about our being tried for man's laughter. I took this at face value. As things turned out nobody prosecuted us on any charge. Adam partly recovered himself, managed to stand unsupported, showed the return of articulate speech by damning us heartily in the most pressing language he could command. I remember exactly what he said.

"I'll get my Uncle Clough to run you over with the Lowthers' car."

We goggled at him in confusion.

"He'll squash you flat in their big Rolls-Royce."

A thrill of fear went through me as I heard this hysterical prediction. To be squashed flat by a big Rolls-Royce seemed a fate suitable for heroes, much better than execution for man's laughter. What a deep well of verbal and moral confusion is the infant consciousness. Mercurochrome, man's laughter, Uncle Clough and his or somebody's big Rolls-Royce. I had never seen a Rolls, but encountered one ten days later when Adam's uncle brought the Lowther family limousine home with him for washing and polishing. Then I saw that to be run over by such a vehicle would indeed be to be squashed flat. The tires were enormous, the biggest I've ever seen on a passenger car. To be crushed by them would be a heroic mode of capital punishment, also painful.

"I'll tell my mother on you. You tried to kill me." With this accusation Adam turned right round and hobbled down the driveway, picking up his pace smartly as he went. His sobs and gulpings faded into the distance. Now we became aware that we were not alone. My mother and my grandmother Archambault were standing at the foot of the back-kitchen steps eyeing us critically. Strangely enough, no punishment followed. My mother simply directed us to put the swing floorboards back in place, which we did at once. As we wrestled the cumbersome component into the correct position we both overheard a remark passed by my mother to Mme. Archambault.

"This is called destroying the evidence," she said in a hushed tone; then she laughed quietly. Woman's laughter, I thought. My grandmother pursed her lips in a characteristic grimace and they withdrew. Nothing further was said about the torments of Adam, in the family or out of it. Uncle Clough and Mrs. Sinclair seemed prepared to let the incident go unremarked. Did they already, when Adam was four and a half, foresee a life of victimization, and a partly conscious need to suffer, for this unusual little creature? Was he waywardly attached to suffering from the very beginning? Had he a deep-seated wish to be hurt? I don't mean masochism as the later psychoanalytic movement explains it. I don't relate Adam's sufferings to his sexual life alone. It is true that not very much later in childhood Adam began to indicate his preference for emotional ties to persons of his own sex, but then quite a lot of little boys did that, as members of gangs or teams or the same class in school, where being made to sit with the girls was considered stinging punishment for little boys. As I have noted elsewhere, being made to sit with the girls was for some of us no true punishment but in fact a distinct pleasure, not that we imagined or wished ourselves to be girls, but that we deeply enjoyed contact with them.

For Adam, however, being made to sit with the girls would

have conferred pleasure of a different order, compounded of close identification with the female gender and social role, the assumption of a quasi-feminine identity, and a wish to appear as attractive to boys as any girl. At four or five or six, the male child's sense of sexual identity is already strongly formed but not inflexible. In many cases identity wavers and flows back and forth between the available poles, often in a series of subtle but detectable nuances, as the enormous wealth of stage and screen comedy about cross-dressing (transvestism, *travesti*) shows.

The fun and fantasy can go either way, just as I could enjoy sitting among the girls for one cluster of reasons and Adam for another. Those groups of reasons would not be entirely separate or discontinuous. We have at least learned that physical sexual identity and gender identification are not founded on the same bases and are easily distinguishable. You can enjoy being made to sit among girls for mixed reasons. I will pass by the question of whether the girls ever enjoy being made to sit with the boys for any reason at all. One thinks of all those hundreds of Elizabethan and Jacobean comedies and romances in which the travesty moves in the reverse direction, female dressed as male, with the predictable response from the audience. Relations between the sexes are always mysterious in their sources and always pressing on the individual conscience. But certain aspects of the person are prior to even this primordial identification. I believe that Adam Sinclair's so-called masochism had little or nothing to do with either sex or gender but was prior to both and more important in his personal history than either.

A rooted need to suffer may be almost purely sexual in its sources — the classic masochism — or it may be more deeply rooted still, in the pure undifferentiated simple humanity and conscience that we all share from the moment of our conception. We all need to suffer, to atone for absolutely primordial guilt, pre-sexual, almost pre-existential. In most of us here below, this need is compensated, as we mature, by others almost as strong, the wish to enjoy, to gratify desire, to grow strong and healthy, to mate, to find ourselves loved. The earliest need remains there beneath the others. In Adam's case it has predominated in his development. When he walked into our backyard on that epoch-making spring day, he exuded victimhood in some very mysterious way. He wanted to be victimized. There was no question of punishment involved; we did not fancy ourselves to be exacting a just revenge on him. We didn't know him. We neither liked nor disliked him. He formed no part of our lives until his first request, "Can I play?"

I can't tell you at this moment why I decided at first sight that this unknown being was one of whom it was permissible to play ugly tricks. Amanda Louise — the kindest of human beings — felt the same, in the same moment, as she later informed me. It wasn't his looks or his speech or his perfectly ordinary clothes and shoes that stimulated this reaction. There was some powerful signal emanating from the depths of Adam's person that absolutely invited mistreatment, but there was no question of his enjoying it.

At that moment Adam's sexual orientation had not yet declared itself. It would be criminal to interpret his subsequent homoeroticism as having been produced out of a fundamental need to be victimized, to suffer. The two motives seem to have been independent of each other. We are wrong to interpret homoerotic wishes as signs of a need for victimization. Such an interpretation creates an excuse for cruelty; it is the resource of the Nazi, and we must shun it. Adam didn't turn towards the imagined safety and shelter of male companionship because of the inner impulse that I have described. He needed in the very first instance of all, before character discriminates itself into distinct motives, to suffer. For this was he sent into the world.

Now I don't profess to understand this, but I can tell you that more than fifty years of experience were required before I began to be critically aware of these matters. The grown man, Adam Sinclair, could take care of himself; he acquired defences and weapons and associations that protected him from his peers. His talent. His beauty. His wit. Hidden emotional resources, friends of parallel orientation, even his riches, helped to form the carapace under which he could continue to live. Like the rest of us, he got by. That's all any of us do, really, but Adam did it in his own way, with a very high proportion of pain and suffering blended into the mixed drink.

Five or six years after the shameful incident of the Sinclair execution, I was lounging on the main drag at Centre Island on a Saturday afternoon with Tom and Gerry Cawkell and Bobby Weisman. I was in the middle of the process of easing my way into gang membership that was necessary to me at that period. I was trying to establish a position in the pecking order ahead of Bobby, on a level with Gerry and some way behind that of Tom, who was a lot older and stronger than me, but not as literate. I needed those guys but was careful not to show it. Anyway, I suddenly spotted Adam Sinclair in the midst of the holidaying crowd, trotting along after one of his aunts. As one, Tom and Gerry focussed their attention on Adam and exclaimed with contempt, "Fucking fruit!"

I was careful not to betray any shadow of acquaintance with Adam or any sympathy with his aims in life. And though I suspected that the Cawkell brothers would not continue very long as part of my social scene — in fact I have not seen them in adulthood — I would not have gone after Adam and taken him by the hand that Saturday, not while Tom and Gerry and Bobby were watching.

"Evil communications corrupt good manners," said some classical moralist, perhaps Menander. Well maybe, but often the supposedly evil communication is somebody we are afraid to associate with because the gang won't like it. Fucking fruit, a damaging label, yet Adam has played a much more important role in my life than the Cawkell boys. Given the right circumstances, I might even risk my life to protect him. I've acquired over the years a certain sense of brotherhood with Adam.

When I agreed to have him as my guest in our family apart-

ment, on this Friday night in 1983, I could feel a link as intimate
and as mysterious as my tie to my uncle and his surprising wife.
At fifty-three I didn't expect my life to twist itself out of the
smooth rut of custom. The trip to James Bay had been as much
as I could put up with. I didn't want any more surprises for a
while, and I was disturbed by the uncharacteristic timbre of
Adam's voice on the phone. Was he getting ready to spring something on me? I felt sure that he was about to ask me to welcome
him into the apartment as a permanent guest, and further that I
would consent to this appeal. I didn't know how Andrea would
feel about it — and where was she anyway, it was getting late —
and I wasn't sure that I could cope. Adam has a quite genuine
celebrity status, lately much amplified and reinforced by his
appearances on *Fate*. Let there be no mistake about it, under
solid direction Adam is a persuasive, compelling actor. I prefer his
stage work to his appearances in films or television. That's only
because I've always experienced him, as it were, as somebody on
a stage delivering lines, even when rolling on the ground and
wailing with the pain of badly barked shins. I like him best
onstage, but recently he had been impressing tens of millions of
television viewers as one of Sadie's illicit lovers in the absurd narrative of *Fate*. Only one of a troop but easily *primus inter pares*.
Now, it seemed, he was about to bow out of this meaty part.

"Habit impels me to inquire after your health," I said after
we'd chatted about this and that for some minutes. "You sound
sort of funny. Sort of choked up."

"I've been bothered by a touch of bronchitis for a couple of
weeks," he admitted. "It's left me with huskiness and some chest
congestion that keeps hanging on. Frankly, I'm having trouble
getting rid of it."

"Playing on your nasal catarrh," I said lightly, repeating a joke
that must have been a century old.

"Oh God, can't you be serious about serious matters?"

A failure to be serious is absolutely the last thought that
occurs to anybody about me!

"I'm all attention," I said. "Speak, O Master of the Lamp."

"What are you talking about? What lamp?"

"No special lamp. Just thinking of Jeannie."

"Jeannie who?"

"Nothing. Nobody you know."

"Well suppose you stop this silly teasing and listen to me. Honestly, Matt, you're getting harder and harder to talk to as you get older. It may be a case of premature senility. They've got a new name for that, Wickenheiser's disease, or something."

"I don't think that's quite it," I said, "and don't you worry about my health, just look after your own, thanks very much."

"That's exactly what I propose to do. I can't take the pace out here any more. I wouldn't admit that to anybody but you, darling."

"Now cut that out!"

"Oh, very well," in a petulant teasing tone, "just as long as you don't repeat what I'm going to tell you. I might be held to be in breach of contract."

"All right," I said, resigned. It had been a long day, and I still had northern scenes shining in my head. Adam on Baffin, I thought, what would that be like?

". . . and I've had to restrict my work because of it. The casting people say that I don't sound like myself, what with this huskiness. Apparently it's affected the pitch of my speech, and you remember how I've always depended on my Shakespearean training and correct diction."

"Yes," I said, glancing at Uncle Philip's watch. Midnight!

"I don't know that I want to film again anyway. I'm fifty-five, can you believe it? I'm getting to the point where I'm not going to be offered leads any more. I've got lines that makeup no longer hides. Lines? More like trenches. I'm going to have to review my options very carefully."

There was a brief condemnatory discussion of casting practices in New York and L.A. "I might do a season in New York. Ibsen, perhaps. I could still get away with Eilert Lovborg, it isn't the lead but it's a strong part, and I could look it."

He was quite right about that. One of the nicest things about him is his artistic honesty; he doesn't kid himself about what he can and can't get away with. Consequently, he has never been badly miscast. I admire that. He would have been a good Lovborg, or Dr. Dorn, wonderful showcases for an actor who is getting on. I remembered when he would automatically be cast in the male lead of any play in which he appeared. And here we were, thinking of him for the *raisonneur* parts, fifth business.

"It's *Fate*."

"What did you say?" I was longing for my bed.

"There are three episodes of *Fate* in the can, scheduled for fall viewing at spaced intervals."

"Only three? I'd have thought they'd have more by now."

"I'm talking about the three in which I appear. My love affair with Sadie comes to a climax."

"What, in reality?"

"No, on the tiny box. They'll keep me before the public down to Christmas. Then I'll have to decide whether I want to go back to work. They haven't exactly written me out of the show; they haven't killed the character off."

"That's a plus."

"The Stalmaster people would always look at tape."

This reference went by me. I'm not very knowledgeable about television production and I don't want to be. "It must be a real jungle," I muttered, but he paid no attention.

"I'm returning to Toronto to get away from it all. I need rest and a new perspective." At this admission I decided to take him in.

I've noticed again and again that when an artist tells you that he or she needs a new perspective on things it means big trouble for somebody. Nobody ever gets a new perspective; you just go on doing what you've been doing. Why kid yourself? I half stood up and tried to wiggle out of my uncle's heavy tweed jacket. I intended to terminate the conversation by almost any means, even if it meant agreeing to any proposal.

"Sadie couldn't have been nicer," he said. "She owns a big chunk of the show, and I've been holding up the shoot with this thing. She wouldn't let them replace me or write the character out of the show. It's an established part of the story line, not one of the principals but a regular all the same. I've been on a dozen times, and there are the three to come. You get worldwide recognition from these things, you know. I'm better known for being on *Fate* than for anything else I've done, Shakespeare, Chekhov, stage, films. It's strange. Anyway, the three fall shows will keep me going until I decide what to do. Meanwhile I'm going into seclusion. That's why I want to stay with you."

I spent another ten minutes trying to convince him that the heart of midtown Toronto, half a mile from the major communications studios and production centres, was not a desert hermitage. He wouldn't hear my objections. Just brushed them aside like cobwebs, and I was too worn out to resist. Finally I admitted that I couldn't turn him down with a clear conscience and that he was welcome to stay in the apartment for a brief spell. I never specified just how brief the spell was to be.

I think it was the reactions from Superior Home Services that embedded Adam in my life. Given daylight to run to, he'll wriggle through the smallest aperture and break into the clear. As soon as he moved in, clearing out Uncle Philip's old room and redecorating it to suit himself, he began to ingratiate himself with the cleaning staff. He involved himself with *dusting*. He seemed to have an endless supply of funds. I expect when you've been famous like that for twenty-five years money just follows you around. Sadie had persuaded him to invest in her little production unit, so he had money in *Fate* that came back a thousandfold, like the seed sown on fertile ground. He started to buy little objects for the apartment, air-conditioning units, video-cassette recorders, sound equipment, compact disc players. I felt the foundations of my life being sapped away; we engaged in a long-running battle about the relative technical merits of vinyl and compact disc. I've collected so many vinyl recordings over the years that I couldn't possibly afford to replace them with compact discs. Anyway, I like my scratchy old LPs.

Muriel and Eleanor from SHS adored Adam. The prodigal son gets the cake and cookies while the stodgy, good stay-at-home brother is ignored by the mob. Eleanor and Muriel were all over Adam; they would do anything he asked. Danny, nominally their crew chief, never had to tell them to take special trouble with Adam's room or the fancy kitchen appliances he'd brought in. They invaded his room with flowers, for God's sake, air-fresheners, clean sheets thrice weekly. They would come in specially to remake Adam's bed with freshly laundered, clean-smelling sheets. Never thought of doing such a thing for me. Even Danny got to like Adam tremendously. He may have had his doubts at the time that Adam moved in, but Adam never patronized him and never made the mistake of trying to tip him. Danny regarded himself as management personnel, or at least as a supervisor. His sense of his own independence and authority made it possible for him to treat Adam on a footing of equality, as one boss to another. This drew Danny's affections towards Adam. All unknowingly, the unbending foreman of a cleaning staff in Toronto was giving in to the same power of attraction that had provided Adam with a thirty-year career as a leading media personality. Throughout his adult life Adam was at the same time private victim and public hero. But he began life as a career victim and only in early manhood evolved his immense powers of attraction. This is a rare evolution. How many beings turn themselves from victims into triumphant heroes? I can think of only one instance in history.

But Danny of Superior Home Services began to pay special attention to Adam's needs, or you might say at first Adam's vacillations. From the time in late June of 1983, when Adam moved into the apartment, until at least two years later, through the spring of 1985, Danny showed from one season to the next a deepening regard for Adam that finally matured into a profound and unbreakable tie. This was lucky as things turned out because he was able to carry the loyalties of Eleanor and Muriel along with him when the time came. Capricious and destined to suffer Adam might have been; at the same time he had an undeniable and puzzling ability to exact loyal support from those around him. I remembered all this time the curious incident of his "disgrace" at the Stoverville Drama Festival of April 1967, and wondered how I could ever have supposed that this emergence from the closet before an audience of a few hundreds would destroy him or threaten his public career. Disgrace in Stoverville doesn't necessarily imply universal obloquy. Sometimes disgrace in Stoverville is just what you need to get you going on some larger stage. The parable of the grain of mustard-seed always surfaced in my mind at this point in my reflections. Very often it is from the tiniest of happenings that the greatest consequences rise up. Adam had been an unquestioned star before Stoverville, but nothing to what he became later. It is the least of all seeds, but when it grows up it becomes almost a tree, and the birds of the air come and nest in its branches. The day that Amanda Louise and I executed Adam we were planting the smallest of seeds.

By the late winter of 1984 Adam had us all trained to do his bidding. We weren't to make phone calls between nine and eleven A.M. because that was when he talked to his staff in New York or downtown Toronto. And we didn't tie up the phone between four and seven P.M. because then it was afternoon in L.A., and he liked to speak to California at that time slot. Why not get a second and third telephone line installed, you ask. As things stood we caused the phone company a lot of trouble while Adam was with us on account of his celebrity. All kinds of people would phone up, at any hour. Andrea and Josh and I simply couldn't have dealt with the number of calls coming in on three separate lines. When I wanted to phone somebody, I got in the habit of walking down to the Rosedale subway stop and using the pay phone there. It was a nuisance and another instance of the powers of the hero-victim. He had us just where he wanted us.

For a long time he was almost always on the phone during the hours I've indicated. I'd hear him wrangling with his personal rep at William Morris in New York or in L.A. on the question of what sort of offers would induce him to go back to work. He was getting all kinds of offers at that time: further episodes of *Fate*, his character having remained extremely popular despite absence from the story line; a possible spinoff series in which Adam's character was to be starred, suggested title, *Destiny*. I guess all media people figure that if it's worked once it'll work twice. They calculate that the mass audience is too stupid to figure out that *Destiny* duplicated *Fate*, or that it loves duplication and reduplication. Darryl Zanuck used to remake the same college football picture once a year for release at Labour Day; nobody seemed to mind seeing it again under a slightly different title. *Punts and Passes*, then *Pigskin Parade*. I suppose if the projected series *Destiny* had been a big hit there'd have been a spinoff from the spinoff called *Fortune* or perhaps *Chance*.

After a while I started to overhear Adam arguing sharply with folks on the other end of the line, seeming to produce proof of his identity. I couldn't at first see why he would have to do this, until I realized after about eighteen months that his very distinctive speaking voice — part of the physical equipment on which his career was founded — had been much altered in timbre and rhythm by some persistent throat and perhaps lung congestion. After a while he sounded like Rich Little impersonating Adam Sinclair. In impressions of Adam there was invariably a kind of hollow echoing tone, a mannerism he sometimes employed himself but which was always exaggerated by impressionists, like Jimmy Stewart's inarticulate delivery or Jimmy Cagney's explosive bursts of phrase. Rich Little always does the mannerisms more than the exact speech patterns of the people he takes off. As he is himself a Canadian he was able to spot Canadian speech habits that Adam had retained, and would stress them in his act, making audiences laugh who had no idea that they were hearing Canadian rhythms or vowel sounds.

When Adam stopped sounding like himself and began to sound like an impressionist, I started to worry about this persistent pattern of congestion. Adam started to feel it necessary to prove to listeners that he was himself, and when he became aware that he was doing this he started to let me or Andrea take his calls. He actually went to the point of showing us proper telephone etiquette in the media world. We were not to describe ourselves as his secretaries. This was because he had legitimate secretaries in New York and L.A. who would be hurt by the suggestion that their jobs were endangered or their functions being undermined. I had had no wish to pass myself off as Adam's secretary, and was distinctly miffed by the suggestion.

"You can call yourselves Mr. Sinclair's personal assistant if you feel the need of a job description," he told me and Andrea early in the course of these developments. "You identify yourself and pass the caller to me. That way he'll know he's really got me."

I couldn't tell whether this self-absorption was innocent or malicious. I had never until then pictured myself as in any degree Adam Sinclair's personal assistant. Yet such was his persuasiveness that once or twice I called myself that when the phone rang, and I took it up in a hurry.

"Good morning! This is Mr. Sinclair's personal assistant speaking." I guessed that some callers thought I was his valet, but what the hell, somebody had to screen poor Adam from the dozens, later on hundreds of appeals that were directed at him. As they mounted in frequency and intensity I began to see how terribly difficult Adam's professional life must have been. Everybody wanted a piece of him, a favour, a service, an introduction, a personal appearance, money, a signed contract. Often there seemed to be an element of coercion and even blackmail in these communications. I might be seated at the phone trying to take in what was being asked. Adam would be capering about beside me, lightly clad in a billowing terrycloth dressing-gown and costly suede slippers, fluttering his palms and whispering commands to me. After a while I could read his intentions from this ritual dance. Some gestures implied flat rejection of the caller and any proposal emanating from her or him; others were inviting and cajoling, transmitting themselves through me by a change in my voice, a warming trend in phrasing or tone. I began to feel like a puppet.

"No, I'm afraid that Mr. Sinclair's month is fully booked. Are you certain that you need to see him personally? Perhaps the matter could better be handled through correspondence. Have you considered that?"

When statements like this were filtered through me at Adam's direction, they always had the same effect on the caller's voice: near-strangulation expressive of irritation or real anger. I might just as well have been some musical instrument of peculiarly aggressive or noticeable timbre as myself. It wasn't what was said, but rather the instigator's intentions, that caused this reaction. Sometimes they guessed that Adam was standing beside me pulling my strings.

"I know he's there. He's got to be there, the monster, and don't you tell me that you can't speak for him. That's exactly what you're doing. You're not a personal assistant, you're a mouthpiece!"

For some reason the most thrusting and exigent callers were women interviewers, caught between suspicion and attraction. They used a strange lexicon when they spoke of Adam to his surrogates, myself or Andrea or Josh Greenwald, who was spending most of his free time with us, or Danny or Muriel or Eleanor. Adam was variously named by this strident clan of women in New York or L.A. or Chicago or Toronto as an aging eagle, a pitiless great white shark, a kinky Robin Hood who took from the rich to give to the very rich, a Daddy's boy. There were dozens of other epithets, not all as inventive as these. These comments gave me a special insight into my old friend's history and lifestyle. You have to have somebody as a roommate before you can understand what he or she is really like.

I'll mention something surprising. Adam loved to do the dishes. Or rather, he loved to clear the table and load the dishwasher. He used to shake dish detergent into the appliance like an acolyte feeding a censer with sweet-smelling incense. He was not much interested, however, in taking the dishes out and putting them away after the cycle was complete. That was my assignment, or Andrea's. The poor man was now in the position of being unable to go out, to have a meal in a public place. People would simply not leave him alone. As I say, they all wanted a bit of him, some sort of contact that might be turned to their advantage. Or they wanted verification of one or more of the absurd rumours that circulated in the city about him and our little family circle. Gossip writers and columnists began to show up on the front steps of our building. Some days they were more numerous than others. Wednesday afternoons and Thursday mornings were favourite times. These people would make offers to Eleanor and Muriel and Danny to get them to reveal all for the supermarket tabloids, whatever "all" was supposed to be.

Our trio of cleaning staff used to arrive at the apartment in a neat white van. The media people somehow got the notion that this closed van concealed round-the-clock surveillance and bugging equipment focussed, as would be natural, on media misbehaviour. Columnists and interviewers and leg-men/women used to circle round and round the van like pumas or cheetahs in high grass. They were sure that the people in our apartment were collecting material for evidence in lawsuits of one kind or another. When Muriel — a completely ordinary middle-aged cleaning expert — emerged from the van carrying a Dustbuster and started up to the veranda, these people were immediately convinced that the small hand appliance was some sort of surveillance device in disguise, some high-fidelity means of eavesdropping on their consultations. They would cluster around her and pull at her sleeves. They would offer quite large sums of money for her "story." As she didn't have any story apart from her familiarity with the best methods of domestic cleaning, she had nothing to tell them. Adam and I felt obliged to add large extra sums as hardship-posting pay to the fees we were paying Danny, Eleanor and Muriel. They gradually turned into important elements of our team, a basic six-person support group informally organized to look after Adam's affairs. It consisted of Andrea, Josh, me, Eleanor, Muriel and Danny. Any of us could prepare a quick meal, take and record a phone call, clean a room, make unobtrusive sallies from the apartment to dry-cleaners, supermarkets, liquor stores, pharmacies. We felt under siege; the whole situation was claustrophobic and the phone calls continued to flood in. Of us all, I think Danny was the most adept at filling in for Adam on the phone, especially with insistent agents.

Eleanor had a telephone manner of immense starchiness, I recall, and was magnificent at convincing genuine business associates that Mr. Sinclair was fully seized of their intentions and would speak to them in due course. I don't know where she picked up this diction; it may have come from watching *Masterpiece Theatre*.

Andrea practised an innocent deception with importunate callers; her sweet, breathy, upper-class-sounding telephone speech readily persuaded callers that they'd somehow got hold of Adam's newest girlfriend or bimbo. They could not concede this unidentifiable young woman full trophy-wife or bimbo status because Adam was known to be married to Sadie. But younger male callers particularly found Andrea a puzzle. She was not known to the tabloids, they knew. *People* magazine had nothing in its files on a Sinclair playmate in her early twenties. Enigma. Her voice revealed nothing but her gender.

Photographers with immensely sensitive lenses began to cover our movements from positions in the shrubbery and among the graceful tall old trees that ringed the property, all of them trying to sneak unposed shots of Adam. I had never had any inkling until this time of the torments to which persons of international celebrity are subjected by the media and the public. There is a warped affection behind this; the celebrity may console herself or himself with the reflection that after all this is love. Few media personalities become famous worldwide without strongly attractive elements to their persons, their images. This is sometimes even true of images created to shock or repel. Frankenstein's monster, Dracula, King Kong.

By the end of the story of the gigantic ape, most of us are strongly in sympathy with him. Adam was no vampire or gigantic ape, but he shared their remarkable ability to exact sympathy from audiences. The character he played in *Fate* was meant in the scripts to be completely unlikable, even contemptible, arrogant, indifferent to others' needs, physically menacing. An Oklahoma oilman named Chris Ohlrig who fought with Sadie's character for control of a vast post-industrial empire and ended as her lover.

In the beginning you were supposed to loathe Chris Ohlrig, and the way Adam played him you should have hated him, but you couldn't. There was a subtext of lovableness that made him endearing. Thousands of viewers wrote fan letters to the character offering themselves as friends or lovers. People would mail in panties! Adam was only on the show a few times each season, but he made by far the strongest impression on audiences of any of the characters. Playing Chris Ohlrig put the topper on Adam's acting career; it made him famous worldwide. In the end he couldn't wangle a quiet restaurant meal or enjoy a drink in a secluded lounge. The moment he sat down, swarms of admirers would cluster around the table and refuse to allow him to eat or drink. He became a regular in the pages of *People*. The supermarket tabs blossomed out with accounts of the last three episodes of *Fate* in which he appeared. That was in 1984. The episodes were repeated in the summer season of that year. According to the tabloids, Adam either was or was not just like Chris Ohlrig: an expert horseman from Oklahoma, born to immense riches derived from the oil industry, a hard threatening man, but fair. None of these tales, crazy and totally incorrect as they were, ever named Adam Sinclair as a gay person or gay rights activist. They seemed to shy away from making such an identification, perhaps realizing that in so doing they would be destroying the mythical figure they had created. Chris Ohlrig had something of the romantic status of Count Dracula or King Kong, those figures of immense but somehow screwed-up potency. Perhaps his sad end would come catastrophically soon, but the tabloids were reluctant to report it or predict it or cause it.

His last appearances on *Fate* were seized on as material for the rumour factories because the actor appeared slightly different than usual. He seemed thinner, a little worn, the hollows in his cheeks more pronounced than before. Was this the effect of makeup, an intentional change in the character's increasingly attractive onscreen looks? Would a leaner, older, suffering Chris Ohlrig be an even more captivating foil for Sadie's character? Could he evoke the pity of that merciless bitch? What was most remarkable in all this fun and games was the total confusion in the public mind of the on-camera Chris Ohlrig and the live human being, the actor Adam Sinclair. I think most people preferred the level of reality of the onscreen character, lean, thin, hollow-cheeked as he might be in his clever makeup, to the suffering man who was living in our family apartment, unable for many reasons to leave it except in darkness, in a state of siege, subject to torrents of misstatements, the slave of his celebrity.

Adam was a prisoner. And so were the rest of us who inhabited the place. We had to have the phone number changed, at first monthly and finally weekly. We had to beg the city police to keep the crowds around the veranda from becoming too numerous and too insistent on the public's alleged right to know. Media people were very well informed about the limits of their powers. They would not prevent the postman, say, or the grocery delivery service from carrying out their lawful occasions. They weren't trying to starve us out; they simply incarnated the dreadful pressure of mass curiosity. By the end of 1984 Andrea had become a full-time telephone attendant. We had a three-line service by then, which allowed her to keep two callers on hold while she dealt with a third. Andrea performed her duties without payment or any thought of reward because she and Josh loved Adam, listened to him tirelessly whenever they could snatch time from attending to his callers; they treated him as a post-modern demi-giant, that terrifying thing, a world celebrity.

About the beginning of 1985 there were, as perhaps there always are, a few personalities whose affairs, often for some purely accidental reason, elevate them to the position of the superstar. Among the two or three who enjoyed (if they could truly be said to enjoy) such celebrity at that time, Adam was for a brief period, maybe nine months to a year, the chief. He was at that time the most written-about person of all.

If you haven't been close to such a phenomenon, you can't form any idea of what it's like, uninterrupted media scrutiny for most of a year. It's like being stripped naked on the steps of St. Peter's. I don't mean to initiate any comparison between Adam and Pope John Paul II, but some time after the events of the mid-1980s I saw a news photo taken in Carmel, California, of the Pope and Clint Eastwood, smiling kindly at one another. The caption was "Two humble men." New social forms are taking shape all around us. I could perfectly readily imagine Adam stripped naked on the steps of St. Peter's. Something very like that actually happened to him, and the rest of us were obliged to participate in the action. Nothing escaped the media investigators. They knew the whole business history of Superior Home Services and the exact date and time when three members of the SHS staff were transferred on long-term loan to Mr. Sinclair's personal service team. They knew Danny's surname before I did, and I'd been dealing with him for five or six years. They knew how much we were paying Danny and Eleanor and Muriel. They knew everything; mystics understand that God sees all.

They solved the riddle of Adam/Chris's personal appearance and possible declining health. Makeup experts employed by the *Fate* production unit revealed under strong pressure that their efforts during production of his final three *Fate* episodes had been to tone down Adam's somewhat fatigued, even slightly wasted appearance. At that point he photographed very dark under the eyes and very hollow in the cheeks and his clothes hung very loosely on him. They succeeded in maintaining his presentable, well-tailored appearance, at the cost of continual readjustments at seams and darts. None of these people had taken an oath of secrecy; there is no Official Secrets Act that compels members of production staff to be silent about the affairs of actors. I don't even think that the media had to pay for much of this information. Anyway, it quickly became public property. By mid-1984 there were plenty of rumours in circulation about Adam's health.

He was alleged to be suffering from an inoperable brain tumour. The effects of brain tumour have been widely advertised in newspapers and magazines. These days everybody has some minor skill in diagnostics. The dreadful afflictions of the rich and famous receive the most minute attention in print and on the box. The X-ray plates betraying the fatal signs find their way into the magazines. The pronouncements of physicians, even though cloaked in guarded language, are at once interpreted correctly by medical journalists. I have far more medical knowledge than I want to have; skill as a diagnostician encourages acute worry about one's own state of health. As Uncle Philip used to say, sooner or later everybody gets a bad checkup. I find myself too ready to examine my own vital signs because of this wealth of medical instruction I've unwillingly acquired. I was perfectly able to see that Adam had no brain tumour; his vital signs were all in another direction. There was no grave and sudden change of character, no precipitate unreasoning angers, no loss of ability to judge the form of narrow spaces. He didn't begin to bump into the furniture. He didn't lose his colour sense; he kept his sense of humour, always faintly tinged with a gamesome flavour of parody. His clothes remained just slightly overstated, just a shade too well cut to be believed. He would wear suddenly surprising small bits of personal jewellery, a tie pin from the Randolph Scott collection dating from about 1933, extravagantly expensive cufflinks, some of them of great beauty.

He had a Mickey Mouse wristwatch that made me laugh whenever he wore it. On the face stood Mickey and Minnie in a compromising embrace, Mickey's arms and gloved palms forming the two hands of the timepiece, which conferred intimate caresses upon the female mouse as they rotated. This watch kept excellent time and only rarely required adjustment. Later on Adam wore it almost all the time, and used to ask me to check it for accuracy against the CBC time signals. It was invariably correct to the second. I don't remember seeing him wind his Mickey Mouse watch; it was a stem-winder, not battery powered or anything like that. I think it may have been an almost mint-condition creation of the very early 1930s, produced with the co-operation of expert watchmakers for some zany Hollywood comic about 1931. Perhaps one of a kind, the work of a famed Hollywood jeweller, it had a face as big as a bread-and-butter plate and could not be concealed under a cuff. Adam wore it as a tease at first, then grew emotionally dependent on this possession. He liked the effect of the surreptitiously pornographic conferred by the slow rotation of Mickey's investigative paws.

"Mice!" he would exclaim. "Mickey gives Minnie a slow feel about once an hour." The first time he showed me the watch he held it up for my inspection. "The mice aren't just painted on the dial. They're executed in hammered silver leaf stiffened by various coloured lacquers. The piece is worthy of Fabergé. The images will last a lifetime. See how carefully they've been painted. And they're raised above the dial so that the hands can pass beneath them. I expect Mickey exists in a state of hourly anticipation."

"Aren't these images strictly protected by the Disney organization?"

"Maybe they are, but who needs to know? They were created very quietly by a designer who used to do animation at Disney. I don't fancy anybody knows about this piece but me and its makers."

"What do you suppose it's worth?" I said idly.

"It's the only one in existence," said Adam. He refused to tell me where he'd got it, or who had given it to him, which made me feel jealous. The watch was obviously a present from one of the people in the background of Adam's emotional life about whom he never ever spoke. I always figured that somebody in his love life, to use a somewhat vulgar phrase, occupied a place similar to that of Jeanne Three Streams in my uncle's unobtrusive emotional history. As time passed Adam began to twit me about the object, and almost to flaunt it.

"I know you'd like it for your own, but you can't have it," he used to say teasingly, often as he was dressing for the day at about ten-thirty.

"Who wants your silly old watch anyway, unless some child maybe, some baby! It's only a kid's toy."

"A kid's toy that's worth a king's ransom." He knew where to flick me on the raw; the phrase conferred a romantic aura on the watch that price and cost could not. Had some royal personage given it to him? Adam had had some strange boyfriends, I felt sure, and I have to admit that I itched to know more about them. At the same time I had to award him points for discretion. At no time did Adam ever reveal specific information to anybody about his male friends or the precise nature of their involvement with him. If I'd been one of the gay community, I'd have felt perfectly safe in Adam's hands, to use a rather questionable expression.

He was discretion itself, which is why I felt it was so unfair when his name began to be circulated internationally by gossip journalism. If it wasn't a brain tumour, they clamoured, it had to be something else, perhaps cancer of the colon. Terribly public inquiries began to be made in the columns about the condition of Adam's intestinal tract. What shape was his rectum in? Was there blood in his stool? It went on like that for a while.

I recollect that just at this same epoch President Reagan was visited by similar suspected illness, whereupon the pursuit of medical information about the president's innards became acutely embarrassing. I concede the right of these miserable journalists to be informed about the health of a nation's chief executive, but I did feel that Mrs. Reagan had justice on her side when she complained of the intensely detailed and specific character of some of their inquiries. Nothing was exempt from their assessment, not even the presidential lower bowel.

I can never understand this impulse. I know that Adam wasn't keen to have his state of health canvassed in the columns or on TV news roundups. For one thing, the difficulty of moving freely, of simply getting in and out of the apartment except during very dark or cold nights made it hard for him to get to see the various physicians who looked after him from time to time. In 1985, as for some time before, doctors were reluctant to make house calls except in very unusual cases; they preferred the patient to come to them. Any such move on Adam's part excited the strongest suspicions among the media about his condition. They assumed that he had something to hide, illness being gravely immoral in their judgment. I was very struck by this at the time. A public figure could act in the most indecent way and the papers would ignore it or praise her or him for it. Being detected in hard-drug use or income-tax fraud, for example, was matter for the liveliest congratulations, but being known to have the symptoms of some serious malady was to incur severe criticism from the media. It became immoral to be sick, but only injudicious or mistaken to act criminally. Adam had to behave circumspectly if he was to have access to medical advice. He couldn't even invite a throat specialist, say, or a pulmonary man to come to the house for a drink or a meal without making news in two hemispheres.

ADAM SINCLAIR CANCER VICTIM?????
UNKNOWN VIRUS ATTACKS STAR OF FATE!!!!!
SINCLAIR SICKNESS RECTAL CANCER?
STAR DROPS FIFTY POUNDS!!! WHY?
ADAM AND SADIE AT BETTY FORD TOGETHER?????

RECENT PHOTOS SHOW SINCLAIR COLLAPSE.
ADAM GLIMPSED IN HOME OF "FRIEND".

The "friend" of course was I. By this time my movements were as rigorously policed by reporters and interviewers as his. Some of Adam's desirability as an interviewee began to rub off on me; the folks on the veranda steps started to tug at my sleeves when I left the building to make a phone call or to run an errand for Adam or simply to get out of the house for a couple of hours. If I'd been entrusted with a communication for Dr. Cotterill at St. Michael's, I had to go up to Eglinton Avenue on the northbound subway, and shake off followers there by changing trains rapidly and then proceeding southbound as anonymously as possible.

The trick was to linger in hiding on the platform, then dart forward just as the subway train was closing its doors, leaving the trackers fuming on the platform as the train pulled out. They might board the following train, but couldn't guess at which of the twenty further stations I might alight. I got quite good at this method of evasion, which I'd picked up from repeated watchings of a famous movie, *The French Connection*, in which a fleeing criminal uses this stratagem to evade pursuit. It worked every time. I don't think that many media people receive instruction in surveillance procedures. Of course things may have improved today.

In this way I was able to carry information from the apartment to the hospital, where I frequently conferred with Dr. Anglin and especially Dr. Cotterill about Adam's symptoms and proposed treatment. I thought at the beginning that his illness was no worse than a bad cold. But the symptoms weren't trivial at all. They were extremely serious. They didn't seem to add up to any known disease, but had the diagnostic status of a syndrome.

"Are Adam's symptoms a linked set?" I asked Dr. Cotterill.

"Far from clear. Persistent fatigue that rest doesn't alleviate. We find that in many disorders, from the most trivial to the fatal. Steady decrease in body weight, with no stabilization. Never an encouraging sign, but again found in the course of many ailments. Enlarged lymph nodes. Hmmmmnnn. Tell me, do you have a really trustworthy scale, a scale of medical quality, a balance scale, in the apartment?"

"All we have is one of those bathroom scales that you stand on and try to read from a height. I wouldn't swear to its accuracy."

"Useless for diagnostic purposes. I'll have the hospital suppliers send you two."

"Why two?"

"One for Adam's exclusive use, the other for anybody else who's staying with you."

Until I met Dr. Cotterill I hadn't credited members of the medical profession with much ordinary common sense or humour. He made me revise my estimate. He's a very humane man who doesn't indulge in evasion or self-promotion, doesn't lord it over his patients and their families and friends and doesn't cloak his words in pseudo-scientific language. He expected the same plain speech and honesty from his respondents. When he was questioning me about Adam's condition, he helped me to feel my way towards the most exact descriptions possible.

"From now on, when we confer, I'll want the most accurate records of Mr. Sinclair's weight that you can get for me. Get him on the scales at the same time every morning, and keep exact records. Fluctuations in weight are always medically interesting."

I didn't have any idea what he was thinking of.

"He can't possibly have TB," I said, "can he? Hasn't it pretty well disappeared?"

"No, it hasn't, any more than smallpox has, but we aren't looking for them."

"What, then?"

"At this point it's a question of noting the symptoms. Do any changes occur to you besides the fatigue and the weight loss? Oh, and the enlarged lymph nodes."

"What would you expect to find?"

"Now, Mr. Goderich, Matthew. May I call you Matthew?"

"Feel free."

"Matthew, I want to avoid leading the witness. Tell me anything else you've noticed."

"His voice doesn't sound the same, and he complains of something that he calls bronchial catarrh. Is there such a thing?"

"Indeed there is."

"I thought catarrh was seated in the nasal passages, not in the throat or chest."

"The terms in this area are perhaps not perfectly defined. Irritated membranes and the production of excessive mucus and associated fluids are found in each of the areas you mention. I shouldn't like to have to disregard these symptoms in any location. What about fever?"

This abrupt transition startled me.

"Adam won't let us take his temperature, but I happen to know that he monitors it all the time in secret. He never reveals the reading, but that's a hypochondriac's habit, isn't it?"

"Hypochondriacs can be as sick as anybody else," the doctor said.

I thought this remark very much to the point. Adam's character included great elements of the histrionic, besides the usual illusions that we are all prone to. Naturally he worried about his health in self-dramatizing terms. He told me once that he'd experienced all known forms of cancer together with many that were unknown to science, like cancer of the hair or of the earhole or of the toes. The likelihood of serious and even fatal illness becomes more and more to be reckoned with as we age. Adam had reached fifty-seven. Time was catching up with the small boy whom we'd cut off at the knees at the time of our own loss of innocence.

The doctor gave me a cordial goodbye. "I'd like to see you again as soon as you've collected some data. You might prepare a detailed set of notes towards a full history, and when I've seen it I'll arrange for a brief hospital stay for studies, or perhaps a series of visits to your home. He never goes out?"

"It isn't that he doesn't, it's that they won't let him. They all want to photograph him or have him talk for tapings. He isn't safe in that situation; he could be misinterpreted."

"Yes, I see. But he isn't too weak physically to go out?"

"I think he's having some pain."

"I've got to leave you now, Mr. Goderich. Matthew. Prepare a full history and get it to me soonest. Then we'll perhaps arrange a brief hospital stay; there must be some way to manage it."

But there was no way to arrange it discreetly. One of the things I admired in Adam was his refusal to sneak about under a false name, with sunglasses or a false beard, in order to mislead media people.

"They made my name important. If it wasn't for them I'd be nobody. As it is, I'm Adam Sinclair and I don't change my name for any reason. It's about all I have to sell."

I considered this just and courageous. The great change in my attitudes and feelings must have begun about that time. I realized that however much the superficial appearance of the romantic leading man might be distorted by illness, the personal reality named Adam remained, unalterably the same as in 1933 or 1976.

I mention 1976 because that was the date of one of our most intimate encounters, that chilly November night when Adam had comforted me in the gay bar on Yonge Street, an unlikely place in which to be comforted. And yet, do you know, his companionship and firm loyalty had meant an enormous amount to me. Loyalty and friendship and length of days and the strangely stated image of my mother all conspired to purge the setting of comic or fantastic qualities. I remembered that when I'd told Adam I'd just left my mother in a nursing home his reaction was horrified and at the same time complimentary. "You don't mean the beautiful Ishy? Not *your mother*? Oh Matthew, oh Matt!" We were standing in wet drizzle on Bloor Street and he rushed me down to the bar in a cab.

We closed that bar; we were there for over six hours, surrounded by Adam's friends, most of whom seemed to me then like comic or grotesque figures executed in a caricatural line. They no longer seem like that to me, more like perfectly ordinary people pursuing the ordinary human needs: love, companionship, shared experience, understanding, a place to go where you'll be accepted cheerfully and without cross-questioning. Those men in that bar had been very decent to me. I had had trouble restraining tears. This seemed to excite broad sympathy in the witnesses at our table.

"The poor guy, what's the matter, then? Is he trying to decide to come out?"

"It's his mother, I think."

"His *mother?*"

This name caused a silence among the listeners.

"Now listen up, you little teases, this isn't something to joke about. This is my old friend Matt, and he's very unhappy. He's just had to leave his mom in a nursing home. This very night. We've just come from there and there's nothing amusing about it. So let's not pester him, okay?"

I thought this summary of the situation very fair, very tactful. A warm small hand, not one of Adam's, stole into mine. It was that of a young man who a moment before had been asking me about twenty dollars and a new suit.

"Forget what I said."

"What was it?"

"About money and clothes."

"Oh sure," I said. "If I can help in any way."

"No, no."

"But I insist."

There was a lot of noise in the place. I fished out two twenties and pressed them on my new young friend. "No, no, take it."

I never knew his name and I never saw him again, but I've always remembered that quick switch from supplication to consolation. He and Adam sat with me for the rest of the night; we left the bar in the small hours and I had to press my companions to allow me to go home alone. Good fellowship and mild intoxication had bonded us.

My last waking thought that night was of Adam's status as natural victim. The night had been a curious reversal of roles in which the natural victim had turned into my protector. I've thought a lot about this since then. I often wonder about the fellow who needed a new suit. Who was he and where is he now? I'd be glad to be able to thank him.

But all that generation, the patrons of the gay bars of 1976, have been gravely compromised, overtaken by terrible events. The chances are high that my kind supporter from the night of November 15th, 1976, is dead or deathly ill.

Less than a decade after that night, in the mid-1980s, a collection of physical signs exactly like those I'd witnessed in Adam began to form a weird litany of affliction heard again and again by internists and immunologists in consulting rooms all over northern Europe and North America: consistent weight loss, persistent low fever, pain in the joints, unshakable fatigue, repeated pulmonary disorders requiring hospitalization. This diagnostic picture grew so familiar to the medical profession that it was clear almost at once, certainly by 1983, that a curious near-epidemic situation was maturing. Some as yet unnamed, and for that reason all the more terrifying, sickness was attacking one of the most readily identifiable social groups in the West.

I can't recall just when the familiar acronyms were first circulated by the media. HIV. AIDS. All I know was that in late 1985 and early 1986 Adam was showing the classic signs that some terrible physical affliction was attacking him. I don't think I could recite the symptoms in the order in which they appeared. I remember his complaints about tiredness. It was only tiredness at first, around 1985, when he'd been refusing offers of work for some time. I thought he'd simply had enough of the terrible stresses of a very public life and that he wanted to get out of the limelight for a while, then perhaps associate himself with some modest, semi-public theatrical venture, assistance to a new Canadian dramatist by financing the production of a new play and maybe appearing in it in Toronto and New York. He was in a commanding position vis-à-vis the agents and producers, and could dictate the terms upon which he would appear on Broadway or in the West End, or in a new TV series or a film. I know that he considered appearing in a terrifying science fiction fantasy that later scared the shit out of everybody who saw it. When it was proposed to him around Christmas 1985, he read the script carefully and told me that the film was going to be a huge success but that he didn't feel up to doing it. By now he was really sick.

Adam had always been able to control his weight rigorously, as a star actor must. He might put on a few pounds when he was resting, but never, he told me, got over 178. When he was involved in a heavy production schedule, he might lose ten to twelve pounds and find himself around 166. He had never gone below that during his career, and at that weight, given his height and frame, he looked youthful, healthy and athletic.

By Christmas 1985 he decided that he should lose some weight because he was just sitting around the apartment, hiding from the media and taking phone calls from people who wanted to exploit him. He was still much written about. Plenty of people wanted to know the "real" reason why he was so unreceptive to offers. The rumour factory was busy constantly. When I tried to leave the building I was besieged by tasteless and illegitimate inquiries that began to be embarrassing and invasive. They said they wanted to be told the exact nature of my relations with Mr. Sinclair. Who was I, anyway? Why was he living with me and — was it my daughter?

They doubted that Andrea was my blood relation. Wasn't she staying with us for questionable purposes? When I insisted that she was indeed my daughter they took a lot of convincing. Wasn't I procuring her to some immoral end? They wanted to know exactly who Josh Greenwald was, and why he could visit

Adam when they couldn't. Eventually it was established that Andrea really was my daughter. They dug out masses of data about her background and training, that she had followed courses in geriatrics and palliative care and later had nursed my mother through a final illness at a well-known midtown nursing home.

What was a volunteer palliative care nurse doing on Crescent Road? Who was sick, what were his symptoms? Why wasn't Adam Sinclair accepting professional engagements? It was more than three years since he had worked. Had he any plans to return to work? Why was I seeing Dr. Cotterill, a well-known specialist in immunology? And again and again, over and over, the drumfire of interrogation, who was sick? What had he or she got? The public had the right to know and it was the interviewers' duty to inform them. They were only doing their job.

They started to make life very difficult for the other people who had apartments in the building, keeping them from using the entrance freely. The people upstairs had to push their way through squads of interrogators. They were extremely forbearing about it. There was an elderly woman, the widow of a bank official, whose tenure in the building went back much further than ours. She was kindness itself when the hurricane hit, never complained to anybody about the ruckus, and smiled encouragingly at me whenever we met outside the building. She was just fine to work with. That's what Adam's troubles turned into, a co-operative work project that soon deepened into a tragic adventure that involved everybody who lived in the building.

Once he got started trimming his weight to the desirable target, somewhere around 168, he found that he didn't have control of the process. Always before he had been able to get down to 168 and stop there. But this time, when he reached 168, he began to shed body fat at a distinctly unhealthy tempo.

This alarmed him, and by God it frightened Andrea and Josh and me! In a few weeks in the spring of 1986, when he foolishly tried to slim down, his weight dropped under 160 and headed towards the 150 mark. Dr. Cotterill had supplied us with the two sets of medical scales he'd promised us. I remember very well the day they arrived and we assembled them. A medical-quality balance scale has to be adjusted very accurately, and like a good bottle of wine it has to be allowed time to settle down in its new residence. You adjust it, leave it alone for a few days, then adjust it again, and you repeat the process until the readings become accurate and consistent, like a good marriage.

Once we had one set calibrated and nicely settled down in Adam's room, we installed the other set in the bathroom and used it as a backup for comparison purposes. None of us used Adam's scales, so as to avoid putting them off balance. We started to keep records of his weight, morning and night. I finally persuaded him to let me record his temperature over two weeks; it was a lousy picture, a frightening picture. We tried to feed him up. We had passed the stage of worrying about how he would look on-camera. It was clear that work in films and television was out of the question, at least for a long while. And there could be no question of his submitting to the terrible ordeal of rehearsing a play for live theatrical performance. He needed some extra weight, but by June 1986 it had become difficult for him to keep his weight at 150. There was a steady slow slippage from week to week, and he continued to run a persistent low fever that occasionally jumped up over one hundred.

He started to be aware of recently formed brown blotches on the backs of his hands and in some other spots. Adam had always had the self-absorption, almost narcissism, that is part of an actor's professional equipment. He always paid close attention to his looks in the same way that a carpenter or motor mechanic might check the condition of his tools. He was now fifty-eight, a time of life when a few sizable freckles on the hands and arms, and even on the cheeks, are normal, nothing to worry about. He used to hold his hands out to me for inspection at his bedside, first thing in the morning.

"Unsightly blemishes," he'd say. I think he was remembering the language of old Fleischmann's yeast advertisements.

"They're not all that unsightly," I told him. "I've got a few of those myself, and I'm younger than you."

"No need to tabulate birthdays," he said stiffly, "and your spots don't look like mine. Mine are slightly raised, and purple at the edges. Yours are ordinary freckles."

I tried to convince him that this wasn't so, but he was having none of it.

"Those are Kaposi blemishes," he said. I don't know where he got the name from. He paid no attention to the editorial or news columns of the papers; he read the arts and entertainment sections and some reviews of books and art exhibitions. He might have heard about Kaposi spots on some mischievous television program. "They're starting to show on my legs, and I think they're on my back, low down. Would you look and see, Matt?"

He was still in bed as we had this conversation. "Roll over," I said curtly. I didn't see myself as a male nurse.

"I can't," he said.

"Of course you can."

"I don't feel strong enough. I feel worn out."

He had just slept for over eight hours.

"Let me get Andrea. She has a lot of nursing experience. She'll help turn you."

Andrea showed me how to reposition a sick adult in bed. Adam didn't seem to mind a young woman handling him in this way. We examined his lower back and legs. He was right. There were many freckle-like marks in the places he'd mentioned.

"Would you like an alcohol rub?" I said. That was something I could manage. We needed the usual grocery items and Andrea knew better than I what to get: it only took a few minutes for me to bathe the skin irritations with rubbing alcohol. This gave him some relief from discomfort. I hadn't realized that those skin marks could cause serious pain. He had some less visible marks on his lower cheeks and under his chin. I think he'd been covering them up with after-shave powder.

"This thing is getting past a joke, buddy," I told him. I was trying to get him on his back again. "I think we'll have to get you in for tests."

"I want to stay here."

"You can stay here any time, for as long as you like, but you ought to consider a short hospital stay for diagnosis."

"Mr. Know-it-all!"

"Adam, I don't know anything about it. I'm not a doctor, but I can tell that you're hurting from something. If you can't roll over in bed there has to be pain involved, isn't there?"

He was silent for a long time. I rubbed his chest idly with the alcohol; it has a cooling cleansing effect, but we both knew it had no curative powers. Palliative, I thought, palliative care. I did not like the sound of the phrase.

"I've got persistent soreness in my muscles and joints."

"And you've got fever, Adam. I can feel it when I rub you. We've got to get you in for Dr. Cotterill to look at."

"You think I've got something bad!"

"I don't know what you've got, but whatever it is, it's bloody persistent. You've been going downhill for months."

I hate that kind of downer talk, but what was I to do? "We'll pick a time when the crowd on the veranda isn't too dense, and we'll sneak you down to the Immunology Unit. That's where Cotterill hangs out."

Always the light touch, Mr. Goderich.

After all, even media folk must eat, if only of the flesh of their victims. We started to take notes on when the hand-held cameras weren't there, and the young women with tape recorders, and the veteran, hard-bitten male reporters who cared nothing for anybody's feelings, including their own. Thursday afternoon was a light period, and later on, Thursday night. The vacation months, when the networks and the newsrooms would be less heavily staffed, might be a good time for Adam to move freely between Crescent Road and the hospital.

At this period, the papers were full of highly technical discussions of immunodeficiency-related illnesses. They were news, and they have remained news, but in mid-1986 I was a complete innocent about these illnesses, and so were Adam and Andrea and Josh. We could see that he was getting sicker and could list the things that were bothering him. It's a sad recital and I won't repeat it, but the tricky element in the case was that his symptoms didn't indicate any single overall cause. We were not competent to diagnose, though we learned a lot afterwards. Oh how we learned.

The happenings that reduced our little support group to desperation were the first two pneumonias, which came about six weeks apart. The first one came at the end of June 1986, taking the form of an almost predictable climax to all the other troubles we'd been noticing.

One evening Adam went to his room early, walking by now with the aid of a stick. He undressed himself and went to bed. He had some fever, I recall, and it was a hot early summer night. He used to wrap himself in heavy bedclothes; he complained often of feeling cold in bed. I didn't understand how he could possibly feel cold on this night. It was the next-to-last day of the month, I think. Canada Day weekend. The media people were feeling the heat and were less noisy and troublesome than usual. I felt sweaty and hot, and hoped that Adam wasn't too feverish. He was quiet at first, but after about ninety minutes I heard a sound that I thought was snoring. It was a bubbling, gurgling sound like a kettle boiling. Adam wasn't usually a heavy snorer, and I was surprised when I heard this unfamiliar choking sound. I went along the hall and opened his door. There was a pleasant faint breeze coming from his window, and there was the smell of a sickroom carried on this air current. The sound I'd mistaken for snoring was really that of very heavy pulmonary and bronchial congestion. He seemed to have filled up with fluid in his lungs such that he couldn't get his breath. I was terrified. He wasn't tossing and turning. He was partly on his back — not a good position — and partly on his left side, as though he'd tried to reposition himself to get some drainage. I heard him strain to cough and clear his chest. It was a disgusting noise, a retching suffocating heave.

Well, he had pneumonia. Neither Andrea nor Josh was in the apartment, and I didn't know what to do. He couldn't speak; that meant that I was in charge of him, and the responsible adult. I rang Dr. Cotterill's number and got an answering service that said the doctor would be home later in the evening. If I left a message he would contact me. I was about the eighth beep down the lineup so I made the message an urgent appeal. As soon as Dr. Cotterill came in he heard the urgency in my appeal and called me right back. I'd been sitting near the phone for ninety minutes, now and then checking Adam's room. I thought he might go out like a light from one moment to the next. Just before the doctor called, Josh and Andrea turned up. They checked Adam's condition and agreed with me that it was pneumonia; they both spoke to the doctor and then handed him back to me.

"I don't care about the reporters and the cameras, we've got to get him into care tonight. We may have been lax in not insisting on hospitalization before now. Get him to Emergency at St. Michael's; I'll book him in before you arrive. I'll meet you there in forty minutes, just around eleven. Try to work him into a sitting position in your car; he'll get a little drainage and be more comfortable. Keep him warm."

It was three years since Adam had appeared on network television, but repeated reruns of his *Fate* episodes, and his old films on TV, had kept him in the public eye. He was still the major star Adam Sinclair. I don't say that this motivated Dr. Cotterill in his handling of the case but it certainly didn't hurt a bit. Ordinarily when you check into a hospital they hold you up while you fill out the forms. You may be expiring but you fill out the forms, and God help you if you're too weak to hold the ballpoint or give the required information. There was none of that when we took Adam down. We eased him into the roomy back seat of Josh's sedan, where he could be seated in relative comfort while

Andrea and I propped him up. The terrible noises seemed to slack off when he was upright. One of the worst aspects of pulmonary or bronchial trouble is the difficulty in lying down; you can't ever find a comfortable position in which to recline. To lie flat on your back becomes impossible after a while, but when you lie face down your mouth and nose drip constantly and there is a tendency to choke on fluid. Lying on either side causes cramping on the underside and overstrains the heart. This is why Dr. Cotterill didn't insist on an ambulance.

This was about ten-fifteen, and the corps of media people was much attenuated. Sunday night, a holiday weekend. There were three people taking pictures, which appeared next day in the Toronto dailies and on the wire services, and there was a TV crew, but only a few print journalists. On the whole they behaved nobly. When we came out the front door, Josh and I were supporting Adam, one on either side. He more or less walked down to the car between us. He was well wrapped up in an old Jaeger dressing-gown, and the breeze was warm and caressing. We had no trouble reaching the car; we didn't have to push through the crowd. In fact they fell back on either side, showing the instinctive human recoil from the presence of the very sick. I remember that a young woman reporter ran to the curb and opened the door to the back seat. This struck me as a generous and humane gesture. She didn't peer into Adam's tormented face and then scribble in a notebook or anything like that.

Adam even managed, in the midst of gasping for breath, and in the grip of a disabling fever, to look this young woman in the eye and smile for her. I was stunned by his ability to overcome dangerous illness, even for a few moments, to be gracious to a media person. I suppose they never lose that instinct to perform; they're never "off." I noticed that he'd donned his big Mickey Mouse wristwatch; the journalist who had opened the door was without doubt eyeing it with great interest. For a moment I feared that Adam was going to offer it to her. I'd always coveted that watch; it was the one element of his fortune of which I was jealous. I would have hated to see it disappear in order to preserve Adam's good relations with the media.

You probably can't preserve a most-favoured-person status with the media when once you evolve from routine, continuing story status to being a hot item. We had Adam into Emergency before the press caught on that the decisive break in the Sinclair case had occurred. Now he was really sick, and observed to be sick and known to be sick. He could now be handled with that strange mixture of persecution and compassion that is actuated by the "public's right to know." I don't believe that there is any such right, where the intimate details of people's personal lives, sickness, emotional crisis, financial woes are in play, even when the targets of the investigation are maximally celebrated. The public has the right to know the details of political decision-making, a right often scouted by giants of administration, politicians, cabinet officers. But it hasn't the smallest right to know the precise details of a grave illness. That's a private matter, or it should be. Anyway, we got Adam into a private room at the hospital almost before the story had turned into hot news.

The next day media attention redoubled itself. Why immunology? Tests for what? At that time the media knew no more about immunological research than the ordinary ignorant citizen. Until the mid-1980s, media coverage of immunological research focussed on the various types of organ transplant, heart, maybe kidneys, and the body's rejection system. There were stories in the Science sections of the major papers, often in weekend supplements, about the biological hazards of organ transplant. After a while the ordinary man in the street — me — could explain glibly why you could accept a kidney only from a near relation, supposing that you required one. Something to do with antibodies. We all knew, or believed that we knew, why bone marrow had to come from a sibling if needed. There were always fantastic tales in the papers about people who were trying to conceive and deliver a baby, so that its already living — and sick — brother or sister might apply to it for one of its spare organs.

Difficult ethical questions about selective breeding would rear their unfamiliar heads in public discussion of these new medical possibilities.

Stories were circulated in the press that Adam had secretly had a heart or kidney transplant and now his body's rejection of the transplanted organ was becoming life-threatening. Various parties came forward during his first brief stay in hospital offering their kidneys as replacements. Nobody offered a heart.

Tests. "In for tests." One of the dominant expressions of our age.

The pneumonia seemed easy to target, and was conquered, apparently, in the first week of July· by the customary drug therapy and nursing attention. But there was an aspect of the case that dictated more technical study. It was something to do with his blood count; his T-cell count was way down. The T-cell, a white cell, Dr. Cotterill explained, is the chief agent of self-immunization. During Adam's first hospital stay his count showed first about 450 — normal level is around 1200 — then dipped to around 400, unacceptably low.

At this period the best testing service for blood was in Ottawa, and was flooded with applications for tests. Dr. Cotterill took the samples he needed from Adam, sent them to Ottawa and let Adam come home with us. He wore ordinary street clothes for the ride uptown, and looked surprisingly good, almost normal, although he walked with an unfamiliar gait because of joint pains and muscular stiffness. On the whole he was recognizably himself, attractive and slender, a very good fifty-eight. I don't know that the reporters knew exactly how old he was; they usually gave his age as fifty-four, when a minimum of research would have allowed them to verify his birthdate. Maybe they were just being nice; that's perfectly possible. He seemed to be in his mid-fifties, and he certainly hadn't lost his figure.

The furore over the alleged heart or kidney rejection died away. He was not known to have had recourse to dialysis. It was true that his blood samples were now publicly known to be worrying, but nobody could infer what the specific worry was. Eventually, however, the results of the initial tests came back from Ottawa. HIV-positive.

I don't think the communication used the acronym HIV. It was only starting to come onstream as one of the most discussed and feared terms of the late 1980s. We didn't think familiarly of HIV the way we did of polio or sickle-cell anaemia or Jerry's kids and TV marathons. There is a thing that might be called TV medicine, that is, the various illnesses that receive late-night TV publicity accompanying appeals for funds. Ailments that have become media big-business and marketing successes. At the end of 1986 we didn't yet include HIV in this high-publicity category. It was still a meaningless polysyllable. Human immunodeficiency virus. And when we looked this mysterious term up in the dictionary we learned that it was one (only one?) of two retroviruses that cause AIDS. One of two? God help us! And what were retroviruses? The modern version of the Black Death? Ignorance and fear now took over in our conjectures.

> *retrovirus*: n. *Biol.* any of a group of RNA viruses which form DNA during the replication of their RNA.

A group? Yes, but mercifully only two of them are involved with the human immunodeficiency virus. Terror leaped out of the dictionary. I was holding Adam in my arms as we read over these concise and dreadful entries. Should we go ahead and look up DNA and RNA? Better not, I thought.

"Oh, go on," said Adam huskily, "we're not going to let the *Concise Oxford* finish us off, are we?"

RNA means ribonucleic acid. DNA means deoxyribonucleic acid. According to the dictionary it is the self-replicating material present in nearly all living organisms, especially as a constituent of chromosomes, the carriers of genetic information.

Adam and I looked at each other; we were undergoing the same process of dim but growing recognition. "DNA," Adam said.

"Of course!" He and I were in the same state of quarter-knowledge that everyone is who reads the papers idly from one year's end to the next. I guess we'd both seen the acronym DNA a thousand times; it had been the big story of the 1960s in biological research. Neither of us had any idea whatsoever what DNA was or what it did. Reading through those terse dictionary entries, amplifying slightly our ignorance, we saw that we had been led into the middle of a terrifying bog. Immunodeficiency, retrovirus, deoxyribonucleic acid. These words had the magical effect of theology on innocence.

"Look," I told Adam comfortingly, "there's a half-word I know. 'Ribo.' Must have something to do with riboflavin."

"Should we look it up?" Adam began to cough, making a weird noise.

"Might as well. Can't hurt."

Well, of course it did hurt. We found riboflavin, ribonucleic, ribose and ribosome, all in a row in this dictionary's dreadful columns. I think the definition of ribosome was the worst,

> *ribosome*: n. *Biochem*. each of the minute particles consisting of RNA and associated proteins found in the cytoplasm of living cells, concerned with the synthesis of proteins.

I looked Adam in the eye. "Shall we look up cytoplasm?"

"Better not. I'm very tired and it looks as though I've got something wrong with my sugars and proteins." He laughed unsteadily, and in a way this laughter was steadying and reassuring. If it was just sugars and proteins (chocolate, peanut butter) there was something to be done about it.

We realized that afternoon that the human immunodeficiency virus might lead straight to fatality, but at least it could be described in the ordinary terms of biology and biochemistry. Riboflavin, I thought, that's been on cereal boxes for years. I felt as though I knew all about these matters and I gave Adam a hug. I said something that had been on my mind for a couple of years.

"It isn't evil. It isn't a curse and it isn't God's revenge for misbe-haviour. Is it? I mean, there's nothing to apologize for, is there?"

We exchanged solemn looks; this was the first time we'd brought things out in the open. We only had the foolish confused layman's terrified suspicions about this biochemical labyrinth. "You can get it in various ways," I said, parroting the papers. "Contaminated needles. Exchange of body fluids. Those are the two you hear about. It's hard to catch, but you can get it from an unlucky blood transfusion."

"That isn't the usual way," Adam said, "and it's nobody's business how I got it. The question is, what have I got and what will happen to me?"

We live in almost unbroken darkness; we have these little pools of information, even of knowledge. Adam knew something about how to put a film together or get a play onstage. I knew ten facts about Giorgione, and I don't know that I'd swear to five of them. But biochemistry and its implications are, like almost all of existence, a mystery to me. The truest words I can speak are: I don't know.

When we were going over Adam's report from Ottawa, as communicated to us by Dr. Cotterill (who may have made cuts and elisions here and there), we didn't know a name for the thing that was destroying Adam. We knew three words but didn't suspect what they meant. Shortly after we received this report, however, we began to see the initials HIV all over the papers. First this celebrity and then that admitted to being HIV-positive. It took us about ten weeks to make the connection, but one morn-ing, as I was going through the papers with Adam, he said very slowly, "That's what I've got. Now I get it! I'm HIV-positive."

Once we knew the name, we felt better. We could see the *Concise Oxford Dictionary* from where we were sitting. Adam kept the big book within reach, and spent part of most days — when he felt strong — chasing definitions around in its pages and making notes. I have his notes. They don't indicate that he ever acquired any true knowledge of what was happening to his blood. What we had was a name, a word, a fear. The newspapers began to provide certain superficial information about HIV. If you tested positive for this virus, a vast body of biochemical information was already in place to predict what was going to happen to you.

By early 1987 this hitherto mysterious virus had acquired the status in public consciousness of a concrete *thing*, an entity, nameable and perhaps even treatable. Statistics, those ghostly information bits, began to come into play. From their chancy revelations we were able to construct a sense of a life lived as a fighting group, with Adam at its centre and the rest of us deployed around him as a support group. It must have been about this time that he had to book into St. Michael's for another bout of pneumonia, a bit harder to overcome than the first. There was some strange development with his lungs, where the right lung had to be collapsed by artificial means for a short time, and all at once the left lung began to collapse on its own. There was great pain involved, like the worst consequences of pleurisy. Fiery sensations of great intensity in the chest cavity, as though terribly inflamed tissues were rubbing against each other without any lubrication. And there was the terrible dread, uncontrollable and final, of immediate extinction.

There had apparently been some confusion about the X-ray plates, or the correct reading of the plates, or perhaps the transmission from one level of authority to another of the right reading of the plates, that caused confusion about the state of the patient's case. It was a very close-run thing. Another two and a half minutes and Adam would have been left without a functioning lung. The feeling of dread was more physical than psychological; it made Adam determined never to go into hospital again. And he never did. From then on we resolved to conduct his case according to the highest standards of home care.

In the minds of many the phrase "palliative care" has bad connotations. Many doctors and nurses who are working in the existing network of hospitalization, with its complex institutional

structure of fee schedules, medical insurance, admissions procedures, aggressive treatment policies, find themselves committed
to last man, last round, fight it to the bitter end, treatment.
Certainly our health-care system needs a certain number of
practitioners who will never give up on a case. They establish
the frontiers of treatment, and heroic measures to extend life
gradually become routine procedures.

But there is also common humanity to be considered, and the
last state of the patient to be looked forward to. If aggressive
treatment, which prolongs desperate pain while allowing a few
more days of life, is the norm for terminal cases, is the sufferer to
have any voice in the choice of treatment, or is he or she simply
to acquiesce in what is being done? Palliative care is not necessarily surrender. To spare the dying some hours or days of pain
at the end of life is not cowardice, not murder. When Adam came
back from the hospital for the second time he swore he wouldn't
ever go back there, and he described the awful sensations of not
knowing whether he could draw his next breath, the fear of
suffocation, with such vividness that he persuaded us to care for
him at home.

"I don't ever want to have to do that again," he said. "I want
to stay here for good. You won't make me go back, will you?"

That was about May 1987, if I remember right. The whole
course of the illness begins to be blurred about this time. We
began to be flooded with current statistical information; certain
orders of probability became clear. If you were HIV-positive you
were incubating an invariably fatal malady known as acquired
immunodeficiency syndrome, the dreaded AIDS.

An HIV-positive person could incubate AIDS for an indefinite
period. By mid-1987 there were already patients who had gone
for as much as three to five years; longer periods have been
observed since. Being identified as HIV-positive threw you into a
crisis situation that might prolong itself cruelly. You might go for
a long time without moving into an immediately life-threatening
phase of the illness. You could even get used to life under these

conditions, like living under the volcano that has erupted before and probably will again.

We have all grown used to living under the imminent threat of nuclear disaster, and this has made us readier to accept the HIV-positive life as a typical human state. Humanity, it seems, is a toxic condition in which your next breath is compromised. The dread is always here and we can't turn it off or deny it. The whole human population has agreed to live like this. Life itself is morbid, a perpetual state of threatened collapse. The race itself is inwardly compromised and the best thing for the environment would be for the compromised human race to disappear soon from the scene. Conservationists and environmentalists begin to agree that humanity is a cancerous growth, a parasitical imposition on nature. It is devoutly to be hoped that humanity will soon disappear, that rationality and imagination will be wiped out of the universe, which will then unroll according to the accidents of the evolutionary process. No more thought. No more worry. No nonsense about God's eternal contemplation of His perfect essence in pure thought. No more emotion. No more love. No more original sin, guilt, salvation, no more Adam. A clean, uncompromised environment. Nature without meaning.

HIV and AIDS are not the gay plague; they have no moral meaning. They are affairs of sugars and proteins, and aggressive medicine can fiddle around with them more or less as one approaches a roulette wheel. Let's give AZT a try, you never know. Azidothymidine. An eye-catching acronym, marketable. And if AZT has a toxic effect, try DDI, the natural next stage. If the process reminds us of monkeys swatting keyboards, and leaves us charged with dread, that's all right too. Farewell, reason!

It takes a while for the sufferer to get to that stage. That's the stage of full-blown AIDS, which is always fatal and may last from nine to ten months. But you don't know when it will start. That's the really hard part. That's what we had to live with on Crescent Road. Adam wasn't going back into the hospital; we agreed on that, all six of us, Andrea, Josh, Danny, Muriel, Eleanor and me.

We got him home, and we put together a medical team that we trusted. I want to say that Dr. Cotterill and Dr. Jackson were wonderful; they didn't insist on aggressive treatment. They respected our decisions and they listened to Adam; they let him have some say about what was to be done. There was awful pain, indignity, terror, madness, erroneous treatment, all that. Sometimes you just have to learn to surrender.

That was at the end; we still had a long way to go before that. We all decided with Adam, and for him, that we would live through this together. It's hard to say how much this meant to me, and for me. That sounds self-absorbed and cruel, but I don't mean it to be. What I got to stand on, what I'd never done before, was be there! I'd always been the little boy, to be protected and cared for. I wasn't with my father when he died. I wasn't with my mother when she died. I wasn't with Linnet when she died. Matthew, the seldom-seen kid. I benefited greatly by being with Adam this time, and we had Andrea beside us. Andrea, my daughter, the little hellhound, as Tony used to call her, became our team leader. She had seen my mother through the gate, and knew how to give injections, attach IV drips and tubes, turn a person in bed. She had a knack for staying up nights. How many nights? Nobody knew yet; we were still in the statistically uncertain state. We might have many years or some years or a few years together; we couldn't know for sure. That was the time when Adam started to talk wistfully about the gay nineties.

"I'll make it. I'll be there," he'd say. He kept his courage up remarkably. And gradually he began to drop out of the news and receive the blessed inattention of the media. The crowd on the veranda thinned out. Some days we didn't get more than two or three interrogatory or abusive phone calls. Business calls had stopped a long time back; it seemed to be an accepted fact in the entertainment world that Adam Sinclair wouldn't work again. After all, he was close to sixty; he was getting hard to cast. It was time for him and his entourage to retire gracefully from the scene, without being pushed. A few pirated photographs of Adam began to appear in the supermarket tabs at this point. When I saw them I was surprised at how altered his looks were. Seeing him every day, you lost the sense of a steady deterioration. I suppose the alterations in appearance were minute, from day to day. You don't notice the aging process in the shaving mirror. But interrupt the daily record for a while and you'll be shocked at the difference when you come back to the daily confrontation with the razor.

Photos of Adam taken in late 1987 show him as what I would have to call emaciated. He could not have appeared on TV or in a film as a leading man. He might have played an elderly invalid, which is what he was. I remember how he commented on this.

"I've never played a sick old man, I wouldn't know how."

"I don't understand you." I couldn't see why he couldn't play it, if that's what he was.

"It's a question of artistic convention," he said vaguely.

I thought this over for a long time. A sick old man might give a lousy performance as a sick old man, unless he happened to be a very good actor; it wouldn't matter how sick he was, as long as he could act. An acted representation of sickness and age can easily be more real than the real thing. It isn't what it looks like! How often have I heard that said of a performance or a narration. When pictures of Adam appeared in the papers, showing him as hollow-cheeked with great dark circles under his eyes, thousands of people simply refused to believe that they were real. "Fake!" "That's not Adam Sinclair!" "That isn't what he looks like!"

Our looks seem to be the realest things about us and the most deceptive. I don't photograph well, whereas Adam photographed beautifully. In a photo he always looked like himself, the same on the screen, like himself. The phrase suggests a mysterious duplicity; a likeness is never exact. It is precisely a resemblance, and a resemblance requires at least two elements, an original and a simulacrum. The status of "being like" is not the status of "being." I've never been any good at thinking logically. I've always been a guesser, and I can't work out the dimensions of the problem of the sick old actor who doesn't know how to play a sick old man. I just know that it's a true problem. Has something to do with self-knowledge and the way others accept us as ourselves. Adam used to get very playful when I asked him about these things.

"I don't know anything about anything," he'd say proudly. "I don't have to know anything. I'm an actor, I can just act it."

"Plato calls that a vicious position," I said. "He says that it's a bad thing that storytellers can make themselves sound like doctors. I suppose that applies to actors too."

He smiled faintly, twisting his huge watch around a thin wrist. I noticed the boniness and felt sad. The watch rotated around the bone very easily, more like a loose bracelet than a wristwatch. He wore it almost every day; his clothes were starting to have an actorish look. I haven't talked about his clothes, but they were one of the things that kept us all going. He was getting progressively less able to move around. He might walk from his bedroom to the living room, and then walk back an hour later to lie down. His breathing was noisy and difficult, so he didn't come and go readily, but he enjoyed getting dressed. He also enjoyed buying clothes. Not for street wear, more like lounging apparel. About this time a whole new generation of sportswear seemed to spring up out of the ground, roomy sweatshirts and turtlenecks in gorgeous colours in soft cottons. Adam loved cotton shirts in these new dyes, crimson, lime, ochre, primrose, olive. He must have had hundreds of them and he enjoyed wearing them. They were easy to get into and didn't hurt his skin, which was acutely sensitive to touch at this stage. Danny and Josh used to help him get dressed. More often than not he'd drape himself in one of his new turtlenecks in a bright colour, with the big Mickey-feels-Minnie watch shining on his wrist. God, those clothes used to arrive daily, in parcels from 800-number dealers in Springfield, Missouri, and Seattle. He could use the phone of course, although it hurt his fingers, and he had dozens of credit cards. He'd spend the early afternoons talking to retailers all over the continent, ordering sweaters and caps and polo necks and traditional cotton broadcloth shirts that he could wear open at the neck, and these parcels would arrive in the mail or by courier. Andrea or Muriel or Eleanor used to bring them in and unwrap them for him.

"Christmas every day." I remember him saying that once or twice.

I was the one who threw out the voluminous bundles of wrapping paper and the shippers' bills. We threw out more paper garbage than anybody in Chestnut Park. Then we got into recycling, to handle the excess paper. Every afternoon, after the shirts and jogging shoes and sweatshirts and sports caps had arrived and been unwrapped, I'd sit in the kitchen and fold wrapping paper, putting it in the plastic pickup boxes that the city provides.

Getting him dressed mid-morning was like witnessing the *levée* of the Sun King. It took ninety minutes because there was always a danger of bruising him or causing him to fall. He could shrug into a soft upper garment but couldn't quite manage to get out of his pajamas and into undershorts or briefs and a pair of trousers or jogging pants. And mind you, this was one of the best-dressed men in the world. This reminded me of the long decline and death in total silence of a world-famous communications specialist, an ironic fate. It's all irony now. Have you had your irony today, I used to ask myself as we helped Adam to dress. Originally we had conceived the ceremony as encouraging, an indication that he was getting up and would be able to socialize normally that day. Scrabble, Monopoly, Trivial Pursuit. Bridge. Muriel and Eleanor were dab hands at bridge, and Adam was for a long time a ferociously deceptive bidder capable of arranging the most criminally favourable contracts for himself and partner. I used to stand near the card table and listen to the bidding. Josh was the designated fourth, and Adam's principal victim. Adam liked to play with Muriel as his partner; he would not play for money in this foursome but would readily wager matchsticks or Q-Tips. He won consistently and so did Muriel. Josh was the big loser.

I asked Josh why he lost to Adam so consistently.

"It's not an architect's game; it's an actor's game."

"How do you mean?"

"Just you watch during the bidding. He seems to have some way of signalling what's in his hand to his partner, especially Muriel. And he always knows what the other couple's body language means. I try to sit perfectly still and give no indication of what I'm holding, and damn him, he can always tell. My hair stands up on my neck or my ears get red or something. He can read me like a book."

I had had no idea that Adam possessed any such perspicacity, and resolved not to play cards with him, certainly not for money and not even for toothpicks. Think of losing all your toothpicks to a movie star! But by now those friendly games were a thing of the past. When some of us gathered in his room to watch him dress, we knew that he wasn't really going to get up. One of us would help him into his trousers, a difficult operation. Try it and you'll see. You can get the legs in all right, but pulling the pants up to the waist is dicey, especially with somebody who has trouble standing erect. Adam used to tease me by letting himself go limp and falling forward, so that I had to put my arms around him tightly to keep him standing up. For a while I thought he was doing it to embarrass me, the position was so much that of a loving embrace.

"Fred and Ginger," he once said, while hanging on to my neck with his hands clasped behind my back. I could hear Andrea giggling from the doorway.

"All right now," I said, "just pay attention to what we're doing." I couldn't really be stern with him, and I wasn't sure that he was really hugging me. He may simply have been trying to stand up. As soon as I'd tugged his trousers into place I

extricated myself as gently as possible from his clutch and drew
the ends of his belt into an accessible position. He stood there
with the rest of us grouped around him. He tugged at the two
ends of the belt, inserting the travelling end into the buckle and
drawing the belt tight around his waist. It seemed as though he
would never finish drawing it tight. One hole and then another
slid through the buckle without the belt's growing tight around
his waist. This went very slowly like a slow-motion film. He
raised his eyes and stared straight at me.

"Matt, you'll have to make some new holes."

He never finished getting dressed that day. We lowered him
back onto the fresh sheets and I took the belt into the pantry
where we kept some household tools. I made four new punctures
in the belt, using a hammer and a punch. As I did this I wondered how many of these new holes he would get to use. Two,
actually. In the end he couldn't get the belt tight enough to hold
his trousers up. By that time the *levée* was a formality. He might
sit up for a while but he didn't walk around. We'd help him put
on a fresh cotton shirt, and that was about the size of it. What
had in the beginning been the complex ceremony we all perform
every morning gradually became shortened and formalized.
Getting a fresh, often brand-new, richly coloured cotton turtleneck over the head became the concentrated essence of the
longer, less conscious ritual.

The dominant ritual of that period was the taking of the quarterly blood sample and its dispatch to the testing service. We
didn't take the sample ourselves. Dr. Cotterill had a hematologist
friend who lived near us; this kind specialist used to come over
to the apartment and take care of the samples. We were
determined that this process should be carried out with extreme
care because this was the best obtainable record of Adam's
progress. The T-cell count varied slightly from one three-month
period to the next but did not indicate potential disaster for quite
a long time. For most of 1988 Adam was at the HIV stage; towards
the end of that year the media began to write about him as if the

condition were routine. By this time several other personalities from the entertainment world and the worlds of sports and politics had identified themselves as HIV-positive. The great public studied these people and their case histories with fascination just short of morbidity. I suspect that pools were got up on life expectancies.

Some of these celebrities displayed great courage and forthrightness about their condition. The posture must have been fairly easy to maintain as long as you were HIV and perhaps in remission. People in this condition came and went, appeared on talk shows, were written up in gossip columns and magazines, were discussed and scrutinized minutely by millions of viewers and readers. Some feminists complained that there was gender discrimination here. Male HIV patients certainly received more coverage than female. Comparisons based on the relative numbers of male and female HIV patients began to be made, but it was hard to obtain accurate counts. No matter how insistently the media might proclaim that no stigma attached to the illness, that the HIV/AIDS sequence was a disorder like any other, those who were receiving care for the disorder were reluctant to go public with it. There was a strange unreadable implication to this reluctance. It was a matter of record and of public conviction and declaration that no health disorder was disgraceful or to be concealed because of possible ostracism. We were past all that! Nobody thought of HIV or AIDS as matter for guilt, not in 1989. And yet there was an obscure moral haze around the subject.

Was the disorder communicable? Did all HIV-positives develop AIDS, and if so, when? If it was communicable, was it very catching? Could you get it accidentally? A very few sad cases of people who acquired the virus in unexpected ways (from a dentist, from supplies of contaminated blood) were much written up. What precautions should be taken against getting it? Sure it was an epidemic, but not an epidemic like the others. I actually received letters damning me for exposing my daughter to infection; one or two acquaintances went so far as threatening me with legal proceedings on this account. Josh Greenwald reported similar communications to himself. He showed me a series of three letters to himself that were indescribably menacing and accusatory in tone. They had been sent to him at his office. The first letter, the longest of three, accused him of conniving at a dangerous course of action followed by his young woman friend. He should compel her to move out of that rotten den on Crescent Road, where a notorious film actor and his boyfriends were hiding out. Josh had no business going to such a place; his girlfriend was at risk. He might as well send her to a leper colony to court infection. This first letter had a terribly frightened, intemperate tone. It continued for three typed single-spaced pages of rant.

The second and third letters were made up of repetitions of rumours that were going around at the time about the incidence of AIDS infections, how widely they were circulating, how terribly contagious they were. How Africa was being swept by them. How the virus had passed onwards to India where it was destroying thousands of lovely male prostitutes in their early teens. The final letter concluded by warning Josh that if anything happened to Andrea the writer would hold Josh personally responsible, and would see that he was duly punished for his negligence and foolhardiness. There were unvoiced threats of legal action, perhaps even physical attack.

"What do you make of these, Matt?" Josh said, when I'd finished reading through these loathsome communications. Unsigned, undated, done in a mint-condition keyboard on the commonest kind of Woolco stationery. The writer could only be identified by some revelatory accident. I went back to the first of the three and looked over the references to myself. They made me feel my neck a bit.

Somebody had been doing a spot of background research on me; the writer knew that I was to all intents and purposes unmarried, or at least without a female partner in my life. There were intimations that my wife had left me because of my long friendship with Adam. The writer thought that something disgusting was going on. He or she showed great detestation of the lives of gay people, making a great show of sexual orthodoxy. The funny thing was, you couldn't easily tell from the wording of the letters whether they had been written by a woman or a man. The writer knew, for example, that my wife had lived with my brother for a long while, and didn't seem to find it shocking. Could that be a distinctively female, or even feminist, attitude? I didn't think so. My feminist friends never took a doctrinaire approach to Edie's departure. Most of them thought that life with me would be safe but boring, and didn't blame Edie for her decision to leave me. A few seemed to think that she had been disloyal, but they were a minority among the eight or nine women who spoke to me about the matter over about fifteen years. I never detected any "feminist position" in favour of all wives leaving their husbands. Rough sympathy was what I got from most of my women friends, and no suspicion that my sexual misconduct had been a factor in Edie's choice. I didn't believe that the author of the three malignant letters to Josh was some rejoicing feminist acquaintance of mine. But they had been written by somebody who knew all three of us, Andrea, Josh and me, somebody probably of their generation.

When I made my remarks about the clean type of the keyboard and the wide availability of the paper, Andrea took me to task for making a game of the matter.

"You sound like somebody in a detective story. I don't think there's any point in going on like that. They're dirty anonymous letters unworthy of attention."

"Don't you think we should try to find out who wrote them and try to defend ourselves?" Josh asked.

"I don't think there would be any point in that," she repeated. "What would be the good? You can't change the characters of people like that. If the person who wrote those letters is over nineteen there's nothing much to be done for him."

"You think it's a man?" I asked.

"Not necessarily. It's somebody who's trying to conceal his or her gender. Why are we talking about these rotten things anyway?" Andrea seldom gets angry and when angry she could be mighty formidable. The new tone in her voice roused Adam, who had been resting in his bedroom. He called out to us as if frightened or in pain.

"What are you guys talking about in there? Is it about me?"

We looked at each other; we could hardly tell him about Josh's three letters, which were meant to be hurtful and damaging. The last one threatened to "go public with the story." What story? There wasn't any story, or there wouldn't be today.

But at that time, late 1988, the public was still massively ignorant about the medical facts in these cases. It took a long time for them to become convinced — if they ever did — that the virus could be communicated only with considerable difficulty, and in specific ways. Later that year a number of professional hockey players expressed alarm at the possibility of interchanges of blood during fights. They said that they were now unwilling to drop their gloves in a fight, which lessened the effectiveness of such action as a crowd-pleaser. A ludicrous instance of irrational fear among a poorly informed small group. It seemed then as though an enormous range of mythical thought was being engendered by lack of accurate public information.

And then there were the real cover-ups and denials of responsibility. A dentist infected a patient and her case drew wide media attention, sometimes a fear-mongering sensationalism. A nun was infected by a blood transfusion. Even more alarming than these cases were the stories that went around about erroneous and incompetent medical procedures, especially those connected with the supply of blood in the treatment of hemophiliacs and transfusion patients. For about five years in the 1980s the Canadian Red Cross seems to have supplied HIV-contaminated blood and blood products to an unsuspecting clientele. In 1984, 1985 and 1986, they were routinely obtaining these products from the United States, even though this implied a higher risk of infection. It later appeared that more than a thousand people were infected with this virus, until the end of 1985 or the beginning of 1986, by this supply of blood products from the Canadian Red Cross. It wasn't till after the turn of the decade, in 1991, that these facts became known. By then, for many sick people, it was too late.

There was nothing to do but go down the hall into Adam's room and try to chat him up about matters that had nothing to do with poison-pen letters. I will say nothing about the two most painful ones that I received, except to note that they were plainly the work of somebody who knew me and the family very well. Somebody who scorned and hated me because of my unfortunate habit of not being around in the crunch. Strangely enough, though they were handwritten in a distinctive script, I never managed to guess their authorship. Nobody I could think of wrote in that spiky, angular, deeply scored fist.

We seemed to be ringed by unidentifiable watchers eager to fasten blame for errors in Adam's treatment on us. When I say us, I suppose I mean me. I was the person who held the lease on the apartment, owned its furnishings and so on. The telephone was in my name. I was Adam's host. For once in my life I was going to be there when needed. I would see the thing through, damn it all. I wouldn't take an appointment in Switzerland or China or Italy.

We all began to be gravely disturbed by the confusing currents of publicity that whirled around the new plague. On the night that we first discussed Josh's three letters, we had to conceal their contents and implications from Adam. When he called out to us asking to know what we were talking about, I think we all felt shame at having left him out of the conversation by gathering in the living room while he was lying down.

There was sharp anxiety in his voice when he called to us. As we trooped down the hall to join him we had no time to invent an excuse for having left him out. We still hadn't been able to put a name to his illness, not right in front of him. For the record, as far as his health was concerned, we let on that we thought he was suffering from an unidentified pulmonary or blood disorder, something like a chronic heavy bronchitis, or some form of anemia, or a persistent mononucleosis. We did not want to come right out with a declaration that he was HIV-positive.

But the three of us knew that this was it, and I think Danny, Muriel and Eleanor knew it too. We couldn't bring ourselves to name it to them. How can you discuss a friend's illness out of his hearing, without having talked honestly about it to him? The moral dilemma was oppressive. I might be talking to Danny about something we needed to get for Adam, a heating pad, or some product to be used in massage, and all the time he would be asking me mutely to spell out for him just what Adam had. After all, it might be infectious. Danny had no way of knowing if he was being exposed to a possibly fatal contagion, but he never expressed such a fear, never asked to have the diagnosis explained to him. He did what he was asked to do, or what he saw needed to be done, without complaint, and he kept his mouth shut as he crossed the veranda. He never leaked any medical information to the press, and I'm proud to say that the rest of us followed his example. We kept silence and did what had to be done as the course of the illness unfolded. But we were perhaps a bit slow to share our cover stories among ourselves; we were frequently uncertain what other members of the support group were thinking. We all saw that sooner or later the medical situation was going to become a matter of public knowledge. A cellular phone could be bugged. A memorandum from a doctor could be filched from a trashbasket. There were dozens of ways for medical information to be uncovered by snoopers on the track of something private that the public might perhaps have some sort of right to know.

The three of us went into Adam's room, which was a good size, and found him sitting on the edge of his bed, dressed in pajamas and his Jaeger dressing-gown, a comfortable old article that he'd bought in Britain in the late 1950s. It was in some

authentic Scots tartan in bands and oblongs of alternate dark
green and purple. It wasn't the Sinclair tartan. I know because I
once asked him about it and he reminded me that his branch of
the Sinclairs wasn't Scots but northern English, a distinction
he insisted upon; some ancient Border rivalry lay behind this
insistence.

There were three or four chairs in the room, and a handsome
desk, besides the big bed, so we all found places to sit down
comfortably. We all noticed that Adam was finding it hard to sit
up straight without back support.

"Wouldn't you sooner take a chair, for your back?" I said.

He gave me an angry look, a real old actor's upstage frown.

"What are you implying?" he said.

This took me right aback. I'd been implying that he was too
sick or too tired to sit erect on the edge of the bed. Actually he
was swaying slightly, as if he had a balance problem. I didn't like
his looks. There had been some sort of deterioration in the last
few days.

"I'm not implying anything," I said defensively. And Josh
leaped in with an invented tale to help me out. No mention of
poison-pen letters.

"We were talking about ways to shake the media coverage
outside. You know those big balls on either side of the veranda
steps, at the top?"

"I know all about big balls," said Adam. It was the last joke I
heard him make. I saw fright in his face. Fright, bewilderment,
inability to take in what was being said to him.

"They've knocked one of those big concrete balls off its column. It's lying in the flower bed," said Andrea. "I don't see how
anybody will ever get it back into place."

"Guess who'll be billed for that!" I said. "Not the Toronto
Sun."

"Was it the Sun reporters that did it?" Josh said.

"They seem the most likely candidates," I said. My voice must
have reeked with elitist feeling. "The Globe and Mail would never

roll anybody's balls off the veranda." Without realizing it I was voicing a deep truth about the Canadian media. There was a flicker of humour in Adam's face. He was letting our story go by.

"I'm very sick," he said all at once. "I'm HIV-positive, you know." It was the first time we'd acknowledged the medical reality, 1988. I still, at that date, didn't fully understand what the acronym implied. None of us in the support group had the full personal contact with the attending physician that the patient had. We didn't enjoy complete confidentiality with Dr. Cotterill. He never said to me in set professional terms that Adam had contracted a specific illness. I think he must have kept his diagnosis strictly to himself, preserved in his professional notes and records, and he never told me the state of the case in so many words. He kept his opinions from everyone but his colleagues and the patient; it certainly wasn't from Dr. Cotterill that the leaks came. Given the strict surveillance that the press and other media kept up, it was inevitable that some investigator would find out the facts of the case. The information could have come from any of half a dozen sources, quite innocently. The address on a blood sample, the names of colleagues consulted by Dr. Cotterill, observations made of Adam's appearance from a distance, by photographs or eye-witnesses. There are no true secrets any more.

"I'm very sick. I'm HIV-positive, you know."

Now each of us knew for sure.

He looked unsteadily at Andrea and Josh. Andrea loved Adam, and ought to have come first in his affections, and Josh was now very close to her. He'd earned Adam's close friendship. I was glad that they were in the room at this moment of bad hard truth.

Adam's teeth seemed to be chattering. "I may be moving into a long remission," he said. I think that's what he said. "Or I may not. At this point it's hard to say. The doctor doesn't know. It might last for years."

Now at last he looked at me as straight as he could, and I could take in the full measure of the change in his looks. He didn't look as bad as he did later, but he looked pretty bad. His neck was so thin. The collar of the dressing-gown was now far too big for him. The bones in his cheeks were formed like big deadly wings. The skin around his eyes was folded and inelastic and faintly bluish. You could smell his skin. Not a sweaty odour but an acrid chemical tang with which I was unfamiliar.

He said, "I want to stay here."

There it was; he would never leave. We were going to be together for as long as it took. That was all right. I knew that Adam and I would be able to handle it. He was having trouble keeping eye contact with me; there was fright and the fear of rejection in his poor face. I remembered that night on my honeymoon when I had awakened from a semi-intoxicated doze to find him in bed behind me. All I'd been able to do, in that extreme position, was make fun of him, hope for Edie to come back and rescue me so that the two of us could ridicule him and chase him from the room.

I had thought of Edie, in that comic context, as the Queen of the Night, a magical figure who intervenes in the opera at crucial moments but doesn't really function in the action. Thirty-five years later I saw in this identification a truth I'd missed at the time. Edie had intervened in the action for a while, then chosen to extricate herself from it. The Queen of the Night might appear again in the final act; there was no way to predict that. But at this solemn moment the person whom I'd loved the longest was sitting across the room from me. Adam had walked into my life long before I'd known Edie or anybody else besides my family, longer than my children or my school friends. He's there on the bottom of page one, a permanent element of my existence.

I said to him, "I won't let you go."

I got out of my chair and crossed the stuffy room to him. I sat beside him on the bed and put my arms around him as gently as I could. So what if he'd made a determined pass at me in the honeymoon bed, was that so awful? Would the sky have fallen if I'd taken him in my arms then? There didn't seem that much distance between the two incidents. I ought to have kissed him then, and I kissed him now. I held the thin chest against my own. I could feel him shaking fast, in a dreadful all-over vibration. I looked him in the eye. This once, God damn it, this once I'd stay around.

"You aren't going anywhere," I said, and I held him close. I kissed him again, pressing my lips to his. The last time we'd kissed was in Stratford in 1953. He said the same thing now that he'd said then: "Oh, darling Matt."

And I started to see something I'd never suspected before, that grew clearer and clearer as time raced by. Uncle Philip had kept a secret love in the interweavings of his life, that his closest friends had never suspected. When Jeanne appeared at the very end of his life its entire context was turned inside out.

If there were any Matt Goderich watchers, my dear lost Linnet must have shown them the way my life went. And now I understood that I was Adam's secret beloved, the great surprise for his intimates, the element they'd never identified in the weave of his history, the big surprise. I had no notion who these people might be, Adam's life having been lived in places remote from my home. There were actors and agents and producers who knew him intimately and had never heard of me. They had been his life, and in their eyes I could only be guessed at as a concealed interwoven thread, and I understood that great love exacts love in turn that can't be denied when the time comes for union. I would not let him go. This dreadful thing that had happened to him menaced me equally. We loved each other and we were going to go through this together.

If I'd been kinder to Adam on that honeymoon night, if I hadn't treated him as a joke and sided with Edie in reducing our relations to a farcical dance, he might never have contracted this illness. Perhaps I was to blame for his present predicament. He never told us where he got it, and we didn't try to find out. He had never received a transfusion and made no use of needles; that left two possibilities that were not subject to discussion. Adam was a gent; he didn't kiss and tell, and for somebody in my position this was comforting. I had heard years before from my dear brother that Adam had talked to him about me, in very affectionate terms, saying that as a child he had imagined us exchanging hugs and kisses. Tony would not have told this to anybody else, except perhaps Edie. It had never been leaked to the gossip columns. Adam's childhood fantasies about me went unrealized for fifty years. Closer to fifty-five, actually.

In all that time, until now, no columnist or reporter had ever publicly linked Adam's name to mine. He was an international celebrity and I was nobody. No wire service ever carried my name. So that when Adam got sick and his diagnosis was discovered by the press towards the end of 1988, the enormous audience for gossipy speculation could make no sense of the link between us. Why was Adam Sinclair hiding out in Toronto with an unemployed art historian? The media never connected me with my father, who, almost forty years before, had been a famous, almost a celebrated, person. But his celebrity status had never rivalled that of Adam or Sadie.

What, the public wanted to know, was a superstar doing in a modest midtown apartment in Toronto, the home of a middle-aged layabout with no reputation and no ties to the entertainment world? By now the number of well-known persons who had been identified as HIV-positive was considerable. The terrible *rite de passage* through which they would move to full-blown AIDS had been closely studied by the world's communications network. Politicians, figures from the sports world, churchmen, people like me in obscure and humble circumstances all passed from incubation or remission into the terminal stage in the fiery glare of publicity. Given these facts, I seemed about to lose my status as Adam's big surprise, acquiring in the process a very inconvenient, and totally unwanted, public identity. I think the worst shock I underwent in the decade was the sight of a blurred and caricatural photograph of myself on the front cover of the most widely circulated supermarket tabloid, with the enormous headline above it, "ADAM'S LOVER?"

Thank God for the shoddy paper and the blurry smeared ink. I don't take a good picture, as they say, and I don't think my dearest pals would have spotted me as the subject of the photo, if the accompanying text hadn't been so specific (if you could ignore some peculiar misspellings). "Matthew Godrick, 58, ex-husband of English woman painter Edna Godrick. Part-time art critic and full-time playboy. Lessee of palatial midtown Toronto retreat of ailing superstar. Boyfriend. Travelling companion." I couldn't read any further; the piece was so loaded with lies and half-truths that I choked over it. I'd never travelled fifty miles with Adam, and I'd certainly never enjoyed full boyfriend status. I noticed an inquiring eye or two cocked in my direction as I slid a copy of this paper off the tall pile beside the doorway of a drugstore. I might have been spotted as the subject of the photograph, boyfriend, boy toy, male bimbo, art critic and companion, and me fifty-eight years old, never before the object of such scrutiny.

This was how I finally understood the awful consequences of celebrity; the communications media finally come to possess you and everything around you. You are in the hands of the fax and e-mail nets and lie in the middle of the information highway. The tabloids and the magazines and TV shows never reviewed their right to say anything they pleased about you, true or false. During the next dreadful stretch of eight or nine months, I can't recollect a single instance of a person in the media checking facts with me. My age fluctuated between forty-five and sixty-five; the colour of my hair seemed especially difficult to ascertain, being described as every shade from raven to ash-blond. I was reported to have visited Cannes and Puerto Vallarta in Adam's company, two places I have never been. I was an art critic, a businessman, of indeterminate gender location, the father of two, or three, or five children. Nobody knew what I lived on. Everybody knew what I lived on. I had inherited wealth. I lived on my wife's earnings. There was a minute nub of fact lurking behind each of these representations, which was simply that the media had never before connected me to Adam. Big surprise, indeed!

LONGTIME DIVORCED MAN TO NURSE SUPERSTAR
ADAM UPDATE: STAR COMATOSE
SADIE WINGS TO ADAM'S BEDSIDE
FATE IN FINAL SEASON?

These inquisitors were like some factory-strength vacuum cleaner; they uncovered everything. Facts about me, often slightly inaccurate, that I would never have believed to be of the smallest interest to anybody, now became public property. My blood group, bank balance in any of several accounts I maintained, annual earnings, total income tax paid for previous tax year, police record (none), medical history, marital status, personal relationship with my brother, career record, abilities as a chief executive of a middle-sized retailing organization, height, weight, results of latest medical tests (blood, urine, chest X-ray) and anything else you can imagine, hat size, shoe size, all were for some reason of the greatest interest just as long as my destiny and conduct could be linked to Adam's life and health.

The shock I'd felt when I'd found out about Jeanne Three Streams was now reversed upon me in the form of the shocked surprise of the whole bloody world. I started *to get fan mail*, at first an occasional letter thanking me for taking care of a beloved idol. These were not the letters of anguished women fans; they were divided equally between the sexes. Several male correspondents described lifelong attachment to Adam's onscreen image, often in the most moving language. He had meant everything to them in the course of their unglamorous obscure lives (their language). I seemed to be their surrogate. For a brief time I became "Matt," the pilot-fish personalist shining in Adam's reflected light. I recall this sort of letter as typical of the late-1988 period. As that year wound down, the media scrutiny grew more and more intense, and the tone of the letters changed. So did

their frequency. The Post Office sent emissaries on three separate occasions to try to arrange with us for a more convenient
means of delivery of the increasing flood of mail. Many parcels
began to be included in the daily intake. Jars of useless medicines.
Royal jelly was a favourite offering. Yeast. Vitamins of every
letter in the alphabet. Baked goods in varying states of preserva-
tion. Many of these gifts originated from kind, decent people; a
few came from cranks. There were no explosive devices, letter
bombs or packaged infernal machines. No revolutionary group
intervened to shorten Adam's suffering or drive us from his side.
There was plenty of hate mail though. We got so we could identify it from the opening sentence, sometimes from the shape of
the handwriting. Hate mail handwriting is either very precise and
clear or very straggly and disordered. Either way is sufficiently
revelatory. Behind the sick mind is the sick soul.

This mail travelled into mental areas rarely investigated by
ordinary people like me. There was much discussion of the transmission of the virus. Hard curiosity gives birth to strangely shaped
images. These correspondents were motivated by a desperate
need to know how Adam had caught AIDS. What body fluids had
he ingested? What postures and acts promoted this transmission?
Maybe I should abandon my indoctrinated prudery and say
straight out what they wanted to know. How did gay men do it?
Did Adam take the penises of other men into his mouth and bring
them to climax by sucking on them? What was that like?

That's basically what they wanted to know. And having
brought myself to this stage of openness I think I can go on to be
even more explicit. The whole sequence of male sexual interac-
tion gradually opened up to us, amazed readers in the sexual
catalogue. Andrea used to examine these communications without turning a hair, but she never asked Adam to explain his
activities to her. How could she? You can hardly approach an old
friend a generation your senior to ask what he or she gets up to
in bed. Poor Andrea! Sometimes I felt that she'd been trapped in
the whole sequence by accident. If she'd had a different father

with different associates, she wouldn't have had to go through all that. By now we were concentrating our forces on making things easy for Adam; none of us was about to ask him what it was like to suck cock.

People's imaginations run in such well-worn grooves. Reading those letters was like sitting through two dozen porn films in rapid dull succession. Nothing reveals the structure of a genre like study of many examples of the kind. In a porn film the first great stage of the narration is accomplished when you are allowed a glimpse of the naked breast, not necessarily the female breast. Then, quite a while later, you are permitted to espy both breasts in motion, later still the whole view of the body naked from the rear, and finally the inexact representation of an act of intercourse. The soundtrack fills with moans and heavy breathing. It makes no difference whether the couple, or couples, are gay or straight; the sequence of the narrative remains invariable, evolving out of a strict code.

The inquiring letters betrayed this strict encoding. They led off with a brief paragraph of moralistic abuse, proceeded to make specific inquiries about sucking cocks, went from there to the niceties of anal penetration and concluded with remarks about more unusual practices that the writers obviously considered shocking and original, never apparently suspecting that they formed part of a dictionary of sexual customs going back as far as the Paleolithic. There is nothing new in human behaviour; the woman or man who invents a new sexy prank will be commemorated by statues in the public parks of the world's capitals, but this is not going to happen tomorrow. The invariability of these letters was the saddest and most striking thing about them; their writers could not imagine any actions out of a very rigid sequence. Cocksucking, fucking up the ass, the narrow repertoire of spinoff practices, bondage, rimming, the infliction of mild or acute pain. Reading about these matters proved drab indeed after the first dozen letters. Imagine spending fifty years as a priest in the confessional, or for that matter as a psychotherapist beside the couch.

This proved to be one of the consolations of the nine or ten months in 1989 when Adam went from the incubation phase into full-blown AIDS. By this time we'd seen it all; every area of unusual sexual practice had been thoroughly ventilated by our little group and there seemed nothing more to be uncovered. Lots of people liked to take other people's penises in their mouths and cosset them orally. After a few weeks this came as no surprise. We began to fall into a reflex so-what-else-is-new response. The best thing about this was that it removed the screen of superstitious awe that we'd been constructing around Adam as though he were some kind of god. It made us see that what he liked to do in bed had nothing to do with awe or horror but was purely human, an expression of the rooted need to be united to some other.

He talked a lot about his body, love, sex, isolation and need in the few months in early 1989 when he could still talk coherently for fairly long periods. He quieted our fears when he revealed how ordinary his needs were.

"I don't think I'm special. I don't think I'm any different from you guys. I used to think being gay made me like a king. It was secret and romantic and elite, and at first I thought that men's bodies, and certain particular men, were the loveliest things on earth. Men had nipples and asses and all those nice things that girls had, and lots more besides. I adored my body from the very beginning; it's the nicest thing in my life, and it always was, the feelings it could give me. They could make my toes curl up with pleasure and there's just nothing like that, the melting feeling where the whole middle of your body goes liquid. The first thing I learned was how to relax and take things up my ass, the enema nozzle or a thermometer. My mum taught me that, but it could just as well have been a nurse or a doctor. Not my dad. He ran off soon, and never had anything to say for himself that I can remember. The sexy thing that got me started was my little asshole and my bum. There's never been a time when I didn't think my bum was the sweetest thing going. When I was six I used to stroke myself between my cheeks and feel terribly excited."

"Did it make you feel like a woman?" I asked.

"I'm glad you asked me that question," he said, like somebody talking to Phil or Oprah, "because I don't know the answer. I never feel like a woman or a man, I feel like me. I don't think I'd feel any different if I related sexually to women. I've tried it with women and I don't feel like myself. There was none of the special pleasure that my body gives me when I'm being satisfied."

"And yet it was your mother who started you."

"Yes, but I never felt anything about her when she was fondling me. It was pure simple pleasure, all around the middle of my body, my asshole and my balls. I got so I could turn myself on by holding back my shit and feeling myself fill up. At times like that I could pleasure myself as much as in any other way. I have an idea that for me sex isn't a two-person thing. Maybe I'm a solitary and always will be."

"What about other people's bodies?"

"They're sweet if they're the right shape." A gleam came into his eye, and I knew that he was going to start to tease me.

This was in the first few months of 1989, when he was on AZT, and by May he was into a state of awful fatigue. He hardly left his bed, let alone his room. The doctors thought that he wasn't responding well to AZT, so they took him off it and he regained some strength. So they'd start again with the drug therapy and he'd relapse into extreme fatigue. We had this conversation at a time when he was on half-dosage and doing relatively well. He got interested in describing to me what his life and his affections had been like.

"Now you, Matt, you're no beauty but you're very, very sweet. You've got very curvaceous legs and thighs, nice little ears, lovely feet and the most endearing bum. It's too bad that they can't be seen. I don't know why we have to wear these stupid clothes."

"Do you like women's clothes better, then?"

"No, I hate the idea of drag. If there's one thing I really bar, it's guys camping around in ladies' dresses. They never get it right, and what's the point anyway?"

"I don't know about that," I said. "Edie and I used to trade clothes for fun. I always enjoyed it and so did she. Before making love."

"Perhaps you're a natural transvestite," he said.

"I wouldn't want to cross-dress all the time, too cold on the legs. I don't see how they stand it in January."

"Oh, Matt, that's so perfect, so like you. A reason for everything. I don't have to have a reason. I never wanted to be a woman or a man either. I just wanted to be myself and have fun. And now look what's happened."

I had the feeling that we'd had the same conversation a long time in the past. I know I had the same uncomfortable feelings both times, so perhaps I hadn't made any progress out of prudery into compassion. I was astonished when Adam started to weep.

"It's so bloody unfair," he said. "I've never willingly hurt anybody in my life. I've given largely to good causes, God knows. I've never been a gossip, I've never embarrassed anybody, and now this!"

Now he began to cry hard. I took him in my arms. It was our first close embrace, the first time I'd ever felt on a footing of true physical intimacy with him, and there was no element of sex or gender involved in the exchange. It was a close meeting of two loving hearts, but there was nothing gay about it. I was terrified and abashed to see him cry. It made me remember the time that Amanda Louise and I had offered to execute him, more than fifty years in the past. These present tears were continuous with those. This made me see that poor Adam had felt close to tears all his life, or perhaps only from the first time he'd encountered me and my sister. We were his fate, the source of all his outcries against injustice.

I hugged him close to me and saw for the first time how wasted his body was; he wasn't an armful. I could almost have put my arms around him twice. His grip was feeble; his strength was gone. I kissed his lips, and felt like Judas.

"That's our second kiss," he whispered.

"It won't be the last. I'm here, Adam, I'll be right here."

"I'd like to make love," he said, "but I just don't think I'm up to it today." He tried to giggle.

"Lie down," I told him, "and I'll get you anything you need. Just ask."

"Could I have a fresh shirt, one of the ones from Gap?"

At first I didn't know what he meant. I hadn't followed his adventures in the mail-order catalogues as closely as Danny and Andrea had. I heard the word as "gap," an open space, a hole or tear. Adam had to bring me up to date.

"It's a line of fine sportswear," he said slowly. "Better quality than Roots or Benetton or Vuarnet."

These last three names went straight by me. I don't pay much heed to marketing come-ons.

"Gap turtlenecks, wonderful cottons," he murmured and then I understood him. I went through several drawers of freshly laundered, unworn or brand-new cottons, and I started to see Gap labels. I selected three turtlenecks, all in gorgeous colours, pumpkin, olive, slate.

"Yummy," said a faint voice behind me. "Can I have the apricot one?"

"Pumpkin," I said.

"Don't hassle me, Matt, the bright orangey-yellow one."

I knew which one he meant. I was just checking his reactions for visual response. We'd been told to watch for temporary loss of vision at this stage, a symptom linked to imbalance in the body's handling of medication. From that point on, he was getting plenty of medication. I hate drugs, which means I'm afraid of them, I suppose. Injections, pills, we're a drug-using society even when we're not addictive. Pop a pill and the fear and pain will disappear. Morphine. The word terrifies me, and yet it's the specific pain-killer used to mask heavy joint and muscular pain. At least you don't have to give it by injection any more; it can be administered under the tongue like a new Eucharist, dissolving in the saliva. This method may be a bit quicker than injection but it can also fail to kick in, I can't tell you why.

I worked myself into position beside him on the bed, so as to get his sweaty, bad-smelling T-shirt off him. This was a difficult thing to do, because moving him caused pain. He had much pain from this point on. It must have taken twenty minutes to ease the dirty shirt off, and then I gave him a light alcohol rub, and a very careful towelling. He smelled like nothing I'd ever smelled before, not a human smell; there was a strong flavour of drugs in the air, how to describe it? It didn't smell like the product of any organic process, digestion or respiration. We all get to know what our bodies smell like in the natural state, during nutrition or recovery from some minor ailment; there's a clear kinship with the odour of animal life, dogs or horses. But somebody undergoing drug therapy in the course of AIDS doesn't smell like a man or woman, a dog or a horse. I can't think of anything to compare it with. If you took a dozen aspirins and powdered them in your palm, and added a little saccharine, you'd be close. A sweet-acrid odour.

He smelled like that quite a lot of the time; sometimes he had a more animal smell, but it was mostly masked by the drug odour. Working his dirty T-shirt off, I got the drug smell overpoweringly. An alcohol rub doesn't get rid of it either. It only masks it until the alcohol evaporates. After a while, ordinary cleanliness can only be intermittent. Finally it's impossible.

I unfolded the fresh turtleneck. It had its own smell of fine cotton, a much more agreeable and acceptable sensation. I had to work the big garment over his head and slide the thin arms into the soft smooth sleeves. His big Mickey Mouse watch, which he now refused to part with, lodged in the wristband as I eased his hand through it. I didn't dare to tug on his hand; he was in tears from the muscular and joint pain. I half-panicked, sliding my fingers around inside the wristband, trying to work it over the big face of the watch.

"Not now, not yet," he mumbled. "You can have it after."

It was like some form of testament or bequest, and I remembered it.

Right after he said that his eyes closed, and I lowered him into a lying position. The turtleneck was all rucked up around his shoulders and his chest and waist were uncovered. They made an alarming sight, skeletal, the skin discoloured and deeply pitted, the abdominal cavity all fallen in as if he had no intestines. You could almost see right through him. I thought that he needed to be covered up, so I called to Danny to give me a hand. Two people were needed for the task, to minimize the risk of bumping him. He seemed to be sleeping now; it would be a crime to wake him.

"You want me, chief?" Danny said from the doorway. He spoke very softly, as though reluctant to intrude on us. I think he understood the very close emotional tie that Adam and I had formed.

"It's the shirt, is it?"

I nodded. All of a sudden I was feeling very strange. I think that I expected Adam to pass out then and there. This was the first such scare but not the last. After that I figured that he could die at any time. But he wasn't sleeping, he was comatose.

We pulled gently at the material of the shirt, sliding it down underneath him. I remember very well how the fresh material smelled, cottony and unused. In a moment we had his torso well covered. We stood up at the bedside — we'd been on our knees together — and exchanged satisfied looks. Then all at once there was this appalling smell, and a squirting, flushing sound. Our satisfied looks vanished and we both choked and put our hands up to our faces, as though we'd been rehearsed. Adam had suddenly lost bowel control, and would now have to be cleaned and changed. I would not have believed that his intestinal tract had contained so much matter and liquid. All of it voided in one rush, spreading and soaking into the bedclothes under him. Now the room badly needed airing, but we couldn't move him in his comatose state, and we didn't want to risk exposing him to a draught of cold air.

"Is he finished?" I said, to nobody in particular. "We'll have to strip the bed somehow." That was the first of many times when we cleaned and washed him, and almost the last time that we had to remove and launder and sterilize his bed linen. The accident was now to be expected from time to time depending on his reactions to drugs, his food intake and the progress of the sickness. The nervous system had begun to come under attack, and the body's control signals became more and more untrustworthy. As we'd never done this before, and as we were both upset by the strong odour, we had trouble over the cleanup. We weren't certain that the spasm, if that's what it was, was over. We weren't afraid that he'd soil more bedding; we had bedding enough for a small hotel. We just felt that he wouldn't have wanted to be subject to these indignities.

All the others were out on various errands, and it was increasingly clear that he had to be cleaned and bathed at once, so we settled down to the work. We removed the pillows, which were unaffected by the accident, and the light blanket and sheet that lay on top of him. The blanket was clean; the sheet was spattered with drops of matter and some fluid. I folded the blanket and put it to one side on a chair. When we saw the condition of the top sheet, Danny left the room without a word and came back with a laundry hamper that he'd lined with a big orange plastic sack. I dropped the sheet in it, then we stood the hamper next to the door. Then came the problem of struggling with the bedclothes while Adam was lying on them.

"Should we help him into an armchair?" I asked Danny. "Would he catch cold?" I was afraid of starting another pneumonia, which would probably kill him.

Danny said, "Let's try to slide the sheet out from under him." Neither of us wanted to handle him, I can see that now. There was a mysterious, perhaps superstitious, awe running through our feelings. We were standing beside a man in the process of being reduced to zero, total nullity. Horror and pity and fear and revulsion were the chief elements in the scene. I know that we both felt this; we were afraid to touch him, but between the two of us we succeeded in removing the contour sheet that was fitted snugly over the mattress. It was in a terrible mess that made us both gag, but we got it off and into the hamper. There was a flannel undersheet, and that too had to be replaced. Fortunately the leakage had not gone through to the mattress, so far as we could make out. We decided that we could leave the mattress in place, and we had just enough sense not to remove the flannel undersheet before we washed and dried Adam. It was terribly like changing and powdering an infant; we used nearly a dozen facecloths to wipe off matter and fluid, all of them being flung into the laundry hamper. Danny supported Adam's legs in the air, while I powdered the groin and the buttocks. We folded a sheet a couple of times and worked it under him. It looked like an outsize diaper, and both of us felt the ghastly but comic aspects of the position we were in, all three of us. From time to time Adam made sounds; you couldn't call them moans or outcries, but they weren't peaceful.

"Cover him up for the time being, Danny," I said, "and I'll clear this stuff out of here. I don't know how we'll launder it."

"I'll take care of it through SHS," he said. "It isn't the first time I've had to cope with it. Lots of sick people have the same trouble. It doesn't always come on so fast."

I trundled the hamper along to the front of the apartment.

"Can you arrange for them to pick it up straight away?"

"I'll tell them it's a Code 70 assignment; that's the right term."

Tricks to all trades, I thought. When Danny had phoned in this special order, and his mates at SHS had agreed to make a special pickup, I rang Dr. Cotterill's office and left a message describing the incident. It wasn't long before he called back.

"We're into a new phase," he said. "I'll start him on a

half-dosage of Lomotil, then we'll see. The Lomotil should
reduce the bulk and the suddenness of the movement. I'll call it
in to your druggist right now, and I'll see that they've got a stock
of adult diapers. You'll want to bring in a supply of them. They're
easy to manage. You don't use pins because they've got an
elasticized waistband, and they're highly absorbent. We never
have any trouble keeping patients clean, not these days."

"Do they have to be laundered?"

"They come in the usual two kinds. Disposable are convenient but expensive. The others are cheaper and can be laundered at home. You won't need too many; it isn't like an infant,
the incontinence is intermittent, and infrequent in many cases. I
didn't think he'd reach this stage quite yet."

An hour earlier Adam had been boasting about deliberately
withholding or controlling his bowel movements to give himself
sexual thrills. Now this form of control of his body had lapsed,
perhaps permanently. I had no idea whether he would recover
any bowel control. I hoped that he would remain unconscious
long enough for the evidence of his loss of control to be removed.
How would he feel about the taking-away of this first autonomy?
His intestinal tract must now be very painful, just as his lungs
and bronchial passages were. I couldn't imagine what the
internal gripings and spasms would do to him. I left the house
quickly, headed for the nearby pharmacy to collect the Lomotil
and a supply of diapers. Can you visualize how hard it is to get
a diaper on an inert, half-conscious adult? But we learned. In a
week or so Josh and Danny and I got pretty good at it. By now
our chief care was to avoid all sudden movement and to be as
gentle as possible in nursing our friend. Everything hurt, the
joints and muscles and lung tissues — what remained of them —
and the nasal and bronchial passages and the stomach and the
intestinal tract. The pain seemed to penetrate into slumber and
even coma; he could feel it in his sleep but was too weak to toss
and turn. There was no threshing about, and very little outcry,
just the steady hurting.

I got out of the house that day, leaving Danny to watch, and went up Yonge Street to the drugstore, where the owner took me into the dispensary and handed me a package in a plain wrapping.

"No need to advertise what you've got here," he said. "Most people wouldn't recognize the name, but you can't be too careful."

I thanked him for his thoughtfulness.

"The other package will be harder to disguise; it's kind of bulky."

It was a parcel of two dozen adult-sized disposable diapers and it made an unwieldy armful. The druggist bundled the object into a big green garbage bag, fastening the top with one of those little red twist-ties. The small red strip was such a homely, familiar object that it almost made me cry then and there. The ordinary and the terrible get so confused together in our lives that finally we can't tell them apart. Mr. Naismith, the druggist, bunted the big parcel across the counter at me. I embraced it and wedged the Lomotil in a jacket pocket. It just barely went in; you could spot it sticking out, and naturally when I arrived back on the veranda the media crowd wanted to know what the two parcels contained. I tried to fend them off.

"Why don't a bunch of you get together and hoist that cement ball back onto its column? You could reposition it in five minutes if you wanted to take the trouble. You're causing damage to property. Here, let me by, you guys. I've got things to attend to."

"What have you got in the parcels, Mr. Goderich? Can we see?"

"They're private," I said.

Somebody said, "Nothing is private."

The gathering insistence of these interrogators frightened me. But to their credit three of the male journalists went down into the flower bed beside the veranda and tried to retrieve the big ornament. It was too heavy, and too hard to get hold of. Afterwards I heard that one of them had aggravated a hernia while doing the lifting. I wasn't grief-stricken about that.

"Mr. Goderich, Mr. Goderich, Matt, just a couple of questions."

The noise rose to a threatening, determined chorus. They had me backed against the front door, with their shoulder-held cameras poking into my face. I think there were about thirty of them that day, maybe more, and they were turning into an angry mob before my eyes.

"Mr. Goderich, who nominated you as Adam's nurse? Where do you get the right . . ."

They rained questions on me without form or order.

"Where's your wife, Mr. Goderich?"

"Are you divorced, sir? And if so, where and when?"

"Isn't it true that you and your former wife have been separated since 1973, over fifteen years? Isn't that a fact?"

"Isn't it a fact that your wife and your brother have lived together in England for most of that period? Isn't it true that your children refuse to see you?"

"No," somebody said, "he's got his daughter inside the apartment with him. We need to know what's going on."

"We need to know. The public has a right to know. We're only doing our jobs."

They explained how they were only doing their jobs for several minutes. They may have hoped to convince me of something. Then they switched to another tack.

"What exactly is your relationship to Adam?"

"Mr. Goderich, are you and Adam Sinclair lovers?"

"Are your wife and your brother lovers? Do your sons refuse to see you? Are you making a hostage of your daughter? What is your relationship to your daughter? Is it molestationary? What is the source of your income, Mr. Goderich? Where do you get your money? Do you have any legitimate earnings of your own? Isn't it true that you live on income from a company owned by your wife's family? What is your profession? Do you have any training in care for AIDS patients?"

"Mr. Goderich, are you and Adam Sinclair gay partners? Are you lovers? Lovers? Lovers?"

I had my back against the heavy front door. I could have pushed it open with my shoulders and legs, but then they'd have followed me into the hall; that would have established their foothold inside the building. I couldn't permit that, so I faced them.

I shouted, "Please listen to me. Listen to what I have to say. I'll give you a sort of a statement."

They seemed surprised, and backed off a few feet.

"Do your cameras have sound pickups?" I asked. I saw some nods. "Just simmer down and give me a hearing. I'm entitled to a fair hearing, right?"

So then they got quiet.

"You want to know if I'm Adam's lover, isn't that so? Isn't that the sort of stuff you think will really interest your audience? I don't need to ask what you mean by lover; we all know what you mean by that. I've known Adam Sinclair since I was three and he was four years old. We weren't lovers then and we aren't now. But if you're asking me if I love him, if he's my oldest and dearest friend, then yes. I love him. I've loved him since I first hurt him in 1933."

I thought that I'd said more than enough, and wanted to wind things up on that note. As I turned to go inside somebody grabbed at me, seizing the garbage bag I was clutching and ripping it down the seam. The plump package of diapers swelled out through the tear. The whole mob saw the lettering on the side of the package. They quickly identified the contents and its uses. I snatched the package back and was able to get inside without asking them to forgo questions about it. Anyway, they'd seen enough to fill columns of print the next morning with speculation about the direction of Adam's illness.

SINCLAIR INCONTINENT?

And of course a companion speculation.

MATT ADAM'S LOVER?

That's as far as they ever went.

By now we were into the stage of experiment with the whole sacred litany of drugs then supposed to be helpful in the treatment of AIDS patients in the closing stages of their sickness. It seems to me now that they formed the basis of a liturgy, a continual vocal supplication directed towards some invisible power, or powers, who might even yet grant a temporary stay in the forward movement of the process. These names were always in our ears; *Lomotil* for control of diarrhea. *Colace* designed to produce the reverse effect. *Ativan* to dissipate anxiety. *Stemetil* to fight nausea. *Acyclovir* for something else, I can't remember what. *Ketoconazole, Motilium*, AZT, DDI, who invents these coinages? The air breathed these incantatory names, sometimes in whispers, sometimes in loud, urgent declarations, and always in this strange new language, not English nor French nor Latin nor Russian. In whose brain does a name like Ketoconazole originate? It has a vaguely Japanese sound, characteristic of the language of super-scientific medicine, a computer-based tongue not originating by any ordinary social process, not even decline and death. The air in the apartment grew suffocating with the stealing odours of broken caplets, crushed tablets, mysterious liquids, feeding formulas, glittery new plastic tubing and oddly scented unbreakable plastic feeders. None of us spoke much in these weeks, but waves of sound penetrated the apartment from outside, like an oceanic surf, the gathering roar of the media.

We tried to find a substitute for the phone, but this was hard to do. If we left our lines open they filled immediately with calls from Adam's professional associates or from simple well-wishers, fans, admirers, or press. We would have had to stay on duty round the clock taking calls and trying to formulate appropriate replies. All this while, you have to remember, Adam's terribly complex business affairs had to be administered. His lawyers and agents had innumerable inquiries which we had to answer as best we could. A few of them could be referred to Sadie's personal representatives in L.A., because of community-property agreements that she and Adam had entered into as a married couple. Some of these agreements were of extreme ingenuity and subtlety, hard to understand if you weren't a tax lawyer and sometimes even if you were. Adam's people in New York kept on sending us money though we never at any time asked them for it. Large cheques made out to me, meant to defray the costs of Adam's lodging and medical care and certain other expenses. I set up a separate account and paid these cheques into it; in a few months they grew into a sizable capital sum that continued to mount. The money is still in that account, and I've taken care to preserve a record of payments made to me, subsequently deposited to this account. I never paid tax on it, and I wish somebody would come and take it away. I don't like having it there. It's a subject for painful remembrance.

Adam was beyond caring for himself; half the time he was asleep or verging on coma. When he was awake he was in progressively greater and greater discomfort, which by around Thanksgiving had escalated into continual acute pain that could be alleviated only by morphine and sometimes not even by morphine. Then there was the looming possibility of what they called — the press, the doctors — CMV infection. To this day, I don't know and I don't want to know what CMV stands for. It's another of the words from the no-language litany, and it menaces the sufferer with temporary or permanent blindness. And naturally it is only treatable by heavy medication. I don't recall which. I don't think it was aerosol pentamidine; that was for pneumonia, I think. Or am I confusing them? Some were given by injection, some as wafers to dissolve under the tongue, some through central-line Port-a-Cath. Nourishment had to be given through IV lines.

The details of the treatment are beginning to fade from my

mind, but some of the phases of the illness haven't gone away. The first onset of blindness was in mid-October. I'm clear about that, because I remember Adam making a joke about being able to smell turkey without being able to see it. He was terrified when his sight went, but at least it was a temporary loss. After that he had vision again, most of the time, almost to the last. He had unpredictable bursts of physical energy that led to his getting up and walking around in confusion, trying to leave his room. I think he was trying to find the bathroom. He did not like being helped to relieve himself, and he actively resisted the diapers, as anybody would have done in his place.

Very late one night, when Eleanor, who was on that night, had gone to bed and I was drowsing over an old copy of *Country Life*, admiring the picture of some daughter of a major-general, who was engaged to the son of another major-general, there came from Adam's room a sudden explosion of sound and activity. He'd gotten up somehow. I forget what combination of medication he was on at that time. But I could hear him banging into chairs. Then he was out the door and into the hall, walking back and forth along it as though he was looking for something. It's a long, rather dark hall. By the time I got to him he was rebounding off the walls from one side of the passageway to the other, his knees flexing and buckling as he moved. He wasn't perfectly conscious; he could speak but he couldn't make any sense, and he didn't understand who was holding him and speaking to him. This was my first sight of the dementia that occurs in these histories. I thought I might be able to talk him down, but he had no idea who I was, or even that somebody was talking to him or holding him. He was very hot, but there was no question of taking his temperature; he wouldn't have allowed it. By now Eleanor was awake; she got dressed pretty promptly and came along to help me. The sight of a woman seemed to calm him. His gestures and his words weren't as disorganized as before. He cried out and wept, then suddenly he grew quiet and let us help him back to bed. Incidents like that were regular for about six more weeks.

You sometimes hear about people in that state being able to recall the distant past coherently, or passages of poetry or historical events that have impressed them. Adam's dementia wasn't like that; it was totally incoherent. His words often weren't words at all, just wordlike belchings or grunts, as if his ability to speak had been destroyed by a neurological collapse. The whole nervous system seemed scrambled, his joints and muscles tending to behave unpredictably. He couldn't walk right, he shambled, and his face gradually grew distorted as the flesh fell away from it, until nobody would have recognized him who hadn't followed his day-to-day progress. He appeared to shrink in size, but this was probably because he looked bent and crouching when he was on his feet. He hunched over in this crouch that shifted constantly. It was plain that these twitchings and leaps and jerks were prompted by different kinds of pain. After a while you got so you could read the degrees of pain from the movements he made. When he was on his feet, if he made sliding, bending movements and dribbled a lot of saliva, he was feeling grave discomfort but not agony. Josh or Danny or I would support him on either side by sliding our arms under his as gently as possible so that he was suspended like a puppet. And he would dance, he would make strange shufflings of his feet in a near-rhythm but not a rhythm hearable by us. I felt almost happy at such times, to help him to his feet and feel him through my shoulder muscles trying to move rhythmically. He was not really conscious of these moments.

If his body moved spasmodically around the solar plexus, cramping itself and jerking uncontrollably, that meant bad discomfort verging on acute pain. It seemed to have a fiery, leaping quality, so far as we could judge from his movements. He could not stand fully erect even with support when these kinds of movements were going on. Twice when we were helping him to stand he experienced an onset of this kind of anguish and twisted himself out of our arms, throwing himself to the floor and kicking and rolling around. He cried unintelligibly at these moments. The collapse on the floor must have intensified the hurting. He had no bladder or bowel control during these sessions. We always had to struggle to persuade him to recline. This type of pain showed the jerky, frantic qualities that in an earlier age would have suggested demonic possession, and now instead showed the degeneration of the nervous system.

This wasn't the worst kind. The worst was when he lay inert on his bed with tubes sticking out of him, the IV feed and the catheter, in a cold dead motionless uninterrupted agony. You could read this as the worst, and yet he survived several lapses into this nearly final state. He would be under very heavy morphine, the dose for the worst, to all appearances at the last stage of all. At these times, which could last for three or four hours, his body would show a strange dead smoothness and exude an indescribable odour that I hope never to smell again. It wasn't repellent or disgusting; it was from another world. I know that I'm a superstitious man in many ways, ready to ascribe unusual happenings to invisible sources, but that smell wasn't earthly, I'll take my oath on it.

And at least four times he came out of this awful state; his fever might alter by a degree and a half, and some colour come into his cheeks, and the unearthly odour grow faint and almost go away. There was no worse pain signal. How his body, under such physical attack, could emerge from a state like that, warm up and live for another few hours, another few days, even allowing a word or two of coherent speech, was a mystery to me. You'd have thought that he was right out of it, but he kept on and on, and you wished somebody would help him out of it.

I don't really understand the idea of palliative care, not for that stage of a sickness when you can't palliate it, when it's going to go on and on without making any sense, without the sense of an ending. The bad thing was that nobody knew how long it would last. None of us minded sitting up nights or giving the medication or keeping him clean. What we hated and feared was not knowing how long it would be. By the beginning of

December he weighed less than ninety pounds. We couldn't weigh him but we could see him growing thinner and smaller by the hour, and his breathing got noisy in the silence. We didn't talk much when we were tending him, but there was always at least one person with him, and usually two. I learned about nursing from Adam. I got to know each lesion and each scabbed and cracked skin surface and the internal vibration that signalled exactly what degree of pain he was suffering. I came to be very familiar with him. I knew his body better than my mother's or my wife's or Linnet's. Late at night I often found myself remembering the heavy pass he'd made at me when Edie and I were on our honeymoon. He'd offered me love. "Matt, darling, I love you so." It came to me with great force, often blinding me with tears, that he had spoken the plain truth when he was wrestling with me in the damp sheets that kept curling around us as we waited for a thunderstorm that was building up in the June skies over Stratford. He had always loved me and I had always turned him away, rejected him and his love, the wrong kind of love.

You can't turn away love; you need any love that's going. To have had Adam in my life has been a blessing. I don't care if there's an erotic aspect to every human attachment. So be it! There is an evil opinion now being circulated that all love is false and an excuse for harbouring false hopes about existence. To love is to essentialize. Love is not to be found in the universe. Love is a human invention, a lie. Love is non-existent. The most human need is a lie, and so is humanity itself. Anti-humanity is the correct view. Only get rid of humanity and things will start to go right for the environment. The cancer of love threatens the planet and Nature.

So what if there's an erotic dependency in every human attachment? I held on to Adam at this time. I would not let go. I mothered him. I didn't just parent him, I bloody mothered him. I cleaned him and I changed him and I held the poor skull to my breast, trying to call out to him. I felt his fever come and go and felt the deep vibrations stop as the heavy dose kicked in. I attached and disconnected tubes and I catheterized him. I wonder who will do that for me. I often folded the poor body in my arms. I remembered from my family folklore that my father had performed the same act for an old man at the point of death in a situation as horrifying as this. I and my father were at one; we learned to love in extreme situations. I never heard my father describe that action; news of it trickled back to me by circuitous routes. But I had a pretty good idea of what had gone on. He helped to bring the sufferer back to marginal life. I didn't think that I would be as effective a nurse as my father. He had more of a gift for it.

And in the end his beloved patient had died in a Swiss hospital.

I don't mean to indicate that I gave round-the-clock care. I had to get away from bedside now and then, to eat, to get out of the apartment for a moment. And they were always there.

"Why isn't Adam in hospital, sir?"

"Because he doesn't want to be treated as a research subject."

"Sir, are you involving a very sick man in some medical difference of opinion?"

"What? What's that? I don't understand you."

"Shouldn't Mr. Sinclair be hospitalized for aggressive treatment of his condition?"

"Have you given up on him?"

"Why can't we see him?"

At that moment my friend was lying comatose and struggling for breath inside. Should I have told them that? What earthly good could it have done? Should we have taken video footage of him, for the medical record? Or co-operated with researchers in the administration of untried drugs? Dr. Cotterill and his associates never made any such suggestion; the idea originated in gossip columns. Until then I'd had no idea of the medical debate between those who favoured aggressive, frontline treatment, incorporating the most advanced research, in which the sick person seems to be treated as a unit in an investigation, and the other people concerned in AIDS treatment who favoured a disciplined caregiver's approach, with drug treatment minimized and the patient allowed to take some responsibility for the course of his treatment. There has been much speculation about the place of the patient in his own care. Should he or she be permitted to smoke, if this has been a long habit? What about the use of liquor? The hard bottom line for this discussion might be summed up in the sentence "He's going to die in any case, why not let him go and enjoy his pleasures as long as he can?" In Adam's case there was no such choice to be made; the full-blown AIDS state developed suddenly, although we should have been better prepared for it. He must have been HIV-positive for at least five years before he went into the final stage. I know that he came back to Toronto not very long after I went to Moose Factory when Uncle Philip died. That was mid-1983. Now it was close to Christmas 1989. Yes. He'd been sick when he came back to Toronto, with bronchitis and energy loss and the other indicators. He must have been HIV-positive then, and his present state was the conclusion of an illness dating back six years at least. He might almost be a textbook case of the etiology of the sickness and its beginnings. I never learned where he'd contracted it. I think Dr. Cotterill heard the story from Adam when they met, but he never offered to tell me about it and I never wanted to know.

What I needed to know, for the sake of Andrea and Josh, and Muriel, Eleanor, Danny, and for myself, was what the risk of contagion might be in the progressive phases of the case. We were running no risk of infection as long as we observed certain basic precautions. You can get it in only three, or possibly four, ways, none of them present in caregiving. I could hold him, embrace him, clean him, kiss him without risk. I would have risked the kisses even if they'd been acutely dangerous. All these matters, and others even more pressing, were being canvassed by the attending throng on the veranda and front lawn. I couldn't believe I was hearing some of the things they asked.

"How long is it going to take?"

Can you imagine somebody asking you that?

"Will he make it past New Year's?"

The joke about the gay nineties was made and laughed about quite regularly out there. I wouldn't be surprised to find that pools were organized, based on estimates of Adam's shortening life expectancy.

"How long has he got?"

They would get into squabbles over whether AIDS was a disease or a bundle of diseases or a syndrome. They never said that somebody had died of AIDS. Always of AIDS-related illnesses, most often pneumonia. I suppose that's as good a way as any to conceal ignorance and terror. AIDS-related illnesses. Something we know about: pneumonia caused by a ghost. AIDS. I don't think we gain anything by inventing these acronyms; they confer an illusory actuality on a blank ignorance. I went through those last weeks of 1989 and I couldn't tell you then or now what AIDS is.

An epidemic? A plague? Some kind of evil? Everybody who discusses it has a different line on the subject. Fifteen years ago it was meanly and callously called the gay plague. There were propagandists who identified it as God's revenge on those who had sinned by their sexual misconduct. But as the years passed and people became afflicted who by no stretch of ethical invention could be accused of any form of guilty behaviour, nuns, doctors, infants, young women, people began to see into the matter more humanely. The origins and progress of the epidemic — if it was an epidemic — were carefully described at this time, say the later 1980s, and by the end of the decade nobody envisioned it as an instrument of divine justice. And yes, it was to be seen as an epidemic, if that word has any medical meaning.

You saw occasional newspaper stories around 1989 to the effect that the number of cases in Canada, say, was tapering off. We hoped that the terrible thing would go away. But it didn't go away, and it isn't about to go away, and there still isn't any cure for it. Prevention is the only defense against this destroyer.

Epidemic warning! Standing on those chilly veranda steps in December, at the end of a terrible decade, I felt myself being swept away in an immensely powerful historical current, the 1980s, the AIDS decade. I had no idea of what was to follow in the 1990s, the ever-increasing numbers, the desperate gropings of researchers towards a vaccine or a pharmacological solution. The realization, as the second millennium wore to a close, that the New Age would see no early medical relief for the sufferers. Use clean needles! Or none at all. Practise safe sex! Or none at all. If you're a surgeon or a dentist, keep your gloves on. If you're in the dentist's chair, keep your eye on what he brings near your mouth. Try not to bleed too freely. Go in fear!

"How long has he got, Mr. Goderich?"

We had no Christmas tree that year, the only time in my life that we didn't put one up. We'd have been vilified in the press if we'd tried to bring one into the apartment. I can just imagine the headlines.

MATT CAROLS WHILE ADAM BURNS

AIDS FOR CHRISTMAS

We kept our heads down. None of us kept count of the last December days. I guess that the unusual quiet that surrounded us for two or three days at that stage was when the media crowd took their holiday weekend. In 1989 Christmas fell on Monday; the media people took Friday till Tuesday off, so we had a few tranquil days when we could come and go fairly freely. Four days. With no uproar on the front steps, we could hear ourselves think; we could hear the struggle for breath. It looked like a last pneumonia would do it. I learned how to give oxygen that week. He didn't have the mask on constantly until the very last. It had to be put in place and the feed adjusted, then taken away as his breathing improved, and reapplied when it grew more laboured.

He made a pitiable sound that I've never heard, before or since. The whole experience was unlike anything else, impossible to describe. I know we got through Christmas Day all right, the Monday, and the media people took Boxing Day off, so that was December 26th gone, with Adam gasping and struggling and then in deep coma and then alive again and fighting for air. He had to prepare each breath individually, one at a time. I don't think he had any lung tissue left to breathe with. It seemed to me that he was suffocating, as though some invisible being was holding a pillow over his face, an invisible pillow from some distant space. And then lifting it just long enough for him to draw a slow breath, then pressing it back down over his nose and mouth. When it got like that it was time to offer the mask. We worked in pairs, Danny and I, Josh and Andrea, with Eleanor and Muriel as a relief team. They were so good in that situation, it was hard to take in, Eleanor and Muriel, I mean. They weren't people we'd known all our lives; there wasn't the close human tie at the beginning. By the last week in December we felt as if we'd all known one another for some long indefinite period. Eleanor and Muriel were middle-aged women from ordinary backgrounds, with modest earnings, who turned out to have the most precious human instincts in rich abundance when they were called upon to show them. They cleaned and cooked and worried and at the end agonized with the rest of us. I don't think I've mentioned their full names until now, and I want to name them and greet them, Eleanor Taliaferro and Muriel Udney. I don't know where you are now, Eleanor, Muriel, but you ladies had what it takes when we needed you.

They were very good to Adam. Not fearful, and gentle, ready to handle him as professionally as anybody could have wished. They grew graceful in their carefulness, more graceful as the need grew greater. Sometimes there had to be six of us in the room, besides Adam. Muriel and Eleanor were adept at not getting in the way while somebody was extracting a catheter or changing an intravenous bottle. The whole scene was like a slow dance, with three couples moving in an unforeseen pattern around a seventh person. And he still kept on, all the way through Tuesday and Wednesday, right up until December 28th.

That morning he was down to one slow struggling breath about every ten seconds. We went to full-mask oxygen supply. The breath action got very noisy, even behind the mask, and there was a bubbling noise from the oxygen itself that I found distracting. I wanted to hear each breath. I don't know where they came from. He can't have weighed eighty-five pounds; his ribs were plainly visible under the rotting skin. What kind of pneumonia is that?

He was very, very cold, and his eyes were partly open but sightless. I remembered the story of my father and I wanted to help Adam to be warm. I stripped off my shirt and my undershirt and lay down beside him. I pressed my warm chest against his side, hoping to raise his body temperature. Then I stretched out full-length beside him with my arms around him. I kissed him on the cracked, split lips. I thought, let him go, Lord. Let him go in peace. His hand twitched, the one with the big Mickey Mouse watch clasped around the shrunken wrist; he moved the hand once, nervelessly, as though trying to find my wrist. He drew a long shuddering breath.

The noise of the breathing stopped. Andrea peeled the damp oxygen mask from the dead face. The apartment was deathly still, only one sound detectable. I already had Uncle Philip's wristwatch on my right wrist. I slid the Mickey Mouse watch off the dead man's arm and onto my left wrist. It was a good fit. In the silence the doubled tickings sounded marvellously clear.

Date Due